THE OTHER SIDE
OF THE KNIFE

By

R. D. Sutherland

ISBN-10: 1721136258
ISBN-13: 978-1721136254

Cover design by Deborah@illuminationgraphics.com

Print layout and ebook conversion by booknook.biz

Chapter One

The light turned red as the tires started to squeal, but Dan only accelerated—every second was critical. At two o'clock in the morning, the dark streets of Amarillo were mostly deserted, and flying through another red light was worth the risk. More than once, he had wished he had a flashing siren affixed to his car like a police cruiser He should; the stakes were just as high.

The call had come at home ten minutes before, jolting him from sleep to full awareness in the space of seconds. "Dr. Parker, this is Jeff Adams in the ER. We have a seventeen-year-old boy who's been stabbed in the chest. I think the blade hit his heart. BP down, looks like he's trying to tamponade. Can you come?"

Dan's wife had pulled a pillow over her head as he flipped on the lamp and started tugging on the clothes already hanging by the door. He normally took the time for a tie to match his coat, a precise full Windsor, but not now. "Have a good day," Dan told Laura, but there was no response. Minutes after the call, he was driving twice the speed limit with the window down, the blasting wind shaking any lingering fuzziness from his head.

His cell phone chirped, and he glanced at the screen. "Pt in OR 2. Prepping."

Dan made the turns without thought, perfectly calm despite his hurry. How many times had he driven this route at top speed? And how many times had he left home in darkness, only to return in darkness again? The streets whipped by, and soon the hospital came into view. The lot was full of cars even at this hour. *Sickness never sleeps*, he often thought. Which meant he rarely got enough, either. The tires screeched to a stop as he threw the car into park in the closest space, not bothering with the assigned spot with his name mounted above it.

He ran inside and all the way to the doctors' dressing room, where he pulled on scrubs and then hurried to OR 2, putting on a cap and mask as he went. As he opened the door to the room, the circulating nurse glanced over and said, "Gown and gloves, no time to scrub. BP fifty."

Dan looked at the supine form on the operating table—a slim young man—and saw he was already prepped and draped. The anesthesiologist, a tall, dark-haired woman named Holly Martin, was ventilating and running two IVs wide open, while the tech across the table held a shiny scalpel in one hand and an electric saw in the other. Without hesitation, Dan claimed the scalpel and began to cut.

The razor-sharp edge sliced easily down through the skin and subcutaneous tissue, and Dan then traded for the saw. The sawblade split the sternum, the long, flat breastbone severing and giving way. Reaching into the split sternum, Dan examined the heart and saw the pericardium—the membrane enclosing the heart—was bluish and tense. Cutting the pericardium, blood gushed out, relieving the tension. Dan gently lifted the apex of the beating heart and saw a squirt of blood out of the edge of the right ventricle with each systolic beat. Using two pledgets, small compresses placed under the sutures, he sealed the wound with horizontal mattress stitches.

Near his elbow, Holly said, "Pressure is coming up. You got here just in time."

Dan held the youth's heart in his hand, concentrating on its shape and feel as it pulsed. Something wasn't right. "His left ventricle is larger than normal, and I can feel a thrill over the outflow tract. Holly, can you do a TEE real quick and see if the aortic valve is leaking?"

Holly nodded, and a moment later she passed the transesophageal probe down the patient's esophagus. She looked at a screen, then at Dan, and although she appeared as calm as he did, he knew her well enough to read the surprise in her eyes. "The echo shows wide open aortic insufficiency."

Dan began barking orders. "Call the nursing supervisor and have her call the heart team and tell them we are going to do an aortic valve replacement. Call this young man's parents and have them wait in the waiting room. Send blood to the blood bank for type and cross for four units."

Holly folded her arms, and now anyone would be able to read her expression. "You know you can't do that replacement. You don't have a consent and his parents are not here to give it!"

"What better time than now? The echo confirms the diagnosis. The parents should be on their way."

A tense silence descended until the phone rang and the circulating nurse answered. She talked for a minute or so, and then hung up and told them, "The parents aren't home, but the night supervisor did reach a house-sitter who said she can get the message to them. They're in Houston at a convention and are expected to take the next plane here."

Dan nodded as if this settled things, but Holly stepped around and glared into his face. "You can't do this without their consent!"

"We can't get consent when they're on an airliner. I feel this is an emergency, so we're going ahead with the operation. I'll take full responsibility."

"You bet you will," she said.

They began. A few minutes later, the heart team entered the room, followed by a young perfusionist named Viola, pushing the heart-lung machine. She said, "Looks like you started without me. The pump will be ready in five minutes. If this goes well, we should be able to start the day's schedule on time."

"You're really going through with this," Holly muttered, not really a question.

"Yes," Dan said. "And if you want to call Dr. Shaw, please wait until I'm done."

The heart team settled into the regular routine, passing instruments, getting the lines from the heart-lung machine, and doing it all in a quiet, efficient manner. After heparin was given, Dan cannulated—inserting a thin tube, or cannula—the ascending aorta and connected it to the arterial line from the heart-lung machine. He inserted another into the right atrium and connected it to the venous line, before motioning Viola to go on bypass—taking over the function of the heart and lungs to maintain circulation of blood and oxygen. The venous line drained blood from the patient into a reservoir, then across a membrane to give up carbon dioxide and take on oxygen, and the blood was then pumped back into the patient. He clamped the ascending aorta and inserted a catheter into the coronary sinus for cardioplegia, intentionally ceasing cardiac activity. The heart stopped.

Once it was cool, he made a transverse incision in the aorta—a perpendicular cut across it—and examined the aortic valve.

"Look at this," he exclaimed, gesturing at the bicuspid valve. "It's infected. Huge vegetations, and part of one cusp is destroyed. He would have died soon, without help from any knife wound."

Dan carefully cut out the infected valve, which would be sent to the lab for smear, culture, and microscopic analysis. He sutured a mechanical valve in its place, his hands steady. He then closed the aorta, unclamped, and watched the heart spontaneously start to beat. After coming off bypass, he closed the chest without difficulty.

It had worked, as he was confident it would. Dan thanked the team, feeling the release of tension in the air that followed any successful operation. He moved to leave the OR, but the anesthesiologist, Holly, called after him. "You can't keep doing this. Deep down, you know it."

He half-turned. "We saved this kid's life twice over. If he hadn't been stabbed, he would have died from the infection. Are you really trying to tell me we did the wrong thing?"

"No, of course not." She met his eyes, and he saw compassion there, though her tone was unyielding. "I'm telling you that you can't keep doing what *you* think is the right thing, every time, and to hell with the rules or what anyone else thinks. Like you're God's gift to medicine. Like you're God himself. It's going to catch up to you."

Dan's gaze flitted to the clock. Nearly five a.m.—patients were waiting.

"Duly noted."

He walked out the door and headed for the doctors' lounge and a hot cup of coffee. It was time for the day to start.

* * *

One cup of black coffee later, Dan Parker went to the doctors' dressing room, took a shower, shaved, and put on clean, light blue scrubs with a white lab coat over them. Next, he began making rounds. Not having residents or fellows on his service, Dan felt it was his professional duty to see every patient early each morning to conduct a brief physical examination, review the chart, and write any orders that needed to be carried out that day. He joked with a few of the more upbeat patients and answered questions for the others.

The Amarillo Medical Center, which included hospitals, cancer centers, rehab facilities, and doctors' offices, was the biggest employer in the area, though still only a medium-sized center considering its 550 beds. Patients were referred there from the smaller towns in the Texas and Oklahoma Panhandles. The facilities contained the newest and most modern equipment, and the hospital where Dan did his rounds was brightly decorated, clean, and innovative in many aspects—always looking for ways to improve. He had often wished he owned a hospital construction company, as the hospital was constantly building or remodeling. He participated in the design on several occasions to make patient care easier and better; for instance, the nurse stations were glazed on three sides and positioned between the rooms, for easier patient observation. The patient rooms were nicely appointed, with attractive art on the walls, top-of-the-line furniture, and HD televisions. Some patients still woke up on the wrong side of the hospital bed, but a comfortable mattress certainly helped.

Following his rounds, Dan began his schedule of operations for the day. Aside from ongoing scowls from Holly the anesthesiologist when they crossed paths, the day went smoothly enough, until he was speaking to a patient in the SICU and his phone chirped with another text message. It asked him to go to the fifth floor to see Mrs. Church, who had an operation scheduled to start soon. He had met her the day before, explaining that her heart had eighty percent narrowing of the left main coronary artery, the left anterior descending coronary artery, and the right coronary artery, along with severe obstruction of the aortic valve —an operation was unavoidable. He walked up two flights of stairs to the fifth floor and knocked on the door to room 529.

"Come in," a weak, reedy woman's voice answered.

Inside, eighty-five-year-old Bessie Church lay in a bed, wearing an expression of utter anxiety that bordered on fear. With hair whiter than cotton, she was thin, almost gaunt, her bony limbs protruding from a full-length, light blue gown. Her veins stood out prominently on her pale skin, like the patterns on an autumn leaf. A tall, middle-aged man with the same sharp features paced the room, arms crossed. He wore a dark, pressed suit, with an azure tie that matched his eyes.

"I'm Dr. Dan Parker," Dan told him.

"David Church." The man extended his hand, and Dan shook it. "My mother still has some questions that need answering."

"I'll try to answer them." He approached the end of the bed and waited as Bessie seemed to work up the courage to voice her fears.

At last she spoke, faintly. "What if I bleed?"

It was not what he had expected. "Why do you ask that?"

"Because I'm a free bleeder, that's why. Look at my arms." She raised them up, mottled with light bruises, as if they were self-evident proof. "Every time I bump myself, I get big blue spots on my skin."

Dan offered what he hoped was a reassuring smile. "Bessie, I've checked your blood clotting tests. They are completely normal."

Abruptly, she sat up straight in the bed and spoke with vigor. "I don't care what your tests show! I've always bled more than other people. Doesn't matter whether it's losing a tooth or getting a paper-cut, I'm telling you."

The clotting tests had been conclusive, and Dan started to protest, but it was clear on her face that this would go nowhere. Instead, he said, "I promise I will be very, very careful. We will take good care of you. And your heart needs this."

She stared straight up for the next few minutes, as if counting the ceiling tiles, so long that Dan had to fight the urge to check his watch. Finally she lay back and folded both hands on her chest, as if ready for burial, and murmured, "Dr. Parker, I am ready to go to the operating room."

Her son approached them, taking full advantage of his height. Over six feet and well-built, he appeared massive next to his frail mother. "I want to know just exactly what you will do to be sure she doesn't bleed." His voice was quiet, but the intent was clear.

Dan met his gaze and spoke firmly, though he softened it with a smile. "Mr. Church, I have told your mother about the need for this operation. But no one is forcing anything. You can decide to have it or not, even get a different surgeon. It's your choice."

After a small pause, David replied, "She did say she was ready."

Dan released a small sigh of relief. "Thank you." After an encouraging nod to Bessie, he turned and left the room. With a little time before they needed him in surgery, he headed down five flights of stairs to the ground floor doctors' lounge.

The attractive lounge featured overstuffed chairs, computer desks, several expensive paintings, and Dan's favorite part—good coffee and healthy snacks. The lounge was empty except for Holly Martin, munching on a protein bar as she leaned against the light blue wall. She was the anesthesiologist scheduled for Bessie's operation, and she watched him with narrowed eyes.

Tall and long-limbed, Holly had a runner's build, and she and Dan had completed a number of fund-raising marathons together. Beyond enjoying the marathons, Dan felt that running kept his back and legs strong so he could operate without getting tired. He liked to run through the connecting tunnel from the parking garage to the main floor of the hospital, then up the three flights to the intensive care unit, and sometimes Holly raced him—and despite his fitness level, she had beat him more than once. Of course, being in her late thirties meant she had a handful of years on him, but he claimed it was merely "ladies first" chivalry on those occasions.

"Dr. Superman," she said, tipping her head in a small bow.

"Don't call me that."

"You love it." She balled the snack wrapper and tossed it across the room to sink into the wastebasket. "I talked to Bessie Church and her son last night. They're worried about her bleeding. I think her risk is high, even though she's got a normal clotting profile. You operate, she may die."

"It's her best chance. That's all we can give her, isn't it?" He filled a mug halfway with coffee. He hadn't really expected an answer to his question, and didn't get one. But as Holly was strolling out, she spoke over her shoulder.

"Dr. Shaw wants to have a little sit-down with you soon. He was going on about it in the elevator. Fair warning."

"Thanks." He drank the coffee, feeling the warmth slide all the way down. It was strong, but not nearly strong enough.

* * *

The heart operating room had pale green walls, multiple built-in monitoring systems, precise lighting, and even a stereo system that could play any music the surgeon wanted. Dan was at home in this room. His musical taste often bounced around from Wagner to Bruce Springsteen to the Beatles, such that he'd heard nurses place halfway serious bets on what tunes they'd be operating to, but today he preferred silence. Only the sounds of people and machines, breaths and beeps.

After starting the operation, Dan let his training and experience take over. It was extraordinarily complex work, but it was also routine, at least initially. He placed Bessie on cardiopulmonary bypass and cooled the heart with cold blood before achieving cardioplegia, or intentional cardiac arrest. He then methodically sewed vein grafts to the coronary arteries. Before proceeding further, he consulted the Somanetics Cerebral Oximeter, a monitor showing oxygenation of each side of her brain; all was well so far. Next he inspected Bessie's aortic valve and found it just as damaged as expected—the three cusps on the valve, or leaflets, were stiff and calcified. He determined the best size of valve and carefully replaced the original with a prosthesis. Finally, he sutured the aorta closed. Dan drew a long breath.

When the aorta was gently unclamped, Bessie's heart warmed. It began to quiver and then gently shake and was defibrillated by one shock of twenty joules. The heart developed a normal rhythm and progressively stronger contractions. Viola, again operating the heart-lung machine, slowed it and allowed Bessie to come off bypass. All business again, Holly expertly performed a transesophageal echocardiogram, which showed the artificial valve to be in position with no leaking, and flow measurements of the vein grafts were excellent. Everything looked good.

But Dan felt a tight strain in the back of his neck, a tension he felt when he sensed that serious problems were about to happen. Bessie was elderly, a small female with poor left ventricular function and a nonspecific history of bleeding. All of these factors could contribute to the development of a coagulopathy, a condition in which the blood would not clot, leading to the patient bleeding to death. Holly slowly gave the precalculated dose of protamine to neutralize the heparin, and Dan hoped he would soon see clot formation.

But as he watched, no clots were forming. Every raw surface in the entire chest wound continued to ooze.

"Where is the TEG?" Dan asked, his voice sharp as he looked around the room. The thromboelastogram would determine the function of each component of Bessie's blood, indicating what component was needed for the clotting mechanism, and they always got it on heart patients after bypass.

"The lab sent word that the TEG machine is broken," said Holly.

A droplet of perspiration ran down Dan's spine as he turned back, and a nurse blotted moisture from his forehead. He knew all eyes were on him, and he did not typically sweat. "Give cryoprecipitate, fresh frozen plasma, and two packs of apheresis platelets. Also give some more protamine and Amacar." It was like shotgun therapy, but he hoped it would work.

After ten minutes of continuous aspiration of blood—suctioning it out—from the pericardial cavity, there was still no sign of the bleeding stopping. Her blood looked like red ink. The only time he had seen such severe coagulopathy was in Iraq, treating massively injured soldiers. Dan said quietly, "She was cool while we operated on her, but she is warm now, and she was never acidotic. I'm going to scrub out and talk to her family. I'll be right back."

Dan pulled off his gown and gloves and walked from the operating room to the surgical waiting room, where he spotted David Church. Dan motioned to David to join him in a smaller, private waiting room attached to the main space.

David was already antagonistic, clearly on edge from worry and fear, each look and movement quick and aggressive. Looking straight into his eyes, Dan said in a calm voice, "Your mother has a severe coagulopathy, which means her blood won't clot. Despite giving her blood products that should have all the clotting factors, she is in risk of bleeding to death."

For a moment, Dan thought the man would actually strike at him. David's hands clenched and his face darkened with anger as he tried to speak. "We told you," he finally managed to get out. "We warned you."

"All of the clotting tests were normal, and she had to have this operation. We're doing everything we can."

Dan could see the anger shift to fear as David processed what was happening, and the man asked, "Isn't there anything that would help?"

"Only one thing I know of. Fresh, warm blood would have all the clotting factors."

"Why haven't you done that?" David shouted.

"Because," Dan said in the most neutral tone he could muster, "all blood is broken down into component parts when it is donated. The bank does not have fresh blood or even whole blood." There had been no problem getting fresh blood in older days, but times had changed. Donated blood was divided into packed red cells, plasma, and platelets, with each part selectively given to appropriate patients according to need.

"Can I give my blood?" David pleaded. "My mother and I are the same type."

Dan did not hesitate. "Follow me," he said, and ran toward the lab. Seeing a technician there, he instructed, "Draw 500cc of blood from this man and bring it immediately to OR 14. Do you understand that? Don't type or crossmatch or do any other test!"

"Yes, sir," the young lady replied, through her shock. "It will only take a few minutes!"

Dan trotted back to the operating room, scrubbed for two minutes, and backed into the operating room door, pushing it open. The smell had changed; now the air was damp with a tinge of anesthetic gas, sweat, and the undeniable odor of impending death.

"Dan, she's sliding," Holly said, sounding grim. "Cardiac output dropping, pressure dropping, and she is still bleeding. I've increased her drips, but they aren't helping much. I also gave her two more units of packed red cells. Did you tell the family she's going to die?"

"Just hang on," Dan said. "Fresh blood will be here in less than five minutes."

"What fresh blood?" Holly peered at him over the drapes, her expression darkening further behind her mask.

"Her son is donating 500cc of blood right now. It should have all the clotting factors and will hopefully stop the bleeding."

Before Holly could protest, the OR door swung open and the lab tech entered, carrying a bulging bag of fresh blood. "Here you are, Dr. Parker. I hope this works, but let me warn you, you are in big trouble!" She stepped to the door and hurried out, as if worried of getting caught up in what they were doing.

"I can handle the trouble," Dan said, directing this comment at Holly.

"Dan," she started, but he cut her off.

"All that matters is that she lives." Dan looked down at Bessie's warm heart and aspirated more blood out of the pericardium. Holly, shaking her head, attached the bag of blood to one of Bessie's IV lines, and everyone watched the red trail migrate down the clear plastic tubing.

The crimson line moved ever so slowly. *It has to work*, Dan thought. Bessie's epicardial sac glistened, the fibrous tissue surrounding the heart, while light reflected off the stainless steel sternal retractor holding her chest open. They watched the blood in her chest cavity, which still had the consistency of red Kool-aid. Gradually, it started to change, gaining the consistency of cold raspberry syrup, before finally turning into sticky globs of deep red clot. Soon after, the monitor showed normal sinus rhythm and normal blood pressure. The bleeding had stopped.

When Holly spoke, her voice was low. "Do you know what you've done? We may lose our privileges over this, thanks to you. We might even be sued."

"This lady's life is more important. I will take full responsibility." No longer sweating, Dan irrigated the wound with antibiotic solution and then began closing the chest. While he worked, Dan caught Holly watching him, and though her eyes did not look angry, her posture was tense.

As Bessie was being taken to the SICU, Dan met with David in the waiting room. The man had been pacing, arms crossed, and he rushed to the door when Dan appeared.

"It worked," Dan said, unable to restrain a smile at the man's instant and extreme relief. "I think she will be fine now."

David let out a choked sound, something between a laugh and a sob, and then he braced a hand on a chair and composed himself. "I thought I was going to lose her. I can barely stand here, I'm so shaky. Thank you, Dr. Parker."

"She is lucky you two have the same blood type," Dan said.

"Yeah, especially since I was adopted."

Dan could not speak. He just stood there and stared at David as what he said sank in. Finally, he said, "You have to know what we did is very illegal. By federal mandate all donated blood has to go to the blood bank to be checked, tested, and rechecked."

"You won't get any complaints from us," David said.

"You're not the ones I'm worried about."

* * *

The day passed. More patients, more procedures, more worried looks from Holly when they passed in the halls. Dan kept expecting a summons from Dr. Golden Shaw, Chief of Medical Affairs, but it didn't come until very late in the day, when Dan could legitimately argue that it was better to wait for tomorrow, and Shaw agreed to meet the next day. Dan felt like a prisoner granted a one-night stay of execution, but he did not regret any of his decisions.

"What a day, huh?" Holly said as she walked by him toward the stairs. "Crazy even for us. Race you to the garage?"

Dan's mouth quirked in a smile, but he shook his head. "Still have some things to wrap up."

"See you tomorrow, then."

She left, and Dan went to his office, in the new office building connected to the hospital, to try to finish for the day. His office was neat, clean, and organized, with maps and framed photos of destinations around the world he had visited with his family. Portraits of his wife and daughter, Laura and Marla, sat on his desk, both sharing the same shiny brown hair and quiet smiles. Through the window, only darkness came in; he had known what time it was, but still it discouraged him.

He checked two voicemails on his phone that had come through during an operation, which he had failed to listen to yet. It had been such a hectic day. The first was from Laura.

"Hey, I'm sure you're busy," she said, "but I wanted to remind you about Marla's recital tonight. You said you'd come. Hopefully we'll see you there." A small pause, during which Dan's heart sank, and then she simply said, "Bye."

The recital was long since over at this point. He would have to make it up to his daughter somehow, although he found this harder and harder the farther she went through high school. When she had been little, an ice cream cone had done the trick, but those days were gone. He started to call Laura back but quickly changed his mind; the apology and explanation would be better delivered in person. Resting his head on one hand, he listened to the other message.

"Dan, it's Kim Konno," the voicemail began. Dan's hand dropped and he sat up straighter. Kim had been his surgical partner for several years, and he was an old friend. "I know it's been a while, but I want to meet up soon. It's important." He sounded breathless, excited. "I've been working on something that I want to share with you, but I want to tell you about it in person. I'll say this much—I'm inches away from finding the Holy Grail of cardiovascular surgery. This will change the world, Dan. This will change everything. Call me."

The message ended, and Dan stared out the window. Kim was probably exaggerating, but then again the man was not one given to hyperbole. If anything, he tended to understate things, so if Kim said it was huge... it would probably be front page on every newspaper in the country.

But it was very late, and his family was waiting. Dan finished some paperwork, responded to a handful of urgent emails, and packed up for the day. As he turned off the computer, his cell phone rang. A nurse was calling, breathing hard. "A patient came into the ER with chest pain, and we found a dissecting ascending aortic aneurysm. The other chest surgeons are all operating already. You're needed in the cath lab if you can come."

Dan started for the door and wearily told the nurse he was on his way. Maybe the world would soon be different, if his old friend was right. But some things would never change.

Chapter Two

Kim Konno gazed at the artificial heart he had just implanted as it sat motionless, totally inert. All looked well, until a small spray of blood squirted from the aortic suture line where he had sutured the graft from the heart to the patient's own ascending aorta. No matter; a quick figure-eight stitch around the leak stopped the bleeding. Kim again stared at the motionless heart, with effort keeping his focus on the operation at hand and not its significance. It wasn't this patient he was concerned about—a medium-sized pig, anesthetized on the operating table—but all those to come.

He turned to the circulating nurse and met her eyes. "Get me some warm saline."

"Already have," she replied, pouring the saline into a silver basin held by the scrub nurse.

Kim took the basin and gently poured the saline over the implanted heart, knowing the master computer chip was temperature sensitive, and the heart started to beat with progressively stronger contractions. "When the heart rate reaches one hundred, start slowing the heart-lung machine," he said. He glanced over his shoulder at the woman operating the cardio-pulmonary bypass machine. "Gradually allow the new heart to take over the circulation."

"Yes, sir. It's already one hundred ten." She reached over to slow the bypass machine.

"Vital signs are stable," remarked the anesthesiologist, a plump, middle-aged man named Bruce Walters. "Nice work, Kim. How many does this make?"

"This is number four hundred seventy-four. But only the last eighty have been successful."

"Eighty successful implants of artificial hearts," Bruce said, shaking his head. "And how many kidneys?"

"Forty." Kim watched as the new heart took over circulation. If all went well, it would give his small, porcine patient its full normal lifespan.

"More than sufficient," Bruce said. "We've got to start sharing this."

"That's enough," Kim said, so sharply that the scrub nurse looked up in alarm.

"This doesn't just belong to you," the anesthesiologist continued. "Like I keep saying, we've all worked on this, and now we're sitting on a goldmine. The world needs it, and you're just going to keep running tests while we wait another *year* or more until human testing is complete?"

"And which exactly are you so concerned with?" Kim started to close up the motionless pig, fighting to keep his hands steady despite his anger. "The world's needs, or the goldmine?"

The room lapsed into silence as Kim finished. He thought the confrontation was over, like other recent occasions, but Bruce sent a parting shot as Kim went to scrub out.

"This will change the world. You can't hold it back." He

stepped after Kim, and when he spoke again his voice was so low that only Kim could hear it. "This is so much bigger than you that if you keep standing in the way, it's going to crush you flat."

Kim half-turned to face him, unmoved. "Get back to work. We have tests to run."

* * *

Worldwide Medical Research, located on the west side of Austin, Texas, employed twenty-three PhDs in biomedical engineering, each with a subspecialty in artificial organ research. They were the brightest Kim could find and attract to Austin with the promise of making medical history, along with a highly generous salary. The impressive facility also employed lab technicians, veterinarians, animal care experts, computer programmers, and security officers. All of them were committed to the goal of developing implantable artificial organs—with the heart being the capstone —which had been the elusive goal of medical research for decades, achieving almost mythic proportions.

Countless people died every year waiting for an organ match; until genetically controlled stem cells could be grown into individual new organs as needed or organs transplanted without rejection, artificial organs appeared to be the next step in medical progress. Their research could change the face of patient care forever, opening the door to a greater symbiosis between man and machine and removing barriers to longer life.

It had not been easy. But after ten years of painful, intense, and sometimes disastrous events, artificial organs had been developed for implantation in humans and prized animals. Horses, sheep, and pigs had been implanted with hearts and kidneys, and artificial membranes for use in heart-lung machines were also developed. Now the FDA had reviewed the research and results of the animal implantations and had approved experimental human implantation at transplant centers in Dallas, Houston, Cleveland, and Tucson. Each center would get ten hearts, but it would be at least a year before the hearts would be approved for general population implantation. Unwilling to wait that long, Bruce and a few of the others were pushing to cut corners and, Kim suspected, sell their research to the highest bidder at the first opportunity.

"Not if I can help it," he muttered, walking the corridors. They could not advance prematurely; they had to be sure the artificial organs were ready. Given the internal strife Bruce was stirring up, he figured it was wise to make appearances beyond his usual circuit. Taking a sharp left, he walked briskly down the hall toward the east wing, which contained the large animals, and soon the dry, pleasant scent of fresh hay reached him. If he closed his eyes, he could almost imagine he was a child again, strolling around his father's farm.

"Dr. Konno, good to see you," a white-coated man said from the first stall, which housed a bay mare with a white blaze. A veterinarian, the man was in the process of examining the horse, stethoscope to its chest. "How is your patient doing?"

"She'll be back to her slop trough in no time," Kim replied, "curly tail and all."

The vet grinned. "Good to hear."

Kim continued down the row of stalls, where the other horses were being groomed, examined, or fed vitamins and protein supplements in their hay. He exchanged greetings with the animal keepers, and all were pleasant. The animals were in good condition, including those that had received artificial organs.

He climbed the stairs to the second floor and found similar

results with the sheep. The soft bleating of contented animals greeted him as soon as he had stepped out of the stairwell. The sheep received careful attention daily, including brushing and shearing whenever needed, with an especially watchful eye on the organ recipients. All was well. One more floor up, the pigs likewise all seemed to be healthy and thriving.

"How's Pinky?" a young animal keeper asked him, her expression genuinely concerned.

Kim smiled. "Number 412 seems to be doing just fine. My pig-ese is a bit rusty, but I think she said to have more carrots ready for her."

The woman beamed that Kim had remembered the animal's favorite treat. "Will do."

It took several minutes for Kim to reach the west wing, passing the turn-off for the north wing as he did so, which contained the operating rooms and intensive care units. Skilled OR technicians performed most operations, but Kim did ninety percent of the heart transplants. He passed a nurse in the hallway, who smiled and exchanged pleasantries with him, no hint of resentment. Maybe it was better than he thought, and Bruce was the primary problem. After all, the nurses—each a specially trained ICU nurse—received twice the salary they would have earned in a regular hospital.

Kim climbed to the fourth floor and headed down a long hallway in the west wing that led to the biochemical research center, where several PhDs and assistants with degrees in biochemistry worked on tissue membrane interface, rejection, and long-term stability of implanted organs. He planned to make an appearance, speak to them about the importance of thorough, methodical work, and gauge their patience with the process. The manufacture of experimental units was carried out on the third floor, another floor was administrative, while Kim's office at the rearmost part of the west wing was the nerve center. From his office, he coordinated the progress of research in each area of all programs and monitored their results.

Kim slowed as he walked the hallway leading into the research center. This corridor, windowless and bare save a row of framed photographs, had been dubbed the "walk of motivation" by one of the research assistants. Kim had figured his team would be lured to the project by the promise of fame and fortune, but as it turned out, most who agreed had personal reasons for chasing this dream—a connection to someone whose life could have been saved by an artificial organ. One of the assistants had hung a photo of her aunt in the empty hallway, "to remind me why I come to work" she had said, and others had quickly followed suit —hanging pictures of grandparents, lost spouses, friends, even children. For weeks, another appeared nearly every day, and he could only guess which of the personnel had slipped into the hallway with a hammer, nail, and framed picture.

Finally, one night after hours, it was his turn to stand in the corridor with a photograph, his heart hammering harder than the tool that he swung. It was a portrait of his father, Tadami Konno —or Konno Tadami, in his home country—a short, gentle-featured man, a first-generation immigrant from Hokkaido. Kim recognized the smile-lines around the eyes that were now creasing his own. In the photo, his father was already confined to a wheelchair by the congenital heart defect that would take his life far too early. All these years later, the image still drove Kim—but not to go faster. No, every time he saw the photo, instead he heard his father's words: *If you're going to do something, do it slow. Do it careful. And do it right.*

"You're failing him, you know."

Kim turned, startled. He had not realized he had drifted to a stop in front of his father's portrait, and he had not heard Bruce Walters approach behind him. His pulse sped up as his hands curled before he even realized how angry the other man's words had made him.

"Touch a nerve?" Bruce smiled without warmth. "You know it's true. Each day you hold this back, you're failing all the people whose lives could be saved by this. All over the world."

"Don't pretend this is about anything but a bank account to you. You know as well as I do what could happen if we rush this or release it too soon." Kim forced himself to relax and take a step back, the right choice suddenly clear. "Which is why you're no longer on the team. Effective immediately. I want you gone by the end of the day."

The man's face paled, but a moment later fury replaced shock and he flushed. "You're a fool, Konno." Bruce backed away, his eyes dark with threat. "And you know what? When the history books write about this, you're not even going to be a *footnote*."

Kim watched him leave, all the good feelings about his team, the facility, and their progress replaced with a sick dread in the pit of his stomach. *Don't let him shake you*, he told himself. *We're so close. It's just scary because it all seems too good to be true. Do it slow, do it right.*

He tried to plaster on a smile as he strolled into the bio-chemical research center, ready to boost morale if needed with the research staff. But he couldn't shake the nausea that lurched in his gut after Bruce's threat. Maybe Kim *was* a fool to think he could just change the world without opposition. Bruce, and others like him, would not just bow quietly out. How far would they go? What else, Kim wondered, was he not seeing?

And more importantly, would he be able to see it in time?

Chapter Three

The porch light on their bungalow in Sleepy Hollow glowed warmly, like a beacon welcoming him home, but Dan knew better than to read too much into that. His wife could be furious with him and still leave a hot supper ready on the stove, his favorite book on his armchair, and the light over the door switched on, no matter how late it got. It was the type of woman Laura was.

Dan unlocked the front door, weariness settled deep into his bones from another hard day. It didn't matter how many half or full marathons he ran for conditioning—the long hours were exhausting. "I'm home," he called softly. Laura's tone in response, he knew, was a much better barometer of how the rest of the night would go.

"In the dining room," she answered, her tone flat. Not a good sign.

Dan found her sitting in a chair at the table in her pajamas and robe, clasping a mug of hot tea with both hands and just breathing in the steam. He draped his coat on the back of a chair and kissed her on the top of the head, but she did not look up.

"Fixed chicken fried steak and biscuits with cream gravy," she said. "Peach cobbler for dessert. I made you a plate and tried to keep it hot."

"Thanks, honey. Sounds wonderful." He stepped into the adjacent kitchen, where he found his dinner still warming on the stove, though it had probably been sitting there for a couple of hours at least.

"Lola misses you," Laura said from the table. "She's been sitting in your chair all evening."

Their dog, a border collie with a typically sweet disposition, was an honorary member of the family—seemingly a rung above their actual daughter, as Marla often joked. Lola frequently slept on the foot of Laura and Dan's bed. "I know these long hours I work are hard on her," Dan said, carrying his plate back in. "I've tried to explain to Lola, but it may have been lost in translation."

"She only speaks dog biscuit," Laura said. "But you should keep trying, or she may need dog therapy. I hear once the damage is done, it's almost impossible to reverse."

"Is that so? You don't think a comfy new doggy bed would do the trick?" He smiled as he sat across from her, but then he saw how serious his wife's expression was.

"No, I don't think you can buy your way out of this. It doesn't matter how many new toys you bring home, or how many times you promise it will get better." She took a long, slow sip of her tea, brushed back the hair that had fallen down, and looked him in the eyes. "When you're gone, you're gone, and you'll never get that time back."

Dan's smile faded. "We're not talking about Lola anymore, are we?"

Laura's gaze dropped as she leaned over her tea, shoulders hunching, looking small and guarded. She let the silence linger a moment before responding. "You said you'd try to go to the tournament. Never mind the recital."

"And I have tried. But I can't just leave for a week, or even a few days, with how busy things have been." Dan sawed into his steak, cutting it methodically. "There's no one to hand my patients to, and it's not like I'm a mechanic who can just let the cars sit in the shop a little longer while I go off to watch some volleyball games."

"It's not about watching the games, it's about watching Marla!"

It was rare that Laura raised her voice, and it surprised him into looking up again from his meal. Laura, a trim woman with light brown hair that reached the middle of her back, had blue eyes that normally shone. But they were dimmed by worry and anger now.

"We've talked about this," he said, groping for any response.

"And yet nothing changes," she shot back. "You leave home every morning at five-thirty and don't get home until nine or ten at night, and then you're so tired you can hardly walk. You haven't seen our daughter in over a week. I can't keep doing everything on my own."

Dan leaned back in his chair, struggling to form an argument that had not been torn apart in past conversations. It was hard to think; all he wanted to do was eat his dinner and lay down. "Why don't we talk about this when—"

"It's always late, and you're always tired," she cut in. "Mitchell Kay's wife told me he works as hard as he can for three weeks, and then he takes the last week of the month off. Why can't you do that? Think of me, think of Marla, to say nothing of your own mental health."

Dan dropped his fork and met her gaze across the table. "That's a great plan, except that Mitchell Kay is a plastic surgeon, which means that all of his cases are elective, while most of mine are urgent or emergencies."

"There will always be a reason if you let there be." She blew out her breath, exasperated. "You work so hard. You give so much, and what do you get in return? You're hardly able to enjoy your own life."

"Careful, that almost sounded like a compliment." He tried to smile and reached across the table for her hand, and she let him take it.

"Of course it did. You know I'm proud of you, and so is Marla... but we wonder when we'll get to enjoy the life you've poured so much into." She let out a short, humorless laugh. "I was flipping past ESPN and they were talking about how much some of the players make, showing their crazy mansions and yachts. They're taking vacations and living the high life, while you're saving lives and then coming home to cold chicken fried steak. It's ridiculous."

"That's not all true," Dan said. "My steak actually stayed pretty warm."

Unamused, Laura jerked her hand from his and began ticking off on her fingers. "You've had four years of college, four years of medical school, four years of general surgical residency, two years of thoracic and cardiovascular surgery residency, and two years in the military. You are smarter and better educated than anybody I know. You work at least eighty hours a week saving people's lives, and you won't make in your lifetime what those sports stars make in one year."

"You think I don't think about that? You think I don't want

31

those things? Of course I do. It's not fair, but people want to be entertained, and they'll pay for it. Nobody wants to be sick. Nobody cares about doctors, nurses, firemen, policemen, teachers, or soldiers until they need them. It's not just me. You'd be amazed how many physicians I know that are having to retire or close their offices because they're making half what they made fifteen years ago." He stopped there, watching her expression, reading the love and frustration in equal measure. She had always supported him, but he saw an anxiety that had rarely reached this level—and it had little, if anything, to do with his income. "But we both know it's never been about the money, anyway."

Laura nodded, wearily. He thought a rebuttal was coming, but instead she stood and with slow movements tugged her robe back into place, cinching the belt. She stepped around the table and slid an arm around him, her head resting on his shoulder; he put his hand over her arm, closed his eyes, and breathed in the soft floral scent of the lotion she had used.

"All I know is that it can't go on like this," she said, so faintly he could barely make out the words. "Something has to give. You're going to have to choose what." She kissed his temple and slipped away, heading toward their bedroom upstairs.

Dan ate his dinner in silence, the food cold now, the house feeling dark and empty without her presence. After a few minutes, Lola, their border collie, came trotting in from the living room and paused a moment, head tilted, watching him. Then she padded on by, to follow Laura up the stairs and lay at the foot of the bed. Dan finished his meal alone.

* * *

This had never been the plan. Saving lives, yes—he first went into the profession because of a burning desire to make a difference, to have some real impact on a hurting world that desperately needed it. It had driven him to serve in the Marine Corps, as a surgeon who volunteered for forward emergency facilities to treat the most seriously wounded soldiers. It had pushed him through all his years of training. He knew the cost would be high; there was always a price to pay, after all. But he never expected what this life would ask of him. It was a commonplace in his profession that stress among all physicians was increasing, but statistics showed that the suicide rate among surgeons was especially high. He understood why.

Before following Laura to bed, Dan stepped into his office and flipped on a brass lamp, the bookie's kind with a green shade, and sorted through the day's mail that Laura had dropped on his desk. Bills, statements, and ads, nothing interesting. He powered on the computer, leaning back in his chair and letting his eyes wander as it booted up.

His framed diplomas took up some of the wall space, along with a case Laura had bought to house the medals from his military service. Laura's diploma from her degree in American literature at Arizona State was hung in here, too; she taught part-time now at West Texas University in Canyon. The rest of the walls were filled with photographs showing Marla tumbling through gymnastics routines as a little girl, then practicing her clarinet in middle school, then scoring points on her high school's volleyball team. She had grown up so quickly, and he felt that snapshots were all he had—quick moments, frozen in his memory, between long gaps where he was absent. It was like he had gotten up too many times from his seat while the movie kept playing, and now he had lost track of the plot. Who was she now?

What did she like? Could he even answer those questions about his wife?

The two of them would be leaving in a few days for San Antonio, where they would be for the volleyball tournament, before the whole team and the mothers went to Dan and Laura's place at Pecan Plantation for five or six days. They would be gone about two weeks in all. A long time away from him, with plenty of time to think and talk without him having the chance to speak up in his own defense.

With a sigh, Dan logged in and opened his email. Most were inconsequential, but one from an old friend, Alex Bear, caught his attention. The subject line read: "No place like home."

Alex and Dan had gone to the University of Texas together and had struck up a seemingly unlikely friendship; Alex, a full-blooded Apache, had grown up on the Mescalero Apache Reservation in New Mexico in the shadow of the massive peak Sierra Blanca. He was the first of his family to attend college, while Dan grew up in a white upper-middle class neighborhood in Fort Worth, Texas, and his advanced education was a foregone conclusion. But the two had grown close, and Dan spent many weekends and vacation days during college visiting the reservation and Alex's parents, George and Sally Bear. After graduation, Alex went to medical school at Stanford and stayed for residency there in cardiovascular surgery; later he joined Dan in Amarillo for several years before moving to practice in Albuquerque to be closer to the reservation and his parents.

A couple of days before, Alex had sent another message, trying to re-connect with his old friend. As Dan clicked open this new email, guilt rose up in him that he had not responded.

Hello Dan,

I hope everything is going well for you there in Amarillo, though I'm sure you are busy. I've taken a little time off to spend with my parents, and there's a lot going on at the reservation, too, even if it isn't the kind of busyness that you and I are used to.

Things are mostly following the usual cycle around here. The herds of deer and elk have come down from the mountain, and the evenings are simply splendid, watching them graze. That family of black bears is back, and I thought I spotted a mountain lion the other night, although it may have been my imagination. I am enjoying the time back home—I'd almost forgotten how beautiful the land really is.

My parents send you their best. They are mostly in good health and still active, finding hobbies to keep themselves occupied. This week the big project is overhauling the house —they've redone the kitchen and are planning to clean out the garage soon. Here's hoping I'm not dragged into helping; the Lost City of Atlantis could be buried in there.

We would all love to see you if you have the chance to fly up sometime. Please give my best to Laura, and tell Marla I caught her last game on YouTube and was blown away by that save in the second half. You've got quite a kid there.

Peace and plenty,
Alex

Dan sat back, feeling burdened rather than touched by the gesture to reach out. Just another relationship he had let slip away. And his friend, though hundreds of miles distant, was more aware of his daughter's life than he was. Meanwhile Laura and Marla, leaving on a trip soon, were aching for his involvement, and something told him that if he waited until they were back, then a window would have closed. Perhaps he was just being dramatic, but what if they decided to stay away? Or what if this tournament was his last chance, and no amount of gifts or promises would gain him another?

He had to find a way to fly out and join them, at least for a day or so. And he should make the time to reconnect with Alex. All of which meant that Dan could not make waves at the hospital, but had to get others on his side and find support to fill in and take up the slack. He needed a different schedule, more time, a change to his life, somehow.

He couldn't possibly do it all. Laura's words came back to him as he turned off the computer, the room plunged into darkness as the monitor's glow faded.

Something has to give. You're going to have to choose what.

Chapter Four

Through the floor-to-ceiling windows of his seventeenth floor corner office, Robert Krum watched the freezing drizzle pour from the dark skies onto the nation's capital. Traffic crawled, while people bundled in coats hurried down the sidewalks, hunched against the elements. Aside from the emergency responder lights, which illuminated the wreckage of cars from fresh accidents, D.C. was painted in dark, gloomy tones devoid of light or life. It was a day for funerals, for suicides, for grief and despair.

Krum loved it.

He turned, checking the time on the quartz and marble clock gracing his claw-foot desk. Two minutes until the next appointment, his most important meeting of the day. He smoothed fingertips down the front of his blazer and checked his tie compulsively. It was impeccable, of course. Outside, thunder rumbled ominously, but it only improved his mood.

The weather seemed a reminder of life's frailty, of the insignificant place that humans occupy in the vast cosmic order of things. So fragile, these little beings, so *mortal*. So apt to break down, so likely to die. Far from depressing him, the reminder was an encouragement. After all, it was what kept him in business.

Someone knocked on the door.

"Enter," Krum said.

"Ellen Blake to see you," said his secretary, a dour, matronly woman.

"Send her in."

Ellen Blake strode in a moment later, and the door was shut behind her. A tall, attractive black woman, Ellen wore a khaki pantsuit and carried a briefcase. Her long hair was pulled back, and her expression was all business—polite but neutral, almost impatient, as if she had other places to be. She shook his hand firmly and took the seat opposite his desk when he gestured toward it.

"Good of you to meet with me," Krum said, "especially in such nasty weather."

Ellen did not smile. "It didn't seem I had much choice. I didn't know that Health Now had such pull with the FDA."

He sat and pushed a crystal dish of mints across the desk to her, but she shook her head. "I have many friends in many places, nothing more," he said. "I apologize if it came across as anything but a request."

Ellen made a non-committal sound in the back of her throat and glanced around the room, taking in the Matisse, the masks from Zimbabwe, the urns from Greece. Krum took a moment to study her, trying to take her measure. She had a straight posture, a rigid bearing; she might be more unyielding than her predecessor. That could be a problem.

"So what is this about?" Ellen asked.

"As CEO, I see myself as the father of a big family. I like to watch for developments that would be good for my children, as it were, all the people who utilize our policies." He smiled benignly, propping his elbows on the desk. Ellen only arched an eyebrow. "So I've been following a certain experimental research facility in Austin, Texas, with great interest. I believe you've been out there yourself. I understand there are self-contained implantable artificial hearts and kidneys. They've had successful animal trials, so they're ready to move to human implantation."

Ellen canted her head to one side. "You're remarkably well informed, Mr. Krum."

"Call me Robert. And yes, I make it my business to be."

"So do I." She unclasped the briefcase and pulled out a sheaf of papers. "I've taken a little dive into your acquisitions and investments, so I know the type of projects that interest you. You've got your hands in pockets all over the world, don't you?"

Krum's expression did not waver. "This is Washington, isn't it?"

"Indeed it is. Since I do inspections for both the FDA and NIH, I assumed you called me out here for some insider information. And there's one fish in the pond right now bigger than all the others—Worldwide Medical Research. You want to know where things stand with the FDA regarding approval for human trials for the artificial hearts. Right so far?"

Though a bit nonplussed, Krum only nodded.

"Personally, I was thrilled to hear about this research." Ellen began fanning papers out on his desk, upside down. "It's potentially world-changing, as you know. I'm fully in support, if the research has been thorough."

"And has it?" As soon as he had asked the question, he knew it was premature. She would only tell him when she was ready.

Sure enough, she ignored it entirely. "Your motives are less clear. From what they say about you, making the world a happier, healthier place is not on your agenda."

Krum clicked his tongue, shaking his head as if offended. "You've got me wrong. In fact, if the hearts are ready for human trials, my company will gladly pay for the transplants once approved. Budgets are tight across the board, but Health Now is a big organization with deep resources, and we will take on this burden to see that the trials do not have to drag out any longer than necessary. Countless people's lives are on the line. That's what I called you here to offer."

He watched her carefully, saw the wheels turning behind her eyes, but guardedly. She was not buying it. He saw it in the tension of her shoulders, in the twitch of her fingers toward the papers, in the doubtful, downward curve of the corner of her mouth. She started to speak, but he plunged ahead before the chance was gone.

"We'll corner the market," he said. "The money we spend on the transplants will be easily made up, that and more, through the prestige and profits of being the first company offering these transplants. People who don't have our insurance will buy a policy just for this reason. We'll be swimming in good publicity, and our stock values will soar. I'll make a fortune." He started to offer her an under-the-table cut, a bribe that she would surely refuse, but he didn't want to overplay his role. She would either believe he was just another greedy CEO, and move forward, or she wouldn't.

"I think we understand each other," Ellen said at length. "And as much as I would like to keep your pockets from being lined any further, it's not worth delaying this life-saving research."

She began to flip over the papers, and he saw forms indicating approval following the FDA's inspection of Worldwide Medical Research in Austin. His eyes skimmed down the papers, seeing stamps and signatures that made his heart go faster. Everything was moving forward.

"The NIH has partially funded this research and has given us an update every six months," Ellen said. "The FDA will approve the implantation of artificial organs after testing shows them to be safe and durable. The whole process will take several years. The estimated cost is one-half to one million dollars for each heart and four hundred thousand for each kidney."

Krum rubbed his forehead, letting out a low breath as if the number surprised him. But it was spot-on with what he had estimated. "Not chump change, that's for sure."

"I've seen how these things go. I know the kind of funds they'll be trying to raise, and the state of the national budget. Medical care of all types adds up to about 40 percent of it, and this thing could stall for the next decade as people balk at the millions it could cost." Ellen leaned forward, her tone urgent now, a sincerity shining behind her brown eyes. "Imagine the number of people with heart failure, coronary artery disease, diabetes, or renal failure that could be eligible for a new heart or kidney. Hundreds of thousands? Millions? The costs will be unbelievable. Without a champion in the insurance field, someone to step up, this might never get off the ground. And people need these."

Krum nodded. "That's where I come in."

Ellen scooped up the papers and slid them back into her briefcase. She snapped it shut and met his gaze again. "Yes. For the good of the American people. And people around the world."

He allowed a truly genuine smile to emerge, and he came

around the desk to shake her hand again. "Ms. Blake, it brings me great happiness to know that we see eye to eye on this. I was simply waiting to hear your verdict on their research, and now that I know a green light is coming, I am ready to throw my entire focus onto this important project."

"I'll settle for a fraction of your revenue," Ellen said. "I'll be in touch." She gave him a curt nod, rose, and left his office.

For the next several minutes, Krum stood unmoving, his eyes on the oaken door Ellen had just passed through, as possibilities ran through his mind. Some were likely; others less so. Many presented risk. Others were safe, predictable, and offered little profit. These were quickly discarded.

He strolled back to the window, gazing down onto the people on the streets struggling through the icy, bitter rain. As he watched, a car hit a wet patch and slid, striking into a pedestrian and then plowing into a lamppost. Krum let out a short laugh. He turned to his desk, ready to resume his work.

It was going to be a good day.

Chapter Five

Something isn't right. The thought bounced around in Ellen Blake's head on the slow, stressful drive back to her office, as slushy sleet ran down her windshield and she steered defensively around the out-of-towners who didn't know how to drive on ice and all the others too rushed to care. Lobbyists, attachés, journalists, and other political hangers-on. Some idealists, others parasites; some crusaders, others thugs. The usual D.C. mix.

Something isn't right. Ellen had dealt with plenty of difficult people in the nation's capital and beyond, so she was surprised at how wholly Robert Krum had unnerved her, though she had struggled not to show it. On the surface, he had acted precisely as she expected him to, given his reputation—like a money-hungry, unscrupulous CEO initially feigning concern for his fellow man and finally making a bargain that would benefit them both. But she could not shake the feeling that this had been precisely what it was: an act. There was something cold and predatory in his gaze, behind the forced goodwill or even the clinical, all-business delivery. Like he was playing a totally different game and just waiting for her to discover that she didn't even hold a game piece, much less know the rules.

A car spun on black ice in front of her, and she gently braked and maneuvered her car around the near-collision, her gloved hands flexing on the wheel. Sometimes it seemed that steering around disasters was ninety percent of her work. She thought her job would give her a small part in bettering lives, in getting life-saving breakthroughs vetted and eventually placed in the hands that needed them. And sometimes it did. But more often it was putting out fires while having her hopes built up and sub-sequently pulverized time after time as greed, red tape, and bureaucratic nonsense teamed up to obliterate the paltry efforts of knowledge and science. Now she doubted every positive develop-ment with the resistance of a skeptical jury placing a huge burden of proof. That had been her initial reaction to the world-changing research being done in Austen; she had to see it for herself before she would believe it was not an overstatement or flat-out scam. Paranoid, her colleagues had mumbled, more than once.

"Maybe I am," Ellen said out loud, flipping the windshield wipers to a higher speed as the sleet poured down faster. "But something's still not right."

* * *

Five hours later, Ellen's head was pounding and her eyes glazing over as she scrolled through website after website on her office computer. Lunch had been a mug of day-old coffee and a stale granola bar she had discovered in a desk drawer. She had canceled two other meetings and postponed a report as she fell farther down the rabbit hole of research she had tumbled into.

Robert Krum's organization, Health Now, was a thriving and expansive insurance company with divisions extending into a variety of market segments and research branches. From what she could tell, everything was done with the appropriate approvals and legal structures to be on the up and up, but she was a bit surprised—even with her background—to see just how wide-ranging its interests were. Through direct funding, partnerships, research facilities, donations, foreign branches, and subsidiaries, Health Now had interests in pharmaceuticals, surgical implants, prosthetics, tissue banks, medical equipment, and experimental procedures. And those were just the publicly disclosed facets.

What really felt off to her were the unstated connections, the picture that began to form as she read between the lines, following seemingly-former employees who worked in international research facilities; so-called third-world street clinics in hotspots of black-market organ trafficking activity; donations to groups supporting looser regulations of tissue sales and acquisitions; and on and on it went, though none of it could be definitively linked to the primary company. She began to feel dizzy, although the caffeine and lack of food likely helped.

Ellen scrolled through the contacts on her phone, considering. *He'll think I'm crazy. She'll blow me off. He won't get back to me for six months.* Finally she settled on a contact at the FBI, agent Lucy Brown. Ellen dialed and sat back in her chair, her foot twitching anxiously.

The FBI agent picked up on the second ring. "Lucy Brown."

"This is Ellen Blake, over at the FDA. I don't know if you recall, but we met at the—"

"I remember," Lucy cut in, friendly but impatient. "What can I do for you?"

Ellen took a deep breath, and then she launched into an overview of her meeting with Krum, his offer to support the research as a funding partner, her uneasy feeling, and the suspicious but not incriminating evidence she had uncovered on the computer. Lucy did not interrupt this time, letting Ellen air all of her concerns and reel off lists of the strange circumstances until she had run out of breath and words. Ellen trailed off, sure the other woman would tell her that it was all in her head.

Instead, Lucy spoke quietly, her words unhurried and firm. "Ellen, this is what you are going to do. You are going to proceed with Krum just as you discussed with him. You are not going to bring up any of your concerns. You will keep copious records of every interaction, including back-ups in a safe place. And you will not call me again, but will wait for me to contact you."

Ellen sat forward, unconsciously peering around to be sure her office door was closed. "You think I've discovered something."

"You didn't tell me anything I didn't already know," Lucy said.

Ellen paused as this sank in. "You've already been watching Krum, haven't you?"

"Thanks for the call. Just do your job, and trust us to do ours. Can you do that for me?"

"Of course." Before she could say anything else, the FBI agent had disconnected, and Ellen was back in the silence of her office. She sat motionless for several long minutes, holding her phone, staring fixedly at the headline on the screen in front of her, partially obscured by another open window.

JOHANNESBURG: CLAIMS OF FOUL PLAY AFTE DISASTER AT MEDTECH FACILITY KILLED RES

Ellen reached a decision. She placed another call. It almost went to voicemail, but he picked up at the last moment.

"Hello," he said.

"Dr. Konno, this is Ellen Blake with the FDA. I inspected your facility a couple of months ago."

"Yes, good to hear from you. How is D.C.?"

"Cold and miserable. What about Austin?"

"Eighty-five and sunny." He sounded tired, despite the good cheer. "To what do I owe this pleasure?"

A few seconds of silence passed as Ellen tried to form her words carefully, unable to shake the feeling that someday she might bé hearing them again in a courtroom. "Listen, Dr. Konno, I truly respect the work that you're doing. I want it to be accomplished and get to the people that need it." She hesitated again. "I can't give you specifics, but I'm worried that your research may be under threat. It puts you in a big league of players, and they don't all play by the rules."

"I appreciate the warning, but I'm not some first-year resident," Kim Konno said. "We have security protocols. We take precautions."

"I'm sure you do, but please take this seriously. Have back-up plans for your back-up plans. Be careful who you trust. And if you need help, know that you have friends in Washington."

"Thank you," Konno said. "I'll be sure to do just that."

An awkward silence followed, and then they exchanged good-byes and Ellen hung up. Recalling Agent Brown's directives, she set about drawing up the paperwork to legitimate her verbal agreement with Robert Krum, officially granting his company their discussed relationship with this new research. It was some time before her heart rate slowed, and before turning off her computer she cleared her browsing history and then deleted the memory cache. Paranoid or not, it was best to be safe.

Chapter Six

There were high points, of course—moments that made it all worthwhile.

When Dan stepped from the hall into Bessie Church's room, he was immediately struck by how strong and alert she seemed. It was a stark contrast to the frail, nervous figure she had been prior to her operation. He listened to her lungs and the prosthetic valve and inspected her chest wound. A review of her lab data showed everything was normal.

"You really look good," he told her. "You can go home tomorrow. Just please take life easy for a while."

Sitting up, she tilted her head in brief concern. "Can I feed my donkeys?"

Dan chuckled. "Sure. Is your son going to be here to take you home?"

"Yes, he takes good care of me. We'll go to the ranch and relax." She smiled. "You don't know what you're missing with the sunsets out there."

"No, I'm sure I don't. Rest up and take good care of your-self."

After leaving Bessie's room, Dan drew a list of patients from his pocket and saw a request for a consultation on a patient named Ted Gibbon. At the nurse's station he looked at the computer history of Mr. Gibbon and the results of his cardiac evaluation. Finding the correct room on the same floor, Dan walked in that direction, thinking about ranches, sunsets, and all the other things he didn't have time for. Could it be enough that people like Bessie lived to enjoy them? If he walked away from this life—or even slowed down—how much could he enjoy sitting on a porch and watching the sky, knowing what it would cost others?

There's a cost either way, he thought, his hand balling to a fist to rap on the door. Someone said to come in, and Dan entered and introduced himself to the couple in the room.

Ted Gibbon was slim, late thirties, with neatly-cropped brown hair beginning to recede. His wife, Julia, was attractive, modestly dressed, and visibly on edge. Over the years Dan had developed the ability to almost instantly assess which people would "pose a greater challenge," as he had diplomatically put it to Holly ("You mean, 'be a pain in the neck,'" she had replied). He tried to tell himself not to judge people on first impressions. But honestly, this sense was rarely wrong.

"Mr. and Mrs. Gibbon," he said, "your cardiologist asked me to see you because of a heart problem. Mr. Gibbon, you need a double valve replacement. You have severe mitral stenosis and stenosis of the aortic valve. The mitral valve is between the upper and lower chambers on the left side and the aortic valve is at the outflow of the left side."

When they both stared at him as if he was speaking Greek, Dan felt it wise to get right to the point. "The valves need to be replaced with artificial valves." He took a moment to let that sink in; Ted nodded agreeably, but the color was draining from Julia's face as he continued. "We can use either tissue valves or mechanical valves, each having certain advantages and disadvantages. And you need to know that there is risk with an operation of this magnitude."

"I don't know anything about heart anatomy or medicine," said Julia, "so I can't ask good questions. Only one thing is important. We are Jehovah's Witnesses, and my husband must not receive any blood. You must understand and agree to that."

Dan looked from the woman to her husband and back. "Do you know that in order to stop and operate on his heart, we have to continuously drain his blood out of his body into the heart-lung machine, oxygenate it, and then pump it back into him?"

"Yes, but that is a closed circuit, and we accept that." Julia stepped over and placed her hand on her husband's arm. "Dr. Parker, we asked, and we know you've operated on other Jehovah's. But many surgeons and even anesthesiologists have refused because they think they'll get sued if they give blood. A lot of people don't understand, but it's very simple. If my husband gets blood he'll be shunned by the church and its members, and we believe he will not go to heaven when he dies."

Dan nodded, listening, but before responding he looked back to the husband. Ted appeared resolute—the expression of a man determined to survive a challenge. Sure enough, when he spoke, his words were low but firm. "Dr. Parker, I'm honestly more concerned about the dying part."

"Ted—" Julia started.

"No, listen, it's my turn. I've had friends that refused blood and the surgeon just let them die. I want to live."

Tears welled in his wife's eyes. "Of course I want you to live, too. You think I don't? But there's usually other medical options, and there aren't any shades of grey on this. You know that."

Silence settled heavily in the room. Finally Dan spoke. "It's my job to help and save people in my care. I only give blood as the last resort if I have no other choice. Almost always I can get by without giving blood, but I cannot just stand there and have a patient die. You can choose another surgeon if you wish."

Julia glanced at her husband, but he shook his head. "Dr. Parker is my choice, and I have faith in his judgment."

"You just can't," Julia said quietly, reaching to swipe her eyes clear. Then, with a stubborn set to her jaw, she added, "He hasn't asked for it, Dr. Parker. He hasn't approved a transfusion."

Dan looked to Ted Gibbon. The man met his eyes resolutely. "I want to live," Ted said. "I hope you understand." Dan thought that he did, and Julia apparently did, too. She turned away from her husband, facing the window, her arms wrapped tightly around herself.

"I recommend mechanical valves because they last much longer than tissue valves," Dan said. "And because I see you have chronic atrial fibrillation, you'll have to take anticoagulants anyway." When Ted nodded, Dan continued. "I can get you on the operating schedule tomorrow, unless you need more time to talk about it."

Ted looked to Julia. Sensing his eyes on her, she muttered, "No, I guess there's nothing more to talk about."

"If you have other questions, have the nurse on this floor call me." When neither said anything else, he slowly walked out of the room. In the hallway, he looked at his watch—not even seven o'clock yet. It was going to be a long day.

* * *

By late afternoon, the tension that began as a tight knot at the base of Dan's neck had spread down to his shoulders. He found himself responding tersely to even the mildest questions. When he barked at Holly for not administering heparin fast enough for his liking, she told him in graphic terms where he was welcome to stick it instead.

And Dr. Shaw, the Chief Medical Officer, still wanted to meet with him today. This could not be good news.

On his way to the coronary care unit, Dan took a call from Dr. Garcia, a cardiologist who wanted Dan to see a patient with preinfarction angina, needing a bypass to his left anterior descending coronary artery and repair of a leaking mitral valve. The interesting part was that this patient had been transferred from prison for his medical care. Dan went to review the patient's history before going to speak with him.

In the prisoner's room, Dan found him restrained by leather straps on his wrists and ankles. Two stout, no-nonsense guards stood near him, each with a holstered .357 magnum. The prisoner was extremely overweight with expansive tattoos covering his arms and chest. His face bore long, straight scars, which Dan assumed were from knife fights.

"Mr. Anchiono, I'm Dr. Parker. I was asked to see you because you have some serious heart problems. An artery on the front of your heart is nearly blocked and a valve is leaking. I'm a surgeon, and I can bypass the blocked artery and repair the leaking valve."

Mr. Anchiono answered in a gruff voice. "What's my chances?"

"With an operation, you have a good chance of being well for many years. Without it you'll get sicker and may die. The operation carries a three percent risk, but I can't guarantee that you won't have a serious complication." Dan paused, stepping nearer, and noted that one of the guards shifted to place himself closer to the two of them. "Mr. Anchiono, I've reviewed your medical history, and you are grossly overweight, have high blood pressure, diabetes, and high cholesterol. You also have a history of heavy smoking. Three packs a day for thirty years are not without consequences."

"You trying to tell me this is my fault?" he replied. Though his voice was calm, the threat behind his eyes made Dan grateful for the restraints.

"I'm telling you that these factors increase your operative risk," he said. "I can't change that."

"Let's be clear," Anchiono said evenly. "Getting me through this is on you, Doc, not me. And I suggest you work carefully because I have some friends who may take it personally if I die on the table. We understand each other?"

Dan closed the remaining distance until they were face to face, ignoring the guards' discomfort and the hand one of them placed on his shoulder. "I do the best I can for every patient, whatever terrible choices he has made with his own life or even the lives of others, and not because I've been bullied into it. But if you don't want the operation, fine by me. I'll tell these guards to take you back to prison today."

For a moment, Anchiono fixed him with a cold stare. Then he made a sound between a laugh and a snort. "Doesn't sound like much of a choice, does it? Sign me up."

"Fine," Dan said. "I'll put you on the schedule for tomorrow. Try to stay out of trouble 'til then."

Dan left the room. Down the hallway, a man with a shaved

head and a stubbly beard immediately rose from a chair and strode right towards him. He was muscular, tattooed, and angry.

"You the guy that's going to cut open my brother?"

Dan bristled, and though he knew he should handle it differently, he did not alter his own course. "Sure am. Step aside."

"Anything happens to him," the man said, "and you answer for it." The man squared off, clearly expecting Dan to move to the side, but he didn't—and they knocked roughly together as Dan shouldered past. The man grabbed his arm, but before he could utter another word Dan had broken the hold and slammed the larger man up against the wall. Behind him, he heard someone shout for security.

"You listen to me," Dan growled. "I didn't give him high blood pressure or diabetes. I didn't make him fat or make him smoke for thirty years. I didn't put him in prison. I will do the best I can and that is all I can do. If you can't accept that, you can find another surgeon dumb enough to operate on him, which you won't find, so he can go back to prison and die."

Dan realized that his hand, clutching a fistful of the man's collar, was pushing him against the wall hard enough to impede his air supply, and Dan eased off as he heard security coming down the hallway. As the man's torso came away from the wall, Dan saw that the framed painting behind him had a crack across the glass now.

"Get him out of here," Dan said to the approaching security officer. He turned and walked away before the officer reached them, the other man staring after him and rubbing his throat.

* * *

Dr. Golden Shaw was a retired orthopedic surgeon who had been a professor of orthopedic surgery at a large university in New York City. He had decided to retire to an area free of smog, with wide-open spaces where skyscrapers didn't block the view. Now the Chief of Medical Affairs at Amarillo Medical Center, he was a tall, gray-haired, generally pleasant man who got along well with nearly everyone.

Nearly.

Dan walked up several flights of stairs to the administrative area, trying not to think too much about what he was about to hear, and found Dr. Shaw's office. He knocked on the open door and then walked in.

"Hello, Dr. Parker," Shaw said, the formal address setting an unpleasant tone for the meeting. "Have a seat."

Dan sat in a large leather chair across from the Chief's massive oak desk. Multiple framed diplomas hung behind Shaw, and the walls were crammed with bookshelves of medical texts. His desk was covered with papers, but neatly organized into stacks.

"Did you assault a visitor in the hallway today?" Shaw demanded.

So much for small talk. "It was self defense. He moved on me first."

"You realize we're here to perform medical procedures," Shaw continued. "Not to judge people's choices. Not to provoke patients or visitors. You know this, don't you?"

"Mr. Anchiono's *choice* was to murder five people, from what I've heard. But yes, I realize. And I intend to operate at the same level I always do."

"The same you always do," Shaw repeated. "Maybe that's the problem."

Dan had been leaning forward, and he forced himself to sit

back, to relax his hands on the chair's armrests. "Is my ability being questioned?"

"Your decisions are. Just last week you gave a patient stem cells during his operation, and then—"

"Stem cell implants into the myocardium have been FDA approved," Dan cut in.

"But not by the executive committee of this hospital!" Shaw put his elbows on the table and began jabbing a finger toward Dan with each accusation. "You gave another patient uncrossed matched blood drawn from her son. This blood did *not* go to the blood bank for testing and evaluation. You did an aortic valve replacement on a minor without consent from his parents. The list goes on. There are complaints about your professional conduct in and out of the OR, both with your colleagues and the way you talk to patients and their families. Do you want me to continue?"

"Who's making complaints?" Dan asked, his heart speeding up.

"I'm not allowed to tell you that."

Dan willed himself to be calm. "Dr. Shaw, please listen to me. I know you came here from a huge medical center with lots of staff. You had high-powered programs with fellows and residents. But here, it's different. I take complete care of my patients. I do the admission history and physicals, all my own operations, dictate the operative notes and also the discharge summaries. I make rounds two or three times a day." He drew a long breath. "I think human life is God given, and it is my job to help and save life to the best of my ability. Everything I do is with that in mind, even if it doesn't follow some stupid regulations."

Something he said had touched a nerve—and not in a good

THE OTHER SIDE OF THE KNIFE

way. Dan could tell by the chief's clenched jaw, the way he folded his hands and spoke low and measured. "That's a nice little sentiment. But you know what I think? I think just because you fancy yourself a West Texas cowboy you have little regard for the rules. Chest surgeons think they're bulletproof, and you're worse than most. You think you're God's gift to surgery and can do anything you want. But here's the catch—you can't."

"I don't think I'm God's gift to surgery. And I'm not going to apologize for saving lives."

"You don't have to apologize," Shaw replied. "You just have to find another hospital, if you keep this up. That's if another will even have you."

Dan could not find a response. Shaw pointed at the door. "Go on. But you are on thin ice, and if you break through you will find out just how cold it is on the other side."

Dan stood and walked out of the office without another word. As he walked down the flights of stairs, plenty of responses swirled through his head that he wished he had the opportunity to give.

I didn't become a surgeon just to let bureaucracy get in the way of caring for people. Shaw probably would have had a ready response for that, too. It had only gotten worse in recent years. The government and hospital red tape showed a total disregard for the physicians actually doing patient care, as Dan saw it. It was no wonder that fewer intelligent young people were choosing to enter medicine.

They were the smart ones, Dan thought. *No one in the medical profession who's interested in a patient's life, not death, has adequately reviewed his charts.*

Chapter Seven

The operating room was quiet, save for the calming notes of Mendelssohn's violin concerto Dan had selected, and all eyes were on him. Sometimes it felt like the expectant hush preceding a stage performance—that buzzing sense of anticipation before the curtain rises, the spotlight prepared to glare down on him alone. Another show about to begin.

Mr. Anchiono had surely been cut plenty of times over his life, but this time he felt nothing. Dan made four small incisions in the left chest and inserted a camera and instruments connected to the arms of the da Vinci, a robotic surgical system designed for complex, minimally invasive surgery. Dan could control it while seated at a nearby console. He took a seat at this console and began moving small handles and turning knobs, deftly manipulating the instruments now inside the prisoner's chest. He dissected down the internal mammary artery, and after opening the pericardium, he found the left anterior descending coronary artery. The da Vinci really was a marvel—it allowed him to carry out the operation with the same precision as if his hands were holding the instruments. Still, it required the utmost care and concentration.

With the man's heart still beating, Dan skillfully sutured the internal mammary artery to the mid portion of the left anterior descending coronary artery. Next, he stood and moved to the patient's side again, where he dissected out the left femoral artery and vein, inserted cannulas, and connected them to the lines from the heart-lung machine. Dan removed the instruments from the patient's left chest, and the first phase was complete.

"So far, so good," he said, more to break the silence than anything.

"Famous last words," Holly added dryly, but he could hear the smile in her voice.

Switching to the patient's other side, Dan made two incisions in the right chest by hand. The nurse attached the robotic arms to fresh, sterile instruments and a camera, and the perfusionist, Viola, placed Mr. Anchiono on bypass. Sitting again at the console, Dan observed the operation on the video remote screen and watched the motions of the robot arms as he controlled them. He occasionally moved the remote camera for visualization in a specific area. As with other operations, he had to be sure each movement was exact; he could not afford any mistakes. If one occurred, he would have to convert the operation to an open procedure by surgically opening the chest.

As Dan operated the da Vinci, the mitral valve—situated between the left atrium and left ventricle of the heart—was repaired by inserting a perfect artificial ring to decrease the size of the annulus, the supporting ring of tissue for the mitral valve between the atrium and ventricle. Testing showed the repair perfect, no evidence of leaking.

"Here we go," Dan said. "No complications yet."

"Still," Holly said thoughtfully, "if he survives, maybe we

should see if this big guy wants to do some anti-smoking commercials."

"Cute."

After the heart was restarted, Viola brought the patient off bypass. Transesophageal echo showed the valve to be competent, indicating an excellent repair. Dan removed all the robotic instruments and closed the small incisions. The total operative time had been two hours and forty minutes.

Dan walked to the surgical waiting room where some thirty people were waiting, including journalists interested in either Mr. Anchiono or the use of the da Vinci system. He addressed the group and explained the operation, before answering questions carefully and as completely as possible using simple, non-medical terms. After heading back to the SICU, he was pleased to see his patient waking up with normal vital signs and no post-op bleeding. He noticed two new guards were in the room and that Mr. Anchiono's wrists and ankles were secured again with leather straps.

"Are these restraints really necessary?" he asked one of the guards.

"Yes, they are," came the quick answer. "He has a history of violence."

"He's also my patient. And it's very important that he doesn't stay strapped to a bed. He needs to sit up in a chair, and he'll need to walk with help. I don't think he'll get far with two armed guards watching him."

The guards nodded but did not respond. One of the nurses, overhearing, said she would get physical therapy to help with ambulation.

"It shouldn't be for long," Dan said to the guards. "If he

continues to improve, he can be discharged in two days. You can go ahead and make arrangements for his transfer back to prison."

"Yes, sir," a guard said.

Dan glanced at the patient and found Mr. Anchiono eyeing him with no gratitude or even friendliness visible. The look was cold and distant. Rather than trusting what would come out of his own mouth if he stayed, Dan left the room.

* * *

Two hours later, Dan was operating again, this time on Ted Gibbon, the Jehovah's Witness. There were no expected complications, but Dan had learned not to rely on that wholly unreliable sense of security. After he opened Ted's chest and placed him on cardiopulmonary bypass, the heart's size and condition were instant red flags to anyone looking; he badly needed this operation.

"His heart is huge," Holly said.

Dan cooled the heart with cold cardioplegia. "He has a lot of damage with the valves getting worse for so many years." As he opened the upper left chamber of the heart to surgically remove the mitral valve, it happened—one of those moments every surgeon dreads. Viola began shouting: "I've got trouble! The oxygenator is leaking blood all over the place!"

Dan immediately stopped the operation and turned to see blood pouring out the bottom of the oxygenator onto the operating room floor. "What's causing it?"

"I don't know. It must have been damaged in shipping. Losing volume!"

"Put bone wax on the leak and cool as much as you can!" Dan shouted back. The blood was continuing to drip and splash, coating the floor like the set of some horror movie. Viola rubbed bone wax on the bottom of the oxygenator and turned the heat exchanger on maximum cold, which cooled the blood being pumped into Ted.

"Watch his core temp, when it gets to twenty degrees shut off the pump and exchange the oxygenator for a new one," Dan ordered. He had only contemplated his words for a moment before reaching the decision. "He might have crossed matched blood in the blood bank. How long will it take you to do the exchange?"

Viola had calmed herself. "Just a few minutes. I should have enough time if he is cool."

At very cold temperature, with the circulation stopped under controlled conditions, a person could survive thirty minutes with no damage to the brain or other organs. Dan had done it before and heard of other cases; in fact, hypothermia and circulatory arrest was a common procedure for resection of aortic arch aneurysms and also in pediatric heart surgery. With the pump off, Dan waited, and he looked over to see Holly watching him, eyes wide above her mask.

"Dan," she began, using the tone for talking someone down from a ledge, "isn't he a Jehovah's Witness?"

"He wants to live."

"But did he specifically approve—"

"He wants to live," Dan repeated, and Holly let it drop.

After the pump had been off for ten minutes, the reservoir was almost empty. Sweat had begun to trickle down Dan's back. Then the circulating nurse hurried in, bringing the new oxygenator from the equipment room.

Viola exchanged the new oxygenator for the damaged one, and as she was making the switch a technician rushed in with four units of packed red blood cells. Dan turned back to his patient and resumed his work. Viola took the blood cell units and added them for volume to the pump along with 500cc of D5W, a mixture of 5 percent dextrose in water. The new units of blood and D5W filled the pump sufficiently for it to start again. While they were working, Dan removed the diseased valve with scissors and scalpel, measured the size of the valve opening, and nearly had a new prosthetic valve sutured in place. Viola started reperfusion—starting the pump again to pump blood into the patient—and core warming, turning the heat exchanger on to warm the blood and warm the patient in the process. As the patient's core temperature rose back to a normal range, Dan finished replacing the aortic valve and closed the chest incision.

"Another successful operation," Holly said. "God help us."

Ted Gibbon was moved to the surgical intensive care unit, and Dan went to the surgical waiting room to discuss the operation with the patient's wife. He found her perched on the edge of a chair, arms wrapped around herself, face pale. She jumped up the moment he entered the room.

"How is he doing?" Her voice was far too loud for the small space.

"Very well." Dan smiled. He was about to continue, but she was already retreating and refusing eye contact.

"That's all I want to know," she said. She sat on the chair again and looked away, a clear dismissal.

"You can see him in about twenty minutes," Dan said. "A nurse will come and get you."

She nodded to show she had heard but said nothing else, though her lips were moving—praying, perhaps. She didn't ask about blood, he knew, because she was afraid of the answer. But at least her husband would be coming home. Dan knew how differently this conversation could have gone—the traumatic news, the sudden silence, the grief, the tears, the anger and blame, the shouts, the denial, the sudden void that disrupts every semblance of life as it was. It was horrific, tragic in every sense. And he had been through it far too many times.

* * *

It took less than an hour for Dan to be called to Dr. Shaw's office again. He had been expecting the summons and honestly would have been surprised if it had not come. He still had ten minutes until the requested meeting—it was not really a request, he knew —and chose to spend them in the doctor's lounge.

Holly found him there, nursing a cup of coffee that was not nearly as strong as the occasion warranted. She snagged a water bottle from the fridge and leaned her back against the counter, crossing her feet at the ankles and watching him as she sipped from it. A good three minutes passed before she broke the silence.

"I've been thinking about that 'caboose' trophy you got for last place in that charity golf game we did," she said.

Dan stared blankly at her, not seeing the relevance to anything.

"Well, if you get your privileges revoked, you'll have a lot more time to work on your swing."

Dan couldn't help a chuckle, although the very thought of losing his privileges made him want to clutch his stomach. "Good to see you're finding a bright side."

"I try." She stepped over and sat at the table across from him, her smile fading. "But sometimes, you know, there is no bright side. No good solution. Not for us, not for our patients. Sometimes there's just no answer, and we have to learn to live with that."

"I'm well aware." He paused. "But there's a difference between no good solution, and no good solutions that I'm allowed to pursue."

"But it's not your decision." She did not sound accusing, only sincere, and she leaned across the table as if she might take his hand. "It's not even your fight. So why do you push so hard? Why do you take these risks, when you don't even know these people?"

"Because they *are* complete strangers," Dan said, his voice quickly rising. "When I introduce myself to someone that I don't know and who doesn't know me, and I tell them I want to cut open their chest... to stop their heart, operate on it, and then put them back together, and then they say, 'Do it,' they are showing faith in me. Trust in me. They know their life will be literally in my hands, and they are willing to make that commitment. That takes unbelievable courage."

Holly listened, without interruption, and let his words hang in the air for a moment before she brushed a strand of her hair back from her face and sighed. "I don't know if you heard about this, but several days ago this kid came into the ICU, seventeen years old, had suffered an accidental gunshot to the head while hunting. No brain function, I mean, it was obvious—most of his brain was downright gone. You know what his parents did? They decided to donate his organs, all of them. So last night a transplant harvest team flew in and took that boy's corneas, heart, lungs, trachea, liver, both kidneys, and bone marrow... even sheets of skin." She sat up straighter. "That takes unbelievable courage, too. To know when to say goodbye, accept loss, and do it with grace."

Holly stood, but Dan reached out and caught her wrist as she passed. "They didn't just accept loss, Holly. They were willing to sacrifice, to pay a personal cost, so that other people would live."

For a moment, he thought she would argue with him, perhaps pull her arm free from his hand. Instead she leaned over and put her other arm around him, giving a quick and uncharacteristic squeeze of his shoulders before withdrawing. Her words drifted to him from the doorway.

"Good luck in there, Superman."

* * *

Dr. Golden Shaw did not appear upset. When Dan entered his office, he found the Chief of Medical Affairs to be calm, quietly reading a report on his desk, and Shaw gestured for Dan to have a seat as he finished. Dan did, and Shaw scanned the final sentences before looking up, his tone all business.

"Dr. Parker, I am placing you under review and on probation because of recent issues. Some of these we discussed yesterday, while others occurred today."

Although he had half-expected it, Dan still found it difficult to draw breath enough to respond. "I have only acted in the best interests of my patients."

"Your intentions and interests are not the subject of my concern. What does concern me is a surgeon who operates on a Jehovah's Witness and places him on cardiopulmonary bypass using a defective oxygenator, and then gives him blood without express consent."

"He told me he wanted to live," Dan said.

"Of course he said he wants to live!" Shaw shouted, losing his composure and half-rising from his chair. "How many tell you they want to die? That doesn't mean you got consent to give blood, which means you've willfully opened not just yourself but this hospital to a massive lawsuit."

Dan tried to formulate a response, a defense that would satisfy Shaw, but all of his arguments—his ethics, drive, tenets, motivations—would be cut down, with little bearing on regulations and litigation. *Lines in the sand are for philosophers, not surgeons*, Shaw had said once.

"You will be requested to appear before a special committee in two weeks to answer the charges and evaluate your fitness to retain privileges at this hospital," Shaw said. "I'm delaying your probation one week so you can get your affairs in order."

"This is a mistake," Dan said.

Shaw waved toward the door. "You're dismissed."

* * *

The trip down the stairs seemed to take a lot longer than usual, his shoes feeling weighted with lead. As he left the stairwell and started down a hallway, his phone rang.

"This is Dan Parker."

"This is Tony Hernandez in the ER. I just wanted to tell you about one of your patients, Mr. Anchiono. He was brought to the ER ten minutes ago DOA. Thought you'd want to know." A small pause, a breath, some shuffling noises in the background. "All I can tell so far is that he tried to attack one of the guards while they were walking the hall, and the other guard shot him twice. Nothing we could do."

"Right," Dan said, and then didn't know what else to say. "Thanks for the call."

Dan hung up and sank onto a nearby chair. He found himself with his head in his hands, eyes closed, while the sounds of the hospital went on around him, seeming to come from far away. Somewhere close by, the guards were being checked out and then sent back to the prison. The ER staff were filling out forms. The prisoner was on his way to the morgue. One moment of terrible judgment undoing everything else. What had been the point of any of it?

Chapter Eight

Ultimately, it was the smile that convinced Kim. Not the warning call from the FDA inspector, not the threats from Bruce Walters, that aggressive anesthesiologist he had fired, and not his own growing concern with the inevitable attention this world-changing research would attract. It was a smile.

This morning, Kim had been working in his office and had reached for a flash drive on his desk, in a small basket where he kept them. There were three, though he expected four—he had purchased a pack of them just last week to fill with data. Surely it was unlikely that anyone would have found a way into his office, and even more unlikely that someone would have stolen from him. And yet.

On the way out the door two days ago, escorted by security personnel who had already revoked his access and would change all the codes within minutes, Bruce had given Kim an inexplicable smile, one that chilled him. Kim hadn't been able to shake it for days, despite the fact that everything seemed secure and was proceeding on schedule; morale had even improved without Bruce's derisive comments. But now, as he stood in the east wing overlooking the horse stalls, Kim knew the smile for what it was: a sign of trouble.

"Good morning," the veterinarian said, in the process of inspecting the hoof of a roan mare that stood patiently, whickering when Kim appeared.

"Morning, John. Everything look good?"

"Mostly. Some bad breath, might be a sign of a developing tooth infection. Looks okay, but I'll keep an eye on her."

Signs of trouble. Wasn't it what they all were watching for, whether examining a horse or implanting a heart? Those tiny, telltale hints that all was not well. Kim continued down the row of stalls, noting the charts, checking that each animal was healthy. The thing was, everything could seem to be fine, and only a small indication would reveal that it all was about to fall apart. You had to trust your instincts.

The call, the threats, the missing flash drive, the smile. The signs couldn't be ignored. Kim turned and walked back down the row to the veterinarian, who was filling out a chart as the mare chuffed into her food bin, munching on oats.

"John, change of plans," Kim said. "I want you to supervise getting the animals ready for transport."

"Which ones?"

"All of them."

The vet's eyes widened. "When?"

Kim headed for the door. "Now."

* * *

In Amarillo, Dan Parker carried suitcases out to the driveway with a heaviness that had nothing to do with the three dozen outfits that his wife and daughter had packed. A big part of him wanted to say *Screw it*, to grab a change of clothes and a razor, jump in the car with them, and light out for San Antonio and a high school volleyball tournament. What would he face if he stayed here? A week of "getting his affairs in order," as Dr. Shaw had put it, and then dealing with a committee that would determine the future of his career—or whether it had a future at all.

Or he could spend time with his wife, reconnect with his daughter, and enjoy margaritas on the Riverwalk. If only that was a viable option. It didn't seem fair... any of it.

"You should do something fun today," Laura said, stepping off the porch with a travel pillow in one hand and a shopping bag full of snacks in the other. Marla's favorites, probably; Dan had no idea what she liked. "Go see a movie or something."

"Yeah, maybe so."

Dan had a rare day off, although he knew from experience that his "free time" could be cut short with a phone call at any moment. It was not nearly enough time to travel to San Antonio —just enough to make him feel guilty for standing around while his family left without him.

"I'll take pictures," Laura added, putting her things in the car. Rather than bitterness, her voice held a resigned calm that he knew was worse. She had given up on things being different. "And I'll text you updates about the games."

"Thanks," he said. "Maybe I can talk to her after them."

"Sure, if you're not in the OR." She pulled a CD wallet from the floorboard, flipped through it, and selected music for the drive with confidence. Leaning over, she cranked the engine and slid the CD into the stereo, which began to belt out the pulsing rhythm of some high-energy pop song Dan had never heard.

On cue, Marla emerged from their house with a gym bag over

one shoulder and her phone in her hand. With features like her mother in miniature, she had her brown hair pulled back in a ponytail and her blue eyes were fixed on the screen in her palm. She smiled at something, dropped her phone in her pocket, and headed for the car.

Dan had not told either of them about what had happened at work: the meeting with Dr. Shaw, the ultimatum, the upcoming probation, the scheduled committee meeting. The possibility of losing his hospital privileges. It was too much, too big, and he could not bring himself to speak the words right before they left —for what if they never came back?

"Be safe," he told them. "And let me know if you have any trouble on the road."

"We'll be fine, Dad," Marla said. She gave him a one-armed, sideways hug, but she was already checking something on her phone before he could hug her back. "Wish you could make it."

"Me too, kiddo." He watched her sling her gym bag into the backseat and then slide behind the wheel. She slipped on sunglasses, adjusted the mirror, and faced forward, already distant.

Laura's arms slid around him, and he held her, letting his breath out, wishing there were words—any words—that would help. None came. She gave him a chaste kiss on the cheek, nodded once as if something were settled, and climbed into the car.

"I'll let you know when we've made it there," she said through the open window. "Enjoy your day off."

"Sure." He shut their trunk, rapped his hand on it twice, and stepped to the side. "Have a fun trip."

Marla shifted into reverse and backed the car down the driveway, reaching over to turn up the music as soon as the tires touched the street. Her mother said something to her that Dan couldn't hear, and already they both were laughing, Laura slipping on shades that matched her daughter's, the road trip officially begun. They remembered to wave when they were three houses down the block, Laura briefly turning to watch him through the back window, Marla's hand sticking out and giving two quick waves before drawing back in.

He waved until they were out of sight, and then he stood there, watching the corner they had disappeared around, wondering what to do now. There was absolutely nothing he could think of that he wanted to do today.

Dan was still standing there when his phone rang, and he pulled it out to see the caller was Kim Konno—that old friend who had said he was working on something big. Dan answered, and an hour later he was flying his Beech Baron toward Austin.

* * *

"You know, I've always envied the freedom you have," Kim said, arm around Dan's shoulders as they strolled down the corridors of Worldwide Medical Research. "Your own plane, the skill to use it, the chance to go wheels up anytime you like and head wherever you want."

Dan couldn't suppress a snort. "Sure, once in a blue moon when I can actually get away long enough to use it, it's great."

"You don't still use the Baron for family trips?"

"Not for a few years now. She still handles like a charm, though."

They had already toured the east wing, which was in the process of moving out the animals to an unidentified ranch; the north wing, which held the operating rooms and intensive care units; and part of the biochemical research center in the west wing. They were currently on the third floor, which handled the manufacture of experimental units. It was all undeniably impress-ive—Dan could scarcely guess the cost of such a place, or the ongoing demands of labor and resources needed to secure the medical progress he was witnessing. Everything was polished, organized, gleaming silver or white, and all the staff were friendly but intensely focused on their work. As Kim had explained, they were in single-minded pursuit of the Holy Grail of cardiovascular surgery: fully implantable artificial hearts.

But even seeing the ongoing research up close, Dan was finding it difficult to believe that the goal was actually within their grasp. Scientists had been trying to make perfect artificial hearts since the 1930s, without success. So far in modern research there had been no satisfactory artificial endocardium, the lining of a real heart. And even if they surpassed that barrier, no one had developed a self-contained power source that actually mimicked the smooth contractility of a real heart, rather than using forceful mechanical contractions in designs that looked like they belonged in a car engine, not a human being. Some devices required carry-ing a battery pack day and night. There were endless hurdles to overcome for a solution that would come remotely close to the efficiency of a real heart.

"You didn't call me down here to talk about my plane," Dan said. "The tour has been amazing, and I hope you succeed, I really do, but...." He trailed off, helplessly shrugging his shoul-ders, unsure what else to say.

"You don't think it's possible," Kim said.

Dan uncrossed his arms, realizing how skeptical he looked. "You'd be doing what no one else has been able to. What science has dreamed of for centuries."

Kim beckoned him over to a couple of chairs, and they sat. After a moment of gathering his thoughts, Kim broke into a smile as he spoke—his voice tinged with the pride he could not quite conceal from his friend.

"The lining is exactly like endocardium," Kim began. "It's smooth, non-wettable, elastic. The interior is better than real endocardium. The aortic, mitral, tricuspid, and pulmonary valves are of the same stuff. We've been in the process of making artificial blood vessels. Think how easy a coronary bypass operation would be if you had small, perfect synthetic vessels."

Dan took too long to respond, and Kim shook his head, as if clearing his thoughts to get back on track. "Anyway, the contractility is done by programed nanobots that can work in perfect synchronicity and can reproduce themselves when necessary. There are special sensors that relay impulses from the main micro-computer driving the electrical system, which drive the nanobots to achieve perfect volume and speed of contractility. The sensors monitor and determine blood pressure, ventricular stroke volume, cardiac rate, pulmonary artery pressure, arterial oxygen saturation, and several more parameters. The unit is exactly the size of a human heart, easy to implant, just like a heart transplant."

"Wait. Hold up a minute." Dan realized he was leaning forward in his chair. "You're talking about this like you've already done it."

Kim grinned. "I've implanted them in dogs, pigs, cows, and horses. All recently and without complication."

Dan fell back in his chair, putting a hand to his forehead. "That's... unbelievable."

"I didn't do it alone. There were the best PhDs I could find working on all aspects of the research."

"I always knew you were a genius," Dan said. "But this, this is something else entirely. This will change, well—"

"The world?" Kim did not sound boastful; if anything, his tone matched the anxiety that was back on his face.

"Yeah. Pretty much." Dan sat forward again, hands folded, watching his friend intently. "How much did it cost to develop, and what would it cost to manufacture the hearts on a production basis?"

"Eight years and two-and-a-half billion dollars to develop. Production cost, probably about half a million each."

"Worth every penny. Can you imagine how many people there are around the world with heart problems, who are healthy otherwise but have no chance of survival? All the people waiting on transplant lists. All those struggling with transplant rejection." Dan forced himself to talk more slowly, to take a breath. "Kim, whoever controls this… I mean, it's like nothing else."

Kim nodded, and for a long moment they sat in silence as Dan's brain spun in mental circles over the possibilities. Kim eventually rose and gestured for Dan to follow him, and he led Dan down more sterile hallways smelling faintly of lemon and bleach.

After several minutes they reached Kim's office at the rear-most part of the west wing. Once they were inside, with the door closed and locked behind them, Kim seemed to lower his guard and reveal how tired and worried he was; his shoulders slumped, his breath came out in a low sigh, and without its smile his face looked drawn and weary. It was probably, Dan thought, about how he looked himself, despite his excitement about the artificial heart.

"I want you to take these," Kim said, passing three flash

drives to Dan. "And these." He gestured to two large black duffel bags on the floor, the zippers open and revealing stacked silver cases inside.

"What's in them?" Dan asked.

"I think you know," Kim said. "Keep the cases somewhere secure."

Dan searched his friend's face. "I don't understand."

"It's probably nothing. I don't want to say a lot. Just a precaution."

Despite the calm words, there was a slight tremor to the hands of a skilled surgeon who had never, in Dan's experience, flinched at anything in his life. Even with his pride of accomplishment, the man was deeply worried about something, maybe even scared.

"Are you giving me the prototypes?" Dan asked. "Why on earth would you do that?"

"Please, just humor me, for old time's sake if nothing else," Kim said. He zipped up the bags, hefted one to his own shoulder, and looked at Dan. After a long moment, Dan lifted the other bag. Kim unlocked the door and checked that the corridor beyond was clear before leading Dan toward a little-used stairwell.

"I can help you get these out without being seen," Kim said. "And I'll be in touch soon about getting them back."

"This is crazy," Dan said, shaking his head. "Why can't they stay here?"

"You think I'm being paranoid," Kim said, placing a hand on Dan's shoulder. "But ask yourself—what do you think people would do to get their hands on these?"

Dan had no answer.

* * *

At Bergstrom Airport, Dan performed his typical, careful pre-flight walk-around exam of the plane: checking oil and fuel levels, tire inflation, clean windshield, ailerons and flaps, rudder and elevator. It was a sleek, red and white, twin-engine Beech Baron, and despite the fact he had little chance to fly it these days, he kept it in good working condition—if not the pristine quality it had once displayed. He stowed the bags from Kim and climbed in.

After placing his cell phone and billfold in the seat next to him, he checked the weather forecast on his laptop. The skies were clear, with little wind. Good; Dan wasn't in the mood to deal with inclement weather. He fastened the seat and shoulder safety belts, ran the engine start checklist, and turned the ignition switches for the left and then right engine. They started in sequence. After engine check, radio check, and takeoff checklist, and clearance to taxi to runway one seven left, he heard from the tower: "Baron 68 Juliet, cleared for takeoff on one seven left."

Dan pushed in the throttles and the engines revved up to full power. The plane accelerated down the runway, and Dan eased back on the wheel, feeling a smooth, hardly perceptible separation from the land as the plane became airborne. He loved this moment, that instant when the earth no longer took hold.

The landing gear was raised and the props and mixtures adjusted. The Baron headed northwest to 81XA, the identifier for River Falls Airport on the south edge of Amarillo, and the Garmin GPS with synthetic vision and terrain warning showed the way ahead. Once the Baron rose to twelve thousand five hundred feet, Dan set it on autopilot and allowed his mind to relax and attempt to process what had just happened.

Kim Konno had been spooked. There was no denying it. This

was a man not given to overreaction, nor false claims. He didn't get unnerved easily and he was not one to daydream or fret.

"Things are what they are," Dan said aloud, one of Kim's common phrases. Not as one hoped—or feared—them to be. Probably a good approach for Dan to adopt himself when it came to the situation with the hospital. But if Kim was not over-reacting, what had him so shaken?

And what would it mean for Dan, transporting these bags back home, with the earth-shaking innovations they contained?

Chapter Nine

He was determined to stay until the last animal left. For hours the pigs, sheep, and horses had been prepped for transport, led down to the loading docks on the side of the building near the staff parking lot, and carefully placed into the trucks and trailers that would carry them to the south Texas ranch where, at least for the time being, they would remain. Kim Konno watched as some of the animals gave their handlers a bit of difficulty—a mare balking at the ramp leading up to the horse trailer, skittishly prancing sideways at the unfamiliar sight; a pair of black-faced ewes protesting with loud bleats as they were piled in with the other sheep; a pig squealing when the handler put it down. The animals had grown accustomed to life in the research hospital, comfortable with their stalls and pens, and who could blame them for their anxiety? Change was hard, even when it was for the best. Soon they would have acres of open land upon which to run, roam, and graze, more than most of the animals had ever seen.

They would thrive on the ranch, he was confident. They were strong, energetic, and hardy. Watching them, Kim could find no indication of which had received artificial hearts. Each seemed the picture of health.

It's the people I'm more worried about, Kim thought. Midnight was long since past, and those not involved with the animal loading and transport had already gone home. Those remaining showed understandable signs of exhaustion, some having worked an eighteen-hour day. They were snippy, irritable, bags forming under their eyes, and the drivers still had a lot of miles to cover. But Kim had been adamant that all of this be finished that day.

"Nice work, everyone," he said, swinging shut the horse trailer's door. "I know you're tired. We're in the home stretch."

A horse's frustrated nickering was the only response. Kim latched the trailer. "And I'll make sure it's made up to you on a Christmas bonus," he added, and this garnered a few waves and a couple of smiles.

The trucks and trailers began to pull out, one by one heading around the building and the parking lot, down the private drive, and toward the main road. At last there were only a handful of employees left who were not traveling with the animals.

The group started wearily for the building, but Kim waved them off. "I'll close it down," he said. "Go home, get some rest."

"Thanks, Dr. Konno."

"Appreciate it, Kim."

They piled into their cars, and moments later Kim was alone in the parking lot. He suddenly felt so tired, a weight settling into his body that threatened to push it to the ground, as if the years had abruptly caught up with him. He needed sleep, he knew. But there were a few things left that he intended to do tonight, and some items he planned to carry down to his car, so he decided to drive his dinged-up blue sedan around the building to a small back entrance that would be a shorter walk from his office. As he slid behind the wheel, it struck him how dark, empty, and aban-doned the whole facility looked—without its people, without its animals, the parking lot deserted—although perhaps it was only his gloomy outlook.

He parked his car near the back entrance. Kim typically took the stairs, but tonight his energy had left him, sapped away by worry and long hours on his feet. He took the elevator instead, leaning against the wall and sighing. The highlight of the day had been Dan Parker's visit, seeing the wonder and amazement on his face when it sank in what they were attempting here. Sometimes Kim could forget just how groundbreaking this was, how many lives it would ultimately save, and the steady widening of Dan's eyes had been an enjoyable reminder. His friend had no idea how far they had come, yet still he was beyond impressed. Hopefully it would stay that way, and Dan would remain excited right through the point that he could return the flash drives and duffel bags to Kim. If nothing else happened first.

"You're just being paranoid," Kim said to his own reflection staring back at him in the mirrored elevator car. He looked a little crazy, his grey-tinged hair in disarray, bits of hay stuck to his shirt from helping with the animals, a brown stain near the collar from some unknown source, worry lines stretching from his eyes.

Yes, maybe it was paranoia and long hours. But he did feel better knowing the animals were safe and the prototypes and data were secure. Whatever other trouble he might be imagining, or failing to foresee, at least he had given the artificial hearts their best chance.

He walked down the hallway toward his office, his loafers squeaking on the floors. The whole hospital seemed almost eerie with no one here, his footsteps echoing unnaturally. Never one for a big fuss, Kim had taken an unremarkable space next to a storeroom for animal food as his office, leaving the fancier, centrally located rooms for other researchers. He had never even bothered to put a sign on the door. Kim reached his office and locked the door behind him, although not quite sure why. He started pulling files out of drawers and taking papers off his desk.

Before long, he was surrounded by piles of paperwork and folders, more flash drives and memory sticks of data, in a disorganized mess. While he didn't want to take this compulsion for precaution too far, there were files that he now felt would be more secure locked away at home than here at the facility, even though he knew that made no rational sense. Of course they were secure here. How could they not be? He was a research scientist, not an undercover agent. It was probably all in his head.

Which was getting heavier by the minute. It was harder to think clearly, to decide what to keep in his office and what to take home. His hands moved slower, his eyelids drooped, and when he sat in the chair by his desk he wondered how he would muster the strength to rise and haul boxes down to his car.

He would rest first, just a few minutes, and then load everything up. Kim folded his arms on the edge of his desk and then settled his head on them, letting his eyes drift closed. Only a few minutes. Then he would make sure the last of the files were safe.

* * *

In his dreams, they were hunting him—unknown, shadowy figures, out there searching. Calling to each other. He was safe as long as he stayed hidden, as long as he remained perfectly still. Their voices drifted in, calm at first, and then angrier as they grew more destructive in their fury. Things smashed, crashed, scattered nearby. His heart rate sped up, and it grew harder to breathe. He didn't hear their voices now. Perhaps they had given up, they had left. He was safe.

No, that wasn't right. His eyes opened. Instantly they watered from the smoke that had drifted under the doorway and was gathering like storm clouds near the ceiling. He was sweating, his hair plastered to his forehead, his arms slick with perspiration where his head had been resting. His shirt clung to him. His office was uncomfortably warm.

For a moment, he could convince himself that he was still shaking off his nightmare, that he had simply dozed off and his mind was still in the grips of the fever dream that had claimed him. But within seconds he knew that something was terribly wrong. The smoke was evidence enough of that. And when he walked to the door and felt the handle, it was warm to the touch.

His office had no windows, no possible exits, so he carefully cracked the door and peered through. The hallway was dim and filled with smoke, and farther down the corridor he could see the glow from something burning. Kim stepped to his desk and snatched up a rag he had used to clean a coffee spill the day before, and he held it over his mouth and nose before stepping into the hallway, hunched as low as possible to avoid the worst of the smoke.

It got hotter as he went, the smoke thicker, and then he started to see the fire—burning behind glass in rooms on the left and right, in offices, in a few places even causing the ceiling tiles to drop down in flaming pieces. It was spreading so fast. Why weren't the fire alarms sounding? Why was the sprinkler system not deploying? It was hard to even think; his head quickly grew foggy, his eyes burning and watering. He reached a junction that he had navigated a thousand times, but never in conditions like this, and as he hesitated—struggling to be certain which way led to the closest exit—a wall collapsed beside him, and a rush of searing heat washed over him, so intense that he fell to his knees. He crawled forward, and when a section of the ceiling caved in, dropping flaming wood and plaster, he moved away from it instinctively, no longer consciously choosing the path to the exit. Now he was simply avoiding the fire and trying to stay alive.

It was harder and harder to breathe as his lungs filled with smoke. There was debris in the corridors, and some of the doors were smashed in, but this didn't seem to be damage from the fire —someone had ransacked the building. He straightened up enough to see through a window into one of the research labs, and he saw that cabinets had been opened, shelves cleared out, materials strewn on the floor. It registered that some of the computers were missing.

Someone did this on purpose, he thought hazily, the importance of this swimming in circles in his brain as he struggled to breathe. *That's why no alarm. That's why no sprinklers. The fire is just to cover their tracks.*

Kim pushed forward, wheezing now, his eyes streaming. The heat was almost unbearable. He thought if he took two rights he would find himself at the east stairwell, which he could take to the ground level and from there find a way out of the building. He was crawling on his hands and knees, but that made it difficult to hold the rag over his mouth and nose, so he aban-doned his makeshift filter and crawled as quickly as he could. His eyes were shut against the burning smoke, the cinders in the air, his nose catching the reek of melting plastic as the fire spread. He crawled blindly ahead, feeling the wall, took a right and then twenty yards later another right, as the sounds of the fire rose to a roar around him. It sounded like the whole building could come down at any moment. But he was nearly there. His hand stretched out, feeling for the stairwell door, but his straining fingers felt nothing but air long after he should have reached it.

The featureless floor looked the same throughout the building —it was impossible to discern his position from the few square feet of flooring he glimpsed when he cracked his watery eyes. Kim put a hand out to the side, found the wall, and braced himself on it as he stood, looking down the hallway's length to try to pin down his location. His face was right in front of a framed photograph, and a couple of feet away was another, and then another. After a moment the horrible realization settled in—he was nowhere near the stairwell. He had taken a wrong turn somewhere, and now he was in the hallway they called the "walk of motivation," surrounded by the pitying gazes of employees' lost family members. He was far from where he needed to be.

It was so hard to breathe. So hard to think. As if from a great distance, he heard the sound of a huge portion of the ceiling collapsing only yards away, and another rush of heat blasted at him, fiery debris showering past and setting his shirt alight. He stumbled but put a hand on the wall to catch himself, straightening, afraid if he went to the floor he would never rise.

His eyes focused on the photograph that was inches from his face, a man in a wheelchair staring serenely out. His father. Patient, kind, and gone too soon. *Do it careful*, he had always said. *Do it right.* Kim had tried to do these things. He had tried. He reached for the photograph, as if he might take it with him, and then the ceiling directly over him at last gave way and released the inferno above.

Chapter Ten

It was just background noise, really. The television ran un-watched in the doctors' lounge as Dan stared with unfocused eyes in its general direction, his mind a million miles away. Actually, it was closer to five hundred miles—the distance to San Antonio, where his daughter was competing today. How would Marla react if she knew her father was not only absent but had been put on probation at work? What would Laura say when she found out? And worst of all, what if the committee permanently revoked his privileges?

"At this time, the fire that destroyed the facility appears to have been an accident," the news reporter on the screen was saying, "although investigations will be ongoing."

It had been a long day already, spent performing the opera-tions that he already had scheduled and making arrangements for someone to cover operations in the future while he was under probation. Word had already spread around the hospital, and the only things that grated on him more than the smug expressions of those who had disapproved of his methods were the looks of pity from his friends.

"You did what you thought was right," Holly had told him, her voice uncharacteristically soft. "That's all any of us can do."

The fact that she had foregone the opportunity to make any snappy cracks about the situation just confirmed the hopelessness of it all. Holly went around the hospital like she had just received her invitation to a friend's funeral—his.

The TV reporter, a chipper young woman, was saying, "The Austin Police Department has now released the identity of the sole casualty of the fire. The lead researcher and head of World-wide Medical Research, Dr. Kim Konno, perished early this morning. It appears he was the only person working at the facility at the time the fire spread."

Even in his mental haze, Dan registered the name, and his eyes snapped to the television. There on the screen, looking serene and wise, was a picture of Kim Konno. Underneath it the text confirmed what he had only halfway heard the reporter state: his friend had died in a fire that utterly destroyed the medical research facility in Austin, where Dan had walked and talked with Kim less than a day before.

Dan sank back in his seat, grabbing at the table and feeling like he might fall out of his chair. It did not seem possible. He had *just* been there. Now it was destroyed? Kim was dead? His gentle, brilliant, kind-hearted friend—ready to change the world —gone because of a stupid, preventable accident.

Even as he thought this, Dan's mind spun down another track. *Not an accident. You don't really believe that. Not after what you saw and heard, not after what Kim gave to you.*

Dan stood, his mouth dry, the room suddenly feeling hot and claustrophobic. He thought of the duffel bags and flash drives sitting in a storage room on the outskirts of town, locked up but far from really secure. It was his brother-in-law's storage unit, which he had a key to, and it was the first place he had thought of to store Kim's things. But was someone there right this minute, having followed him to it and now loading them into an unmarked van? Had someone seen Dan talking to Kim, or figured out where he flew off to? Had someone been listening in on their phone conversations, or decided to ransack Dan's house?

Now you're the one being paranoid, he told himself. And yet, he was sweating.

"It will all work out."

Dan spun, startled. He hadn't heard Holly enter the room, but she stood by the counter watching him. She stepped closer, eyes widening with worry when she saw the perspiration dampening his forehead.

"My friend," Dan managed, gesturing at the screen. "He just died in a fire in Austin."

"Oh, Dan," Holly said. "I'm so sorry. In the middle of everything else—"

"I've got to go home for a little while," Dan said. He was already heading for the door.

"Of course. I'll let the others know what's going on, and we'll try to cover." She squeezed his shoulder as he passed.

"Thank you." In the hallway, he wiped his sleeve across his forehead and headed for the closest exit.

* * *

From the front driveway, the house in Sleepy Hollow looked peaceful. But something about it felt off—the uneasiness that Dan had felt during his speedy drive back from the hospital only increased when he took in the complete stillness of his home. So he went through the gate and around to the back door, where he found the glass smashed in, the door ajar. Despite his fear, he had not really expected to find it that way, and for a moment he could only stare at it as he processed what this meant.

He pushed the door open and listened, but the house was utterly silent. Inside, the devastation surrounded him—furniture shredded, glass smashed, books in piles near overturned shelves, lamp pieces scattered on the floor. He glimpsed the kitchen and saw the refrigerator open and emptied, dishes broken, the door to the microwave torn off. And turning toward the stairs, he saw a small, motionless pile of black and white fur beneath a slashed cushion that had been tossed atop her. Lola. He crouched beside the dog, tears filling his eyes, and confirmed what he already knew. She was dead.

Walking across scattered papers and magazines, he up-righted a chair and collapsed into it, feeling unable to take any more in. He sat with his head in his hands and struggled to organize his thoughts. All he could think was what might have happened if Laura and Marla had still been home... what it would be like if it was more than the family pet waiting to be discovered. This took his thoughts down such dark paths that he finally forced himself to stop thinking and continue on through the house.

Dan rose and headed upstairs to the bedroom, which had also been ransacked—the mattress slashed open, Laura's collection of angel figurines in pieces, everything knocked to the floor and smashed. Next door, in his study, many of his folders and binders were gone, others were in a jumbled mess on the floor. The desktop computer was bashed open, with the hard drive removed, and his laptop was missing, as were his planner and every flash drive from his desk. As he stood in the midst of it, his cell phone buzzed with an incoming text message.

He checked his phone, his breath seizing up as he expected some threatening ultimatum, a terrible continuation of this unfolding nightmare. Instead, it was a message from his old friend Alex Bear.

Dan, don't know if u got email about my dad. But it's serious. Pls call if you can. Thks.

Dan stared at it. Email? He had been so consumed with the developments at the hospital that he had not checked his personal email in a day or so. He pulled it up on his phone and found another email from Alex that he had sent the day before, marked urgent.

Hello Dan,

I don't know if you've seen my last email, but I wanted to send you news about my father. I figured you would want to know.

Starting yesterday, my dad has grown sick with fever, sweats, and cough. My parents were cleaning the garage, sweeping it out and throwing away junk, and I believe he breathed in dust from deer mice droppings that had the Hanta virus. Of course, you know what that means for him. I tried to explain it to my mom, but she didn't want to listen.

From what I've heard, the University of New Mexico has the best results and the largest series in the treatment of the Hanta virus. I want him to go to Albuquerque as soon as possible, but he insists he will not leave the reservation. You know how he is.

He's always been impressed by you (more than by me, I think!) and has talked for years about how you're one of the few doctors who knows what he's talking about. He respects you, Dan. So maybe he would listen to you.

I know I'm asking a lot, but if there's any way that you could travel to the reservation and talk to him, it might make a difference. I don't have to tell you that time is short.

Your friend,
Alex

Dan read through the email a second time, and by this point he needed to sit down again, but his chair had been ripped open and broken. His legs were unsteady, and he put a hand on the edge of the desk. It seemed that his world was falling apart. On top of everything else, George Bear, who had become nearly a second father to him, was sick and probably dying from the Hanta virus. The window for intervention was desperately small. What would be next? A sudden fear gripped him about his wife and daughter. Surely they were safe, out of town and traveling with other families, but he had to be sure. He typed a quick message to Laura.

Just checking in. Everything OK?

He stood in the midst of his wrecked study, staring at his cell phone, waiting as the seconds and then minutes ticked by. He willed a message to appear, wanting it more than anything. None came. Maybe Marla was in the middle of a game, maybe they were at a crowded restaurant, maybe Laura was taking pictures and hadn't seen his message....

The phone rang. He answered immediately, not even looking to see who was calling.

"Laura?"

"Dr. Parker," came an unfamiliar female voice. "This is Special Agent Lucy Brown of the FBI. I have some questions for you. Is this a good time to talk?"

Dan did not respond. The phone threatened to slip from his hand. The Austin facility burned down, Kim Konno dead, his home ransacked, priceless prototypes transferred to him, and now the FBI was calling. If there had been any doubt about the danger he was in, those few words from Agent Brown had dispelled it.

"Dr. Parker?"

"Sorry," Dan said, squeezing the bridge of his nose. "Actually, this isn't a good time."

"Sorry to hear that, but this won't take long," she persisted, friendly but firm. "I need to speak with you about a fire early this morning at Worldwide Medical Research in Austin. Did you know about that?"

"Yes," Dan said slowly. "I heard it on the news."

"Right. And has Kim Konno been in touch with you recently?"

For a moment, Dan did not know how to respond. Realizing he was taking too long to answer, he said, "Kim is an old friend... was an old friend. We stayed in touch."

"You sure did," Agent Brown said. "We see from phone records that you spoke just yesterday. What did you talk about?"

"Do we have to do this now? I've just heard about his passing from a news report, and I'm still reeling from it." He looked around at the destruction, wondering if he should mention it, and get the police or FBI down here. It felt like the wrong move.

"Of course. I'm very sorry for your loss." Agent Brown's voice was professional, neutral, and yet he heard what sounded like genuine compassion in it. "Dr. Parker, I do need to ask you more questions, but let's do it face to face. Can you come down to the FBI office? It's on Taylor Street. I can meet you at whatever hour is good for you."

"Sure. Fine."

"What time?" she pressed.

"Seven o'clock this evening. I need to take care of some things."

"That's fine. But stay in town."

"Thanks for the call, Agent Brown."

He disconnected. Part of him wondered why he had not opened up to the FBI agent, told her about his fears, about the prototypes he'd been given, and about the ransacking of his home. But what if the FBI wanted to confiscate the hearts, or to blame him for Kim's death since he had them now? Or what if the investigation meant the research would never see the light of day, and Kim's death would be for nothing? He needed time to think, to figure the best path forward, but there was not much time available to do it.

He went to the closet in their bedroom, found an empty suitcase, and started grabbing clothes off the floor where all the drawers had been emptied. Dan snatched a few toiletries from the bathroom and tossed them in the luggage. He finished packing the bag in five minutes and headed back downstairs. As he locked the front door behind him—which seemed like a pretty pointless gesture, although it felt best to leave the house as much as possible like he had found it—a message buzzed on his phone.

Doing fine, it read. *Marla is killing it on the court. Took some videos. Wish you were here.*

It was from Laura. At least for the moment, they were safe—and perhaps the best means to keep them that way was to maintain the distance between them and himself. He put the suitcase in his car's trunk, slid behind the wheel, and sent one more text message, this one to Alex Bear.

Got your email. Sorry for delay. Will fly to NM today.

It was probably a crazy plan, but it seemed like the best he had. The FBI's questioning would have to wait. He would keep his family safe, help his friend's father, and put some space between him and whoever was after him and the prototypes.

But first, he needed to swing by a certain storage unit.

Chapter Eleven

They were a step ahead of him.

It was the only explanation. First, they had ransacked his house, helping themselves to anything they wanted—even if the artificial hearts were not there. Now they had beaten him to his hangar, and as he stood outside the door, staring at the broken lock, he was on the verge of screaming. Was there no escaping these people? Maybe it was better to run into the protective arms of the FBI, spill everything, and let them sort it out....

Except for Alex's father, dying of the Hanta virus. Dan had called Alex and told him he would be at the Sierra Blanca regional airport in two hours, as it would take an hour to drive to Riverfalls Airport, get the Baron out of the hangar, and do the preflight, and then another hour for the trip to Ruidoso. But had anything happened to his plane?

Dan jerked open the door and went straight to his Beech Baron. If it was possible to love an inanimate object, he loved that plane, and the thought of someone damaging her made white-hot anger surge up in him again, so thick that for a moment he could not think of what to check first. They might have damaged or taken the radio, transponder, GPS unit—any number of things.

Forcing himself to move slowly and methodically, Dan carefully inspected the plane. Everything seemed to be intact and unchanged. He checked the tires, engine oil, fuel, control surfaces, windshield, pitot tube, landing gear, and propeller blades, even looking for nicks in the leading edges. It all looked normal. Gradually, his stress receded, his heartbeat still quick but his hands no longer trembling.

"They didn't hurt you, did they, girl?" he heard himself say, running his hand along a wing. Maybe they were simply looking for him, or checking to see whether he had stored any of the artificial organs here. Dan retrieved the duffel bags from the trunk of his car and deposited them in the baggage compartment of the Baron. He still had not opened the bags, but he could feel thick packing through the sides, so the organs were hopefully well insulated and protected for travel.

Dan checked the weather between Amarillo and Ruidoso, which was under the influence of a meeting between a warm, wet front from the gulf driven by a strong high-pressure cell in Louisiana and a cold front being pushed by a high-pressure cell in the upper West. The outlook predicted marginal ceilings between Amarillo and Ruidoso with rain, possible icing, and possible thunderstorms. However, the front had passed Sierra Blanca and that area was clear. Ceiling tops at eleven thousand feet, northwest wind fifteen to twenty knots.

Dan filed an instrument flight plan for twelve thousand feet that would take him over the storm in bright sunlight and then provide a visual approach to Sierra Blanca. The engines started in sequence, as readily as ever, and he performed all his checks methodically, although he was eager to get in the sky—to put some distance between himself and whoever was after him. When the plane was at last accelerating down the runway, and the time came to draw back the wheel and go airborne, it was as if a switch flipped inside and he was able to breathe again.

Dan raised the landing gear and adjusted the props and mixtures. Everything looked good. He relaxed his grip on the wheel, feeling the tension ease up in his shoulders and back. He contacted Amarillo Departure, established radar contact, and was handed off to the Albuquerque Center.

"Albuquerque Center, this is 68 Juliet," Dan said. "Do you have the weather at Sierra Romeo Romeo?"

"68 Juliet, weather at Sierra Blanca is clear, five miles visibility, wind three hundred and fifteen knots."

"68 Juliet, thanks." Dan settled back in the soft leather seat, checking engine instrument readings, fuel flow, and the Garmin GPS. He felt the Baron had never flown smoother or better. Finally, something was going right.

* * *

When Dan was twenty-five miles from Sierra Blanca, he activated the radio. "Albuquerque center, 68 Juliet requests descent to eleven thousand."

"68 Juliet, cleared to eleven thousand feet," came the reply.

Dan throttled back the engines to descend. He might have several minutes of instrument weather, he figured, and then he would break out in the clear and see the airport. It would be a welcome sight.

The explosion in the left engine rocked the plane so hard that Dan was thrown against his safety belts. Instantly the plane veered as the autopilot disengaged and the aircraft started a steep downward spiral. His hands locked on the wheel as his eyes jerked to the left engine, which was covered in flames and billowing smoke as it hung down from the engine mounts. He cut the power on the left engine, feathered the prop, and shut off the gas. Instincts were kicking in, the steps coming automatically. Hard right rudder, level the plane, watch the airspeed indicator and altimeter. There was far too much drag from the left engine.

"Albuquerque center, 68 Juliet," Dan called. "Mayday, mayday—" He let the call for help fade into silence as he realized that all electronics were gone. No radio, GPS, engine ignition, or autopilot.

Fly the plane, he thought. *Fly the plane. Basics!*

Turn indicator, airspeed, altimeter. He was going down. Through the windshield, partially obscured by clouds and smoke, he caught glimpses of the ground below, its features and buildings quickly growing larger as the plane continued to plummet. Should be about ten miles from the airport, he thought. Right engine running on magnetos, at least some power. Down and down. Watch airspeed. There was the airport, about five miles. He looked at the distance, gauged the remaining altitude, and knew the hard truth: he was not going to make it.

There, off to the side, was an open field next to an arroyo. *Power off, gear up, going to hit hard.* He steered for the field, only precious seconds left, fighting to keep the Baron steady and controlled as it plunged lower and lower. The ground rushed up at him. Dan braced.

The impact onto the hard, rocky field threw him to the limits of his inertia safety belts as dirt sprayed up over the windshield. The plane continued to plow ahead, digging a furrow in the field as it tore forward. The cockpit shook, the sound horrendous, smoke filling the cabin now, until finally the plane jerked to a halt.

Dan couldn't see anything, but he knew he had to get out. The engine was still on fire, too close to the gas tank. Pain on his face, in his leg. The door wouldn't open, the frame too bent. Glow from the still-burning flames cast everything in a red haze. He couldn't get out.

The passenger windows, he remembered. On each side, these windows could drop out for emergency exits. Dan crawled painfully into the back seats, swiping a hand over his face to clear his vision. He pulled the lever to drop the window on the right side and then dragged himself through it and out. He fell head first out of the plane, landing roughly on cool, dry earth. On his hands and knees, he crawled to the baggage door and pulled it open. He reached inside and hooked an arm through the strap for the closest duffel bag. Dan crawled away, unable to walk and dragging the bag with him, while his left ankle sent sharp pain up his leg with every motion. His ears were ringing, his head hurt, and he kept needing to wipe blood out of his eyes. When he was mere yards away, another loud explosion knocked him to the ground—the earth itself shaking, vibrating right through his palms, the heat washing over him. The left-wing gas tank had exploded, and seconds later the gas in the right wing followed. Dirt, rocks, and parts of the destroyed Baron blasted into the air and struck him as they flew.

Dan's vision threatened to close off. He fought the blackness back, reaching out and dragging himself hand over hand, his fingers clawing at the dirt. He pushed with his right foot, his left foot in too much pain to use. Smoke curled around him, blood obscured his vision, and he lost track of his distance from the plane. Many minutes could have passed, or maybe just a handful of seconds. It was impossible to tell. Every muscle ached, and just as he thought he could crawl no farther, would just lay there and hope for rescue, a blurry shape appeared above him, haloed by dark smoke.

"Hold on, Dan," the figure said. "I'm going to get you out of here."

Dan knew that voice. Strong arms lifted him, and he was carried to a Jeep and laid down in the back seat. A thick, coarse blanket was wrapped around him.

"Get the bag," Dan choked out.

Hurried footsteps receded, and then the bag was dropped in the back of the vehicle. Dan tried to sit up, swiped at his eyes and blinked, and through the side window he could see flashing lights approaching down a small road. For some reason, the sight filled him with panic rather than reassurance. He still did not want to get pulled into official custody, and more than ever, he did not know whom he could trust.

"An ambulance will be here in a minute," the other man said, reappearing in Dan's field of vision, and this time Dan could make out his face. Of course. Alex.

"Just drive," Dan said. "Please. Get me out of here."

Alex started to argue, but he nodded and jumped behind the wheel. The Jeep's wheels spun in the loose dirt, and then the vehicle lurched forward, tearing across the field. Its four-wheel drive handled the rough terrain easily, plowing through bushes and across rock and sand.

"Don't know how you reached me before they did," Dan said.

Alex looked over his shoulder and grinned. "Well, they use

roads." He faced forward again, swerving around a scrub-covered hillock of dirt, the Jeep bouncing and painfully jostling Dan's ankle. "Sorry. Almost ran you over when I drove up, you were so covered with debris. I was waiting for you at the airport, and as soon as I saw that smoke trail, I took off. What happened?"

Dan's head was still spinning, and he found it impossible to think clearly. What *had* happened? "I don't know. The left engine exploded and it was downhill after that. Thanks for getting me. Thought I was going to die."

Alex whistled. "Well, you got the plane on the ground and survived the impact. That must have been some mighty good flying." Alex looked back at him again. "Or maybe you were just lucky."

Dan had never felt less lucky in his life. He propped himself up enough on one elbow to look out the window, and he could still see the flashing lights of the first responders, but they were smaller now, dwindling away. The smoke from the crash was still clearly visible, though, rising like a black plume into the sky. Still aflame, the plane's wreckage resembled the set of a disaster movie.

"Not your best landing," Alex said.

"What's that they say, any landing you can crawl away from is a good one?"

"I'm pretty sure it's 'walk away.'"

"Minor detail."

Dan's head and ankle still throbbed, but he felt safer in Alex's jeep. Here was an answer to the question of whom he could trust. The Jeep jittered and jerked as it bounced across the uneven ground, until finally it left the field and found a road, the ride instantly smoother as the tires gripped pavement. Dan lay his head down on the seat and pulled the blanket tighter around himself, starting to relax.

Until Alex spoke up. "I think we're being followed."

"Is it the ambulance?"

"Sorry, but no." Alex reached over to pop open the glove box and pull something from inside—not a good sign. "No, it definitely is not."

Chapter Twelve

Alex did not slow down. The Jeep turned onto another road, but Dan could tell from his friend's frustrated exhale that their pursuers were continuing to trail them.

"Three motorcycles," Alex said, glancing in the rearview at Dan. "All black. Think I know the gang."

"Friendly?"

"Not in the least. You in some kind of trouble?"

Dan wiped blood from his eyes again, and the jolts from the road continued to make his ankle throb. "Yeah. You could say that."

"Hang on. They're closing." Alex gripped the wheel with one hand, the other out of sight and holding whatever he'd withdrawn from the glove box. "Dan, don't move."

The rumble of the motorcycles' engines grew louder, nearer, until the powerful vibrations were enough to rattle Dan's stomach as the bikers drew alongside the Jeep. Dan forced himself to lay still rather than raising up to look out the window.

Alex leaned out and called, "Help you gentlemen with something?"

One of the bikers hollered back. "What you got inside?"

"Dead body from the plane crash," Alex said.

"Some reason you didn't wait for the ambulance? You don't look like you work for the morgue."

"Listen closely. I'm Apache, and this man was the closest thing I've ever had to a brother." His protective tone—just short of a threat—was the best thing Dan had heard in a long time. Even if it was part of a ruse. "So I'm taking him to be buried on the reservation, a special honor. I don't expect you to understand."

"Oh, we understand fine, Kemosabe. Pull the Jeep over."

From where Dan lay, he could see Alex's shoulders tighten, whether from stress or the slur. But he slowed and then pulled to a stop by the roadside. As the vehicle halted, his words drifted back, so faint Dan might have imagined them: "Don't even breathe."

The side door opened. Dan had not closed his eyes in time and he found himself staring at the door, head half-propped by the bunched blanket wrapped around him, so he fixed his eyes on a point on the horizon and stared, unblinking, his breath caught and held. Blood covered his face from the laceration on his forehead, and it stained his clothes and the blanket.

The biker, standing at the door, was a huge man clothed in black leather. His beard was trimmed short, and despite his rounded gut his arms looked like they could pound through walls. Narrowed eyes swept over Dan, taking in the blanket-wrapped body, the blood, the unseeing stare.

Dan fought to stay motionless, his lungs beginning to ache for air, his eyes burning with the need to blink. The man continued to look at him, and Dan knew he had only seconds left before giving in.

"A'right, then," the man said. "Take him to your little dung-hole and burn him, scalp him, whatever it is you people do with your dead."

He shut the door. Dan closed his eyes and drew a breath, as quietly as he could.

The motorcycle engines revved again, and then they were pulling away, and seconds later the thrum of their motors was lost to the distance. Alex cursed lowly, opened and shut the glove compartment, and turned around to look over the seat at Dan.

"You okay back there?"

"I think so. Who were those guys?"

"Call themselves Spikes," Alex said. "Cycle gang with members in every state. They're not just bikers, though... rumor is, these boys are bad news. Involved in drug-running, kidnapping, arson, murder, you name it. Them showing up here, right after your crash? Can't be coincidence."

Alex didn't come right out and speak it, but the question was implicit. Dan owed him an explanation. "Let's just head to your parents' house," Dan said. "I'll tell you everything."

* * *

Between Ruidoso and Tularosa, New Mexico, in the Sacramento Mountains, lay the Mescalero Apache Reservation. Towering over the northern edge of the reservation was Sierra Blanca, a twelve-thousand-foot-high peak teeming with wildlife. Massive herds of deer and elk roamed the mountain and nearby valleys. Large black bear, mountain lions, coyotes, and fox were abundant on the ground, while magpie, ravens, cardinals, and hummingbirds roamed the sky. Nearby, Dan knew from past experience, was a clash of more than rock and earth, or ground and air, but of cultures—of old and new, heritage and so-called progress. Some parts of the mountain were still considered sacred by the Apaches, and many of them still followed the old ways. They held religious ceremonies and athletic events there in the shadow of the peak, where the most famous Apache, Geronimo, was spoken of in reverent tones by confident young men, like youths looking for heroes the world over.

Alex's parents, George and Sally Bear, embodied this clash themselves, like no other couple Dan had known. Alex's mother embraced new developments and opportunities with the same wide-open arms and smile that she offered to any stranger who graced her doorstep. But his father, Alex joked, would have been a much happier man if born three hundred years ago and saw little to celebrate in the centuries since then. Despite this, George and Sally's marriage worked in a beautiful way that only they, perhaps, truly understood.

The Jeep traveled through the reservation, Sierra Blanca rising beyond the windshield as high and imposing as Dan remembered it. It struck him afresh with awe and wonder; or maybe it was just the recent brush with death. He talked while they drove, Alex listening without a single interruption, until Dan had told him the entire story of Kim's scientific breakthroughs, the artificial heart prototypes, the fire at the facility, Kim's death, his own house's ransacking, the call from the FBI, the break-in at the hangar, and the mid-flight engine explosion. It sounded so crazy to Dan that he hardly believed it himself.

"Wow," Alex said, once he had at last finished.

They drove for a few more miles until Dan could not take the silence any longer. "That's it? That's all you have to say?"

"I dunno, I think 'wow' sums it up pretty good."

"I should have stayed in Amarillo," Dan said. "I should have cooperated with the FBI."

"Maybe. Maybe not."

They drove on. Alex was sharp, a deep thinker, although few people guessed it when they first spoke to him. The questions were coming—the perspectives Dan had not considered, the steps he could take—but not until his friend had been given a chance to mull them over. There was no point pushing him until then.

"I'm not just running," Dan said. "I haven't forgotten your father. Hanta is every bit as urgent."

Alex nodded, and though his voice was relaxed, his hands were tight on the wheel. "Despite how you got here, I'm glad you came."

Deep in the reservation, the Jeep at last pulled up before a small, neatly-kept house. It was surrounded by a thriving garden, full of bird-feeders and tiny wind chimes, their sound like gentle rain. Alex helped Dan out of the Jeep, although he was already feeling better; the pain in his ankle had shifted from sharp agony to a duller ache, and when Alex examined it, they both agreed it was likely a sprain and not a break. The cut on his forehead had stopped bleeding, and the rest were scratches and bruises that would heal with no lasting damage.

As Alex examined his injuries, Dan got his first good look at his friend, who hardly seemed to have aged in the past few years since they had seen each other. Alex Bear, at 130 pounds of solid muscle, stood five feet three inches tall with skin like polished cherry wood, a broad face, and deep brown eyes. He had grown up on the reservation, which perhaps why he seemed as perfectly at home here as he did in a big-city hospital's operating room.

Before walking away from the Jeep, Alex reached through the window to the glove box and withdrew a gun, which he tucked behind his back, mumbling something about being careful. Then he stepped around to a water pump, found a towel his mother had left out while gardening, and used it to clean Dan up until he looked almost presentable.

"Can't look like I'm bringing hobos home," Alex said. "Even us savages gotta have standards, eh Kemosabe?"

"Those guys were idiots," Dan said.

"No doubt. I mean, your act fooled them, and it wasn't exactly an Oscar-worthy performance." Alex walked up to the front step and knocked twice to be polite.

"Hey, you try not blinking or breathing while some psycho biker stares you down."

"I think I would have had the brains to close my eyes."

"Are you kidding? My stare is what sold it."

The door opened, and a short, dark-haired woman appeared, her muscles well-toned and plenty of laugh-lines creasing the corners of her eyes. She ignored her son completely and wrapped her arms around Dan.

"Thank you for coming," she said. "It's been too long."

"It's good to see you, Sally."

They followed her inside, where it was clear that Mrs. Bear had continued to defer to her husband's wishes for their home; the décor was traditional, embracing the tribe's rich heritage, from paintings to pottery, baskets to beadwork, with shelves holding Native weapons and instruments.

As she led them through the house, she told Dan, "He's been sick for about two days with fever, sweats, and cough. He can't eat, he's short of breath." She looked at him, unable to mask the fear in her eyes. "He's getting weaker. He can't even get out of bed."

Dan put a hand on her shoulder. "Has Alex told you what he thinks?"

Her eyes darted to her son and back. "Hanta virus. He said when George was sweeping out the garage, he inhaled some of the dust, maybe from mice droppings. Deer mice, they live in the garage."

"That's right," Dan said, as gently as he could. "It's a viral infection that causes the lungs to fill up with fluid, called pulmonary edema. He's in respiratory distress." Dan hesitated, in obvious discomfort. "It's usually fatal."

"So what do we do now?" Sally asked. She tried to remain calm, but Dan could see the tears she was holding back.

"The University of New Mexico has the best results and the largest series in the treatment of the Hanta virus," Dan said. "We need to get him to Albuquerque as soon as possible."

"That's what I keep telling them," Alex said.

"No," Sally said. "He won't go. He told me he wouldn't leave the reservation. He said he'd rather die."

"That might be exactly what happens," Alex said, his frustration finally spilling over, and when his mother made a motion to hush him, he shook his head. "I don't care if he hears me."

Dan squeezed Sally's shoulder. "Let me see him."

She led them down a hallway lined with photographs of Alex as a grinning, athletic boy, and into their bedroom, where George Bear lay fully clothed on the bed, eyes closed and breathing rapidly. Although a much larger man than his son, at the moment he seemed small and weak, as if the body draped on his large frame no longer really fit him.

Dan stood at the bedside, his hands resting on the edge of the quilted coverlet. "Hello, George. It's Dan Parker." There was no response. After another minute of silence, he heard Sally step into the hallway, and then soft crying. Alex came over to stand beside him, and if it was difficult for Dan to look at the man laid out on the bed, wracked with infection, he could only imagine how painful it was for Alex.

"I respect him too much not to honor his wishes," Alex said. "But I can't just let him die."

"Maybe I have something that can help." Dan turned to face his friend. "It's experimental, and I didn't even develop it, but it might be his best chance."

"Are you talking about that bag I put in the Jeep?"

"It might have something in it that could save him." Dan started for the door. "That is, if it survived the plane crash."

Chapter Thirteen

Robert Krum loosened his necktie, undid the top button of his shirt, and tugged at the sweat-dampened collar. The air felt close, oppressive, thick with moisture. The smells and sounds of a crowded Indian market drifted his way, nearly overpowering the scents of fenugreek, eggplant, curry, and chutney from his Gujarati Thali—a full platter of food on the sidewalk-fronting table before him. There was heat to match the humidity, pedestrians hurrying around him, bicycles and taxis rattling past, and it all combined for an assault on the senses. He hated it.

Hated the whole area, in fact. The restaurant was near King's Circle, Matunga, in north central Mumbai—part of what they called *Brihanmumbai*, where the city ended and the suburbs began. It was a border zone, in some ways, and not just between the urban density and suburban sprawl; this was a solidly middle class district, yet it was within a stone's throw of the second-largest slum in Asia, in Dharavi. The slum had been pictured in plenty of Hollywood and Bollywood features, famous for its unfathomable expanses of poverty-stricken humanity. There were opportunities here for those who looked, of course. Krum had acquired a leather belt there for a very decent price, and thankfully the slum was good for other things, too, or he wouldn't be here sweating bullets and eating overcooked basmati rice.

As a man approached, Krum took a lengthy swig from a bottle of water and set it next to a folded newspaper on the table. The man sank into the chair opposite him and waited for Krum to speak. He was middle-aged, hard-featured, with his head shaved and jawline sporting a three-day stubble. The man was more appropriately dressed for the climate, with light khaki pants and a loose, short-sleeved shirt.

"Do you know how I feel about my condo on twenty-second street?" Krum began. He dabbed at his mouth with a napkin. "It's a penthouse. Madison Square Park Tower. It's got floor-to-ceiling glass walls, and I can look out across Manhattan, see the Flatiron Building, Chrysler Building, it's all right there. Sixty-fourth floor. It's forty-eight million dollars very well spent."

"Sir, I don't—"

"Now ask me how I feel about coming here. Ask me how I feel about having to fly halfway around the world to sit here, soaked in my own sweat, talking to you."

The other man had looked calm and composed when he sat, but now his own forehead was damp, and he wiped a hand across his face. "Mr. Krum, I can assure you it's under control."

"That's good to hear, Lee. Because for a minute I was starting to worry that you were stupid enough to have risked exposure for the entire organization." Krum flipped open the newspaper on the table, and the other man's eyes lowered to scan a headline near the bottom of the page, where Krum's finger tapped at the words *MORE MISSING IN DHARAVI*.

Lee lifted his gaze, looking scared now. "I'm telling you, it's not attracting attention to us."

"Isn't it?" Krum raised his eyebrows.

"People go missing in the slum all the time. That's nothing new."

"And yet, you've managed to make it news worth reporting by the *Times of India*, a paper that nearly three million people read." Krum folded the paper back over, tucked it away inside his coat. Intentionally, his hand hesitated inside the coat long enough to make Lee flinch when he pulled it back out, but it only gripped his wallet. Krum pulled out a 500-rupee note and dropped it on the table, Mahatma Gandhi's irritatingly serene face now beaming up at him.

"Here's what we're going to do," Krum said. "Your four top men can be added to the missing by midnight tonight, or you can. It's your call."

Lee blanched. "Sir… those men are needed to run operations. We can't keep hitting the numbers without them."

"Sounds like you've made your decision, then."

"No," Lee said sharply, halfway rising from his seat. He settled himself back onto the chair. "No, they're gone. I'll make the call."

"Good. And I'll be by tomorrow to explain personally to your remaining staff just how important discretion is in our line of work, since it seems you can't grasp the meaning of the word. You're dismissed."

Lee nodded and stood, still sweating. "We'll be ready for you."

Krum waited until the other man had stepped off the sidewalk before calling to him once more. "Lee. Don't make me have to come out here again."

"No, sir. You won't."

Lee disappeared into the throng of people bustling past, and Krum was left with the remains of his meal and a building frustration at what seemed to be the general depletion of intelligence in the world. How many other mistakes were being made—in Tokyo, Sao Paulo, Beijing, New York, or Mexico City? How much suspicion was being raised where before no one cared? He had offices in a dozen cities, but he rarely visited any of them outside of D.C. and New York, and he liked it that way. But, desperate times. This might call for visits to more of the satellite operations in far-flung whirlpools of urban decay.

Then there was the chest surgeon, Parker, the one connected to that bungled job out in Austin for the artificial hearts. It should have been so easy, but the organs had disappeared. They would turn up, that was just a matter of time, but the whole thing left him anxious, that edge of nausea fluttering in his gut like when he forgot to leave the ice out of his drink in one of these third-world dives.

His men had found Parker's hangar easily enough, and under his orders had installed a small explosive device, difficult to spot. It had an internal barometer that activated when barometric pressure increased to a certain point, so when the pilot started a descent in the plane the increase in pressure would set off the bomb. Simple. Yet there was a report that someone apparently pulled Parker from the wreckage, and although the men put in place to confirm Parker's death had done so, the whole thing felt off to him.

Krum pulled out his phone and dialed, not caring whether he woke the other man up.

"Go ahead," came the answer. Hunter sounded wide awake.

"Your man told me Dan Parker is dead. I want to know that he made sure."

"Well, he saw some Apache carting him off to bury him. The doctor was all covered in blood and wrapped in a blanket in the back seat. He was dead."

"Did your man check his pulse? Did he make sure?"

"No, I don't think so. But he's created enough dead bodies to know one when he sees it." Hunter paused. "There something else you want me or the Spikes to take care of for you?"

"No. Not now, at least. I'll call when there is."

Krum disconnected. Jack Hunter had sounded confident, but Krum remained doubtful. How could he trust the word of a few bikers when so much was at stake? He propped his elbows on the table and opened a web browser on his phone. Krum searched for reports in the Ruidoso, Albuquerque, and Amarillo newspapers about the plane crash.

Although there were plenty of articles about the crash itself, there was nothing about the death of the pilot. No obituaries for a prominent Texan heart surgeon who had died in his airplane. Dr. Dan Parker seemed to be missing, that was all. Perhaps this could be explained by the Apache who had apparently taken the body for burial on the reservation, and had maybe failed to notify any other authorities as of yet. It was a possibility. But this seemed unlikely to Krum, and he was well-used to calculating chances, likelihoods of some event. His whole business, the whole industry in fact, was predicated on it.

Better to deal in near-certainties where he could. There were ways to assure that Dan Parker, if he was still a loose thread that continued to dangle, would be cut off. He would send some of his own men to the reservation to make this a certainty, he decided, and to see if this Apache friend had any idea where the hearts might have been taken. Then both of them could find shallow graves out under the starry sky and Krum could sleep more restfully at night.

He stood and stepped away from the table, one hand rising to flag a taxi as the other dialed another number. A car pulled to the curb, all black save for the bright yellow roof. The phone dialed. It connected, but there was only silence on the other end.

"I have a job for you," Krum said.

Chapter Fourteen

As it turned out, Kim Konno's well-justified paranoia extended to his packing of the experimental units, which he had arranged carefully in the duffel bag. Addressing any conceivable impacts during travel—apparently including a plane crash—he had packed the hearts and the experimental oxygenator in individual containers with thick buffers to protect them. He could not have known what the next hours would bring, but he had prepared for it as best he could, Dan thought. *God rest his soul.* Dan had packed the flash drives carefully into this bag as well.

"Is that them?" Alex asked, at his shoulder. They stood at the back of the Jeep, where Dan was examining the contents of the bag. "The artificial hearts?"

"They don't seem to be hurt." Dan ran his finger along a cracked casing that housed one of the hearts, but the organ itself seemed unfazed. "From what I can tell, everything survived."

"Except my dad doesn't need a new heart."

Dan zipped up the bag and started to hoist it onto his shoulder, but Alex snagged the strap to carry it for him. Dan let him, as he was hobbling a bit when he walked due to the sprained ankle.

"There's something else Kim told me about. Another one of the research projects in Austin was extracorporeal membrane oxygenation, or ECMO. They developed a very special artificial membrane that allows blood to exchange oxygen and carbon dioxide just like normal lung tissue." Dan limped along next to his friend, but put a hand on his shoulder to pause when they reached the front door. "Your dad's lungs are filling up with fluid and not oxygenating his blood, right? But if we can oxygenate his blood for four or five days, he has a good chance of recovery. The experimental membrane system is in the bag, along with an in-line rotary pump. Kim said it works on large pigs and calves, so it should work on a person."

Alex looked at Dan with a combination of hope and disbelief. "Pigs and calves? Are you serious?"

Dan attempted a weak smile that he hardly felt. "It may be the best chance he's got."

They stood on the doorstep while Alex processed this, and Dan allowed his friend the time to mentally chew on it. Sally spotted them through the open door, hesitating on the step, and beckoned them in. They both plastered on smiles and Dan raised his hand in greeting, but they didn't move yet.

"All right," Alex said, his voice low. "Tell me what you need."

"I know there's a small medical clinic here on the reservation. Go there and see if you can get some sterile dressings and chlor-hexidine. We'll need normal saline, IV bags, and IV tubing. What else… Versed for sedation. An oxygen bottle. A Foley catheter. Seven and one half gloves and a tray. You have all that?"

Alex nodded. "I won't be gone long."

"Good. I'll keep your parents company."

Transferring the bag to his friend's shoulder, Alex headed for

119

the Jeep. "Just don't tell my mother any more stories about your death-defying operations. She already thinks you're a better doctor than me."

Dan laughed. "A woman of taste."

"Yeah, bad taste."

Dan headed inside and hobbled to the living room, where he set down the bag and sank onto the couch. Sally brought him a glass of iced lemonade and sat in the chair opposite him, trying to look relaxed but still visibly on edge, seeming unsure what to do with her hands. She kept brushing strands of hair away from her face, fussily, and her eyes were red.

Dan leaned forward, setting the lemonade on a coffee table. "Sally, did I ever tell you about the dead-on-arrival stab-wound patient we got back on his feet in twenty minutes? He was stabbed in the chest but we still saved him."

* * *

It was two hours later, and late evening. Outside, the glow of the sunset was fading into the dusky greyness of twilight, and the day shift of wildlife was settling down to rest while the night's creatures prepared to scurry forth. In the Bear household, all was quiet and watchful.

George rested comfortably in bed with a slow IV Versed drip for sedation, while Kim's artificial membrane unit functioned as planned, providing his blood with desperately needed oxygen. Dan had told Sally how the unit had been used for patients in other types of respiratory failure with success, and he had tried to explain to her how it worked—by the unit taking blood from a three-stage percutaneous catheter placed in the right internal jugular vein, oxygenating the blood, and the rotary pump delivering the blood back to the right side of George's heart. But Sally's eyes almost immediately glazed over, and he knew that in honesty she cared not a bit how it worked, so long as it kept her husband alive. It could be held together by paperclips and chewing gum so long as it did the job.

"The unit's so small," Alex said, seated in a chair on the other side of the bed. He was on the edge of it, hands on his knees, watching his father. "It's battery-powered, isn't it?"

"Yes." Dan stood at the foot of the bed, nothing left to do now that he had examined the patient. "Really lightweight, too. Quite a device."

George was perfectly still, but Dan thought that just perhaps some of the life seemed to be returning to him—a slight change in his color, or the relaxation of his body, or maybe just that ineffable something that he could sometimes sense when a patient was turning a corner. Or maybe it was only his imagination.

"I'll slow the Versed, and when George wakes up we can help him walk, even with the unit running," Dan said. "All we need is a portable IV stand to hang the oxygen bottle and the unit. He can be awake and mobile."

"Is he going to be all right?" Sally asked, perched on the bed and holding one of her husband's hands in hers. "He's been sleeping for hours, even before you got here."

"Well," Dan said, "this isn't a million-dollar ICU, but I hear some faint breath sounds in both lungs. His mucous membranes and fingernails are pink, so he's oxygenating. He is making urine, so his kidneys are working, and he has good pulses in his feet, so his blood pressure is okay. All of those expensive monitors in an ICU are good, but here the basics are what's important."

"How do you know he won't die in spite of your treatment?" Sally said, finally turning her gaze to Dan.

"I don't," he said, answering slowly. "But I have hope."

That seemed to be something she understood well, far more than technical devices and medical procedures, and her unvoiced gratitude shone in her eyes. Alex caught Dan's attention and tilted his head toward the hallway, and Dan took the hint.

"We'll give you two some privacy," he told Sally.

Dan and Alex walked down the hallway to the living room. Alex stepped to the couch, where a crutch was propped up, and passed it to Dan.

"I know you're walking better, but I brought this back for you. If you play your cards right, and milk it for a while with Laura, maybe it will get you out of taking the trash out for a few days."

Dan smiled and accepted the crutch. "I don't think I'll have any such luck. I called her while you ran to the clinic, and she wasn't too happy that I'd flown to New Mexico without telling her, never mind that I crashed the plane."

"She was probably just shaken up by what might have happened," Alex said.

"I guess so. She wanted me to come meet her and Marla, but I told her I need to stay on the reservation for a bit, to help your father."

Alex nodded. "She'll understand."

"Someday. I hope."

Alex strode to the back door and out into the yard, and Dan followed. He leaned on the crutch to walk, as much out of tiredness as anything, as the sprain was not nearly as bad as initially feared.

Outside, the stars were just beginning to come out, pinpricks of light in the vast blackness, while shadows were starting to pool thick and dark around the garden and the scrubby woods beyond. Somewhere close by, an owl hooted, and the plaintive sound was comforting to Dan—otherworldly, but also gentle, almost longing. One whole part of the sky was blocked out by the rising mass of the mountain, mostly visible by its dark outline against the darker heavens.

"Thank you for coming," Alex said. "There's any number of places you could have gone. But you came here, and you helped my dad. Whatever happens, I want you to know how much that means. To this family. To me."

Dan shrugged it off, taking a few paces deeper into the southwestern garden, where juniper bushes and cactus bloomed. "No problem. You'd have done the same."

Alex stepped after him, his voice uncharacteristically somber. "Whatever's going on with these hearts, I'll have your back on this. We owe you. I've got friends on the reservation police—you say the word, and we'll bring the fight to whoever is after you."

"You don't owe me that much," Dan said.

Alex smiled. "What's a little favor between friends?"

"You call that a little favor?"

"You need help, and I don't care whether you want to take it. My dad's got a real shot now, so it's time to talk about you," Alex said. "I don't think it's smart for you to stay here."

"Where am I going to go that's any safer?"

"Over the mountain. The highway is probably being watched."

Dan stared at him. "You're serious."

"I'll guide you. We'll start at first light, and I'll arrange for a car to be waiting on the other side. Best way to get away clean and figure out your next move."

Although the idea of scaling Sierra Blanca to shake off pursuers sounded absurd in his head, the more Dan mulled on it, the more sense it made. They stood for a moment, just listening to the quiet of the gathering night, mixed with the chirp of insects and the faint rustle of wings taking flight. Dan felt himself calming, breaths deepening. Maybe Alex's plan could work. When his phone rang, it startled him, a jarring sound breaking the peace.

It was the same number that had called him at his house, after the ransacking. The FBI agent—Lucy Brown. Could it really have been earlier this day that they had spoken? After a moment's hesitation of what to do, he let it go to voicemail. When the phone beeped its notification, he put it to his ear to listen.

"Dr. Parker, this is Agent Brown. I need you to call me. I heard about the plane crash and want to make sure you're all right." There was a pause. "Others here think this shows your guilt, that you're mixed up in all this, but I think you got scared and ran, and I can understand that. I can help you. I just need you to trust me, and the sooner you do, the better it will go for you. Call me at this number, any time of day."

The message ended. Dan stood staring at his phone, the glow overly bright in the gloom, until Alex asked him, "Everything okay?"

Dan couldn't answer, and when he looked up his eyes fixed not on his friend but on a point in the trees where he had sensed motion. Something ducked out of sight. Not an animal.

"No, I don't think it is," Dan said quietly. "And we're not alone."

Chapter Fifteen

Dan shifted his weight, turning to get a better vantage of what —or who—had ducked behind the trees, when the first shot was fired. It was silenced, so the only sound was the impact as the bullet collided with his metal crutch, spinning it from Dan's hand. It took only an instant to process what had happened and what it meant. They were shooting at his legs to disable him, which meant they would try to take him alive. Alex might not be so lucky.

"Get down!" he shouted, and at the edge of his vision he saw two men now, moving out of the trees and toward them with guns upraised. Dan and Alex hunched over and ran. The men both fired as they approached, gravel flying up around Dan's and Alex's feet, bullets ricocheting off garden stones, planters bursting in sprays of soil and roots.

Rather than heading for the house, Alex continued past the side of it, and Dan understood and agreed—they would not wilfully put Alex's parents in harm's way. They tore through the garden and over the line of rocks that marked its edge, as around them bullets whined past. Pain raced up from Dan's ankle, but it supported his weight. The moment they were far enough that the house was no longer a backdrop, Alex drew the gun from behind his back and began to return fire. The shots went wide, but the men pursuing them paused, crouching behind a trellis and a stone bench.

"They're after me," Dan said, "but they might kill your parents if they go inside to find the hearts."

"Toward the mountain. Follow me."

Alex ran into the scrubby woods bordering his parents' land, and as the trees grew more thickly, the darkness deepened. Sure enough, the two men ran in pursuit, and as their quarry fled, they seemed to care less whether they disabled or killed. The buzz of passing bullets continued unabated, sometimes thudding into tree trunks as Dan and Alex ran past. Alex blind-fired behind them a few more times, but he was more focused on leading the men away. Dan followed as quickly as he could, gritting his teeth from the pain in his ankle and pushing through it, determined not to slow them down. The ground began to incline upward, the soil becoming more rocky, and he realized they had reached the lower slope of the mountain.

What started as a gentle rise in the ground quickly became steeper, and a couple of times Dan lost his footing and caught himself on his hands. Some of the rocks strewn in the dirt were small boulders, and directly ahead the main mass of the mountain completely blocked out the sky. The quiet of the settling night was all around them, broken only by their breathing, the whine of passing bullets, and the loud reports of Alex's gun as he fired back. Dan had not been counting, but he knew his friend would be out of ammunition soon unless he had an extra magazine tucked somewhere.

"We can lose them farther up," Alex said. "Maybe double back."

"Can you call somebody? Get help?"

Alex shook his head, aiming and firing back down the slope at the men, who flattened behind trees. "Always lose my signal up here. You can try."

Dan checked his phone. No signal, but the glow was like a target in the gloom, and he dropped it back in his pocket and sidestepped as two shots struck a rock he had just been standing by. He ran farther up the path, Alex falling in step beside him and then passing him, leading the way higher. Here, on the upper slopes, there was not much room to maneuver—the path clung to the side of the rising mountain, switch-backing left and right, affording the option to either go forward or back. They climbed higher, breathing hard, and then leaned over to look down the slope. The two men were still in pursuit, and Dan grabbed his friend by the shoulder and pulled him back just as the men fired up at them.

"You go," Alex said. "I'll hold them here."

"Like hell," Dan answered. "How many rounds you have left? Three or four?"

Alex ejected the magazine, checking it in the pale moonlight. "Two. Maybe you should take this, Mr. Marine Corps."

"That was a long time ago." Dan winced, his ankle throbbing as they stood still, as if the pain had waited for them to stop before it could catch up. "What are our options up here?"

"Let's see, aside from death by gunshot, there's death by rattlesnake, mountain lion, bear, rockslide, lightning strike, falling into a crevice...."

"You're just a ray of sunshine," Dan said.

"Wait," Alex said, leaning forward just enough to peer down the slope again. "They're splitting up. One of them is heading back down." He aimed with the gun, but already the man was under cover of trees farther down the mountainside.

They stood for a few seconds, each searching for a solution. Dan spoke first, though he had no answers to offer. "We can't let him get to your parents' house."

"Come on." Alex turned and ran up the slope, and Dan hurried after him as best he could. Below them, they could hear the sounds of the man still in pursuit of them, scrambling up rocks for a shortcut and then running doggedly along the path.

Dan and Alex reached an open, flat area, still low on the mountain but well out of the trees, covered in grass and strewn with small boulders. Above, the trail continued on, considerably more steeply, cutting up the face of the mountain and all but invisible in the piles of rock. Off to the side, the ground dropped sharply away, and behind them the trail wound back down the mountain, where the gunman was in fast pursuit.

"There's a ledge I can drop to," Alex said, pointing to where the ground dropped off. "And I can scramble down from there, a shortcut down the slope. If I hurry I can beat that guy back to my house and be ready for him. Maybe call for help as soon as I get a signal."

Dan stepped to the edge and looked down. Maybe Alex knew what was below, but it was mostly dark, and he knew he would slow his friend down if he attempted the quick descent that way. Besides which, the second gunman could fire on them from here if he reached the plateau before they had descended far enough for cover.

"Keep going over the mountain," Alex said. "The reservation

isn't safe. I'll deal with this guy and then put the hearts someplace nobody will find 'til you're able to come get them."

It seemed insane. Cross the mountain alone, at night, with a sprained ankle and a murderous gunman after him? Maybe Alex read his expression, because he pressed the gun into Dan's hand and squeezed his shoulder.

"Just follow the trail," Alex said. "It's faint at times, but look for the markings and cairns. Rock piles. When you get to a fork, keep left. You can hike down the other side and down to Tularosa. Head to the Walmart parking lot, I'll have a car waiting. Call me from there."

Dan tucked the gun behind his back. It had been a long time since he had felt the cold, heavy weight pressing there. "You going to be all right?"

"I know this mountain better than you know your living room." Alex smiled. "I'll be fine. Now get going."

Alex moved to the edge, crouched down, and dropped out of sight. Down the slope behind him, Dan could hear the gunman coming up the last switchback before the area where he stood, and knew he had only seconds of lead time now. He turned and ran, following the trail up the mountain.

* * *

How did I find myself here?

The thought kept coming back to him as he ran, ignoring the pain in his ankle, bracing his hands on rocky outcroppings when he nearly lost his balance. His eyes scanned up the trail so he would not lose precious time searching for the way when it became faint, which happened repeatedly, the path vanishing into a small field of thin grass or huge piles of rocks he had to scramble across. Always, when he looked, there was a marking painted onto a stone, or a small tower of rocks to mark the way, and soon he found the path once again. He had lost track of how long he had been climbing, but his breathing was more labored from the altitude, and the air was colder up here. He was thankful for the marathons he had run and the endless days spent on his feet, for at least his legs were holding up, if sore. Below, he could make out the lights from the reservation, including George and Sally Bear's house, already looking small and distant. He hoped desperately that everyone was safe there.

The weather had begun to change, the clear night giving way to thick grey clouds rolling in, and now the first tiny, stinging droplets of rain were striking his face and hands as he pushed on. Every so often he heard the man pursuing him, his grunts of effort or the skitter of pebbles that his boot dislodged, but so far Dan had managed to maintain the distance between them. His pursuer could likely climb faster, but had to work even harder to keep from losing the trail or his prey.

Dan thought about crouching behind a boulder, waiting, and shooting the man dead when he appeared. But despite the circumstances, a big part of him recoiled from the idea. He was in the business of saving lives, not taking them. And he only had two rounds left, so if he missed, or only wounded the other man, he would be out of chances. Even if he managed to stop the man after him, there was no telling how many others might be waiting at the bottom of the slope now, or at the Bears' house. He would have to hope that Alex and his friends could keep George and Sally safe, and the artificial hearts and flash drives, while he escaped over the mountain as Alex had wanted him to.

It got darker as cloud cover obscured the moon. His head felt strange from the lack of oxygen, and his body started to ache. Ahead, the mountain peak rose, looking deceptively close. The summit could not be that much farther but he knew that it would be harder than it looked to reach it. The raindrops got fatter, harder, starting to pelt him now as he pressed forward, having to spend more time on hands and knees to scramble up. Electricity built around him from the gathering storm. The path was getting harder and harder to find, and even as he followed it, the trail grew narrower and more treacherous—steep drop-offs to one side, slippery scree that slid out from under his boots, and sharp rocks protruding from the mountain like teeth from an open mouth.

His boot slid out from under him, the loose rocks carrying him down three feet until his hand snagged an outcropping and he stopped the slide. Rocks shot off the edge of the trail, falling so far he didn't hear them land. Heart thudding, Dan regained his footing. He climbed upward, no longer seeing the path, searching for markings. He could hear the gunman, very close now, but it was so dark with the clouds and rain that he could see almost nothing behind him.

But up ahead, he saw the fork that Alex had mentioned—signified only by two small cairns of rock, one off to the right and likely heading to the summit, and another to the left, the way Alex had said would take him down the mountain. A few more steps, and his pursuer, not knowing the land, would hopefully choose the wrong path and be diverted. Dan climbed toward the left-hand cairn.

Bullets pinged off the stone directly by his head, causing a small slide of gravel. Dan half-turned, and now he could see the other man not twenty yards back on the trail, his gun up and firing, little bursts of light from its muzzle the only giveaway. He was too close for Dan to turn and climb. Dan drew his own gun, aimed for one of the man's running legs, and fired. Missed. Bullets kept ricocheting off the rock wall behind him.

One round left. Dan took careful aim and squeezed the trigger. The gun fired, and the man cried out and fell on the trail, clutching at his leg. But then, instead of turning back, instead of dropping and clutching his leg, the man dragged himself up, recovered his gun, and staggered forward—firing at Dan. Even as Dan turned to climb, the gunman took another lunging step, but this time his feet slid completely out from under him as the ground gave way. He clutched at the rock face, fingers scrabbling for purchase, but in seconds he had lost his balance entirely and tumbled off the side of the trail. Dan heard his scream and then a quick, sickening impact.

Part of him wanted to just keep going. But he moved back down the trail to where the other man had fallen and peered over. The man had not fallen far—maybe twenty feet—but he had landed on a sharp outcrop of rock. Over the building storm, Dan could hear the man's quiet gasps of pain.

If he was careful, Dan could climb down to where the man lay, bracing himself between two large rocks. He made his way down slowly, testing each step, until he was able to kneel by the man's still figure. The first lightning flashed above, arcing between the clouds, and in the glare Dan saw that the man's hands were empty, the gun having fallen somewhere farther down the slope.

"What a stupid," the man said, and then coughed, his fingers pressing to his leg. Blood seeped around them. It was several seconds before he could finish. "Stupid way to die."

Dan reached into the man's back pocket and withdrew his wallet. Jacob Reid. Perhaps not his real name, but possibly. "Why are you people trying to kill me, Jacob?"

"Just a job," the man said.

"A job." Dan tried to feel compassionate, to embrace the same feelings that made him want to save the life of every patient who crossed his operating table, regardless of what choices the person had made before then. But it was a lot harder this time.

"Gotta put food on the table somehow," Jacob said. His hands moved from his leg to a gash in his side, where he had landed on the rock.

Dan pushed the man's hands aside, ripped and balled a length of the man's shirt, and pressed it firmly against the wound. "There are better ways to make money."

"But not faster." Jacob sank back against the rock. He cursed, his eyes now closing against the rain.

"Don't give up yet," Dan said. From what he could see, the man's injuries from the fall were not immediately life threatening; the real danger lay in blood loss from the leg wound.

"Not worried about me, Doc." Jacob's voice was thin, weak.

Something about what the other man had said prompted Dan to lean a little closer, his tone softening. "You have a family."

"Yeah."

"Tell me about them." Hands moving quickly, Dan removed Jacob's belt, looped it around his leg just above the gunshot wound in his lower thigh, and cinched it tightly. The blood had pooled thickly on the rocks, the pelting rain unable to wash it away quickly enough, but with the makeshift tourniquet the flow slowed dramatically.

Jacob spoke faintly as Dan worked. "A three-year-old. Min.

We adopted her from Korea, and she was supposed to be healthy." He kept his hands against the balled fabric at his side. "But she's sick."

"Tell me."

The man's words came slowly. "Gets tired. Tired a lot. She squats down, and her lips turn a little blue."

Dan nodded. "Has she been diagnosed?"

There was no answer.

"Jacob? Stay with me."

Dan elevated the injured leg, propping it on a rock. The man's eyes were closed, but he was still breathing, and when Dan eased him into a halfway sitting position, he groaned. Dan checked his side and back, which were badly bruised—possibly even some broken bones—but he found nothing lodged or penetrating.

Dan slapped the man's face lightly, and his eyes opened. "You have a phone?"

"Pocket…"

Dan dug inside Jacob's jacket until he found it, and he leaned over to protect it from the falling rain. As he figured, there was no signal.

"We can't call for help, but they'll come looking for you. Keep the leg up. Keep pressure on the cut on your side until it stops bleeding. You should be okay." Dan started to replace the phone, but on impulse he scrolled through Jacob Reid's messages and call log, not sure what he was searching for.

There were no incriminating text messages, just some that appeared to be from his wife, but there were recent calls to and from someone named Robert Krum. He made a note of the area codes of other recent calls so he could look them up, but one stuck out to him—512. Wasn't that Austin? He had seen the number when he looked up the address for Worldwide Medical Research. Before it burned.

"You're going to tell your boss that I have the hearts," Dan said. "You hear me? Tell him the Bear family has nothing to do with this. They're not targets."

Jacob's head turned to the side, eyes closing again. "You don't know what I'm going to do. You've got no idea."

"No, I don't," Dan admitted. It was true. Kneeling there in the rain on the side of the mountain, Dan could only guess what this man would do if Dan let him live. "I can hope, though."

Around him, the rain poured down, and the air crackled with electricity moments before another bolt of lightning blasted in the clouds above, alarmingly close. Dan replaced the phone, stood, and turned. He reached for the first handhold to pull himself up, but as he gripped the rock, he looked back.

"Your daughter has Tetralogy of Fallot," he said. "It's a congenital heart defect. You need to get it corrected with a pediatric heart surgeon."

He could not make out the other man's expression in the dark, but he saw his attacker nod, just staring. The lightning flashed again, and Dan began to climb.

Chapter Sixteen

When Dan awoke to utter darkness, he felt sudden disorientation and then fear—he had no idea where he was. Every inch of him ached. He rolled over and sat up, palms resting on cool stone, and the events of the previous night surged into his clearing thoughts. The memories did nothing to make him feel better.

A cave. I'm in a cave on a mountainside, waiting out a storm, because people are trying to kill me for something I didn't even create.

Not the best way to start a day.

He groaned and stretched, his eyes still straining for some indication of light, some clue to the contours of the caves, but the blackness was complete. He had not intended to fall asleep, had stumbled into the cave in the downpour not long after he began the descent from the path's fork near the summit. It was an escape from the icy rain pelting him, and although he had worried about wildlife likewise sheltering within, the stone warren had been empty. A short tunnel curved to the right, ending in a bare chamber. He had lain down, occasional lightning flashes illuminating the space perhaps twice the size of his living room at home, and had apparently passed out from exhaustion.

His clothes were mostly dry now, though the cuffs of his

pants and shirt were still damp. He was hungry, but most of all he was terribly thirsty. Once he made it down the mountain, finding water would need to be a priority.

Dan stood and tried walking with hands outstretched until they met the wall, but then he did not know which way to go, and for the next few minutes it led him nowhere. Rather than take the time to follow it around, he used his other senses; he could hear air moving over the mouth of the cave, and when he went toward it, he passed into the tunnel and soon saw a dim light ahead. He reached it and emerged onto the mountainside, the path continuing on and down the slope toward Tularosa. It was still dark, a dazzling spread of stars visible now that the storm had blown by, its clouds dissipating. But the horizon held the pale glow that promised dawn approaching.

The trail was peaceful, and he was able to appreciate the mountain's beauty now that no one was chasing him—at least, that he could see. After half an hour of hiking across mostly scrub and rock, he reached the timberline about the time the sunrise broke the horizon and began to paint the land in warm shades of pink and orange. The trees, stately and tall Ponderosa Pines and New Mexico cedar, were lit golden; the insects, birds, and small animals woke up and began their day, skittering through the underbrush or flitting through branches overhead. The world came alive around him.

Going down the mountain was easier than going up, although the constant downward grade did wear on his knees. Still, the activity helped work out the soreness from sleeping on the cavern floor, and he found his body waking up even as his mind did. He indulged in what seemed a reasonable amount of anger and even self-pity, but then he did his best to tuck this away and focus on the problems at hand, mentally turning them over and over as he hiked.

By the time he reached the base of the mountain, emerging at the trailhead and from there finding his way to the closest road, he had a plan in mind.

* * *

The road led into Tularosa, and just as Alex had promised, a car waited at the edge of the Walmart parking lot. It was a battered old Ford Taurus, dark green, and the only car at the farthest end of the lot, so Dan figured it was the one left for him. Rusted holes pock-marked the fenders, the right side was dented in, and the paint was flaking off, but he found the keys tucked up in the driver's side wheel well. He slid in and started the car, and he could not believe how smoothly the engine ran, given the car's exterior. Dan caught a glimpse of himself in the rear-view—face filthy and stubbled, hair matted, mud caked around his collar, shirt torn and speckled red.

Weary and dehydrated, he trudged into the store and found the restroom, where he washed up as best he could, rinsing dirt and blood from his hands and arms. Then he purchased a sandwich and two bottles of water, paying cash.

The cashier raised her eyebrows at him. "You look like you need more than water and a sandwich," she said. "You need me to call you a doctor?"

"I am a doctor," Dan muttered, snagging the bag and heading for the exit. He had devoured the sandwich and drank a whole bottle of water before he had even reached the Taurus, and he had to restrain himself from downing the other bottle, too.

In the car, he found the store's Wi-Fi signal and used it to search on his phone for information about Robert Krum. Head of Health Now, a major insurance company, but with ties to global interventions in medical research, tissue banks, organ transplants, and more… mostly it seemed above-board, but as he dug deeper, he found complaints, lawsuits, investigations, and strange gaps in information. He found his suspicions growing. Could this man be responsible for the loss of Kim's life, and the attempts on his own? For putting Alex and his family in danger?

Alex. Surely he was safe, and it might be a risk to call him, but Dan had to know. He dialed, and Alex picked up after the first ring.

"Dan, tell me you're okay," Alex said.

"Yes, I'm fine. I made it over just like you said. You and your parents safe?"

"We're good. I got the drop on that guy just before he headed into their house. I got the gun from him, and he ran, managed to get away. I didn't want to go too far from my parents in case there were others."

"I don't blame you." Dan released a long breath, feeling some of the tension easing up now that he knew the Bears were safe.

"Some friends came over to help keep an eye on our place. I took the ECMO out of Dad, and he's recovering well."

"And the duffel bag?"

"Safe for now. I'm going to hide it today until you can come back for it."

"Thanks, Alex. I owe you big."

Alex gave a little laugh. "Oh, I don't know. You saved my father's life, so I think we're pretty much even. You figure out your next move yet?"

"Have a few ideas. I'll be in touch. Meantime, make sure you and your parents are safe, all right?"

"These friends of mine don't mess around. Unless somebody sends an army, we'll be fine. Stay safe, Dan."

"You, too."

Dan disconnected, and then, before he could lose his nerve, made the next call. He had no idea if this was his best option or the worst possible decision he could make, but he knew this—he wanted to find, and help to stop, the people responsible for everything that had happened, and he needed help in order to do that.

She picked up right away, and she sounded tired, but sharp—like she had been up all night but was still at the top of her game. "Agent Brown. Is this Dan Parker?"

"Yes, it is. I think we need to meet."

"So do I. Tell me where and when."

"Tularosa. There's a bakery on St. Francis, I'll be sitting out front. Can you meet me at four o'clock?"

The most fractional pause. "Yes. I can fly into Alamogordo-White Sands Regional and drive up from there."

"Just you." Dan continued with as much authority and inflexibility as he could muster. "I don't want to see anybody else. If I do, I'm gone. You offered to help me, and I'm choosing to trust you."

"Dr. Parker, if I wanted to take you in, I can promise that you still wouldn't see anybody else." She let that sink in. "But I meant what I said. It's not too popular in my office to follow your gut, but my instincts tell me you're not the enemy here. I'm choosing to trust you, too."

"Fair enough. Have a good flight, Agent Brown."

"Save me some sweet breads."

Dan hung up and sat for a few minutes in the car, just staring at the dashboard without really seeing it. Just days ago he was a cardiovascular surgeon with no greater concern than whether the chief of medical affairs would pursue suspension because he had chosen to put his patients' needs first. Granted, that was a big concern—his livelihood, his career, and his passion—but now it seemed small in comparison to the safety of his friends and family, and his own. Not to mention securing a medical break-through that could change the world. And here he was sitting in a parking lot in a car that wasn't his, waiting to meet with an FBI agent who could easily toss him in a federal penitentiary and throw away the key.

Well. Nothing to do that would change any of that now. The die was cast.

Dan drove until he spotted a cheap, unremarkable motel, The Desert Inn, where he used nearly the last of his cash to rent a room. It was dingy, painted tan, the type where you parked in front of your door. Two stories. He used a different name, and when they asked for ID he apologetically explained that he had left it in the car, and the unsmiling lady behind the desk waved it off. She passed across the key and Dan exited the office and climbed to the second floor. Behind a faded turquoise door he found a somewhat-grimy room with a generically Southwestern print on the bedspread and wallpaper, a TV that didn't work, and stains on the carpet that he did not want to think about.

But it had a shower and a bed, and although they were as run-down as the rest of the establishment, Dan had never enjoyed either more. By mid-afternoon, he was clean and moderately rested, and he spent the last of his time before the meeting with

Agent Brown reading up more on Robert Krum and Health Now.

About thirty minutes prior to the scheduled meeting time, he drove the short distance and parked a block up from the bakery. He approached cautiously, searching for any indication that others were in place, but saw nothing. As Lucy had said, he probably wouldn't even if they were there, and although his heart hammered to simply stride up—even in a public place like this—he eventually resigned himself to whatever chain of events he had set in motion. He walked down the street until he reached the bakery, where a couple of small tables with chairs were set on the sidewalk out front. Dan took a seat and prepared to wait, but he did not have to wait long.

Behind him, the door to the bakery opened, a bell above it jingling. A short, blonde woman in jeans and a black jacket held the door open with one hand, the other clasping a couple of Mexican baked goods wrapped in a paper sleeve. She held the door for another customer coming out, and as she did her jacket fell away from her side in a way that allowed Dan to glimpse the handgun strapped to her hip. It somehow seemed intentional. The woman let the door swing shut and slid into the chair opposite Dan, wearing an easy smile.

"Dr. Parker, I'm assuming." She extended her hand across the table, the paper crinkling. "*Pan de paño?*"

Chapter Seventeen

Dan wasn't sure what he was expecting, had not put any conscious thought into it, but as the woman slid into the opposite seat and offered him a pink icing-topped sweet bread, he knew that whatever his mental image had been she did not match it. She was official-looking enough; her golden hair was secured in a neat bun, her cream-colored blouse was modest, and the gun he'd glimpsed beneath her jacket certainly bore the stamp of authority. But her eyes were crinkled with laugh lines at the corners, and her smile seemed unforced, like they were sharing a glass of iced tea on the front porch watching fireflies. Her blue eyes sparkled—cowgirl eyes, shiny as rhinestones—and she had pink icing stuck to the corner of her lips, which were a pale coral shade. Her age was hard to place, as she seemed youthful, her short figure fit and toned, but as he watched her he felt sure she was quite a bit older than she looked.

"I already had one," she said. "Help yourself."

A bit disarmed, he found himself picking up the *pan de paño* and taking a bite, the sweet taste crumbling into his mouth, as she lounged in her chair and rested an arm casually on the table.

"It took a lot of courage to meet like this," she said.

He felt his guard dropping further, and it startled him. He met her gaze directly. And then he saw it, and only because he was looking—a steely edge in her eyes, an unflinching iron core that lay behind the sunshine and roses. No mistaking it—every word and move this woman made was carefully calculated.

"Are you wearing a wire?" he said.

The agent sat straighter, noting the shift, some of the pretense falling away. "Would it make a difference?" She wiped the icing from the corner of her mouth, sucked it from her fingertip, and produced a pack of cigarettes from inside her jacket. Lucy tapped one out, taking her time with it, drew a lighter from her pocket, and lit up with a long, smooth draw. She offered it to him, the smoke curling between them.

"Gracious, no," Dan said. "You have any idea how many people I operate on with lung cancer?"

Her eyebrows arched. "A lot?"

"None. I'm a cardiovascular surgeon, not a surgical oncologist."

Lucy let out a laugh. "Is that doctor humor?"

"Okay, actually, I do a lot of lung resections for a variety of reasons. But point is, most lung tumors are inoperable." He was trying to mimic her casualness, to show he was at ease as much as she. He wasn't sure if it was working. "Out of a hundred people with lung cancer, maybe fifteen or twenty will still be alive five years later."

Lucy smiled widely. "I'll probably die an early death anyway. Might as well enjoy it."

The expression on her face, the twinkle in her eyes, were undeniably charming, but Dan felt manipulated again. He tapped his fingers on the table as she smoked half her cigarette, the two of them just taking each other's measure. Dan decided that he was not offended by the woman's calculated moves—but he would not want to cross her. Despite the easy smile, something behind those blue eyes was as cold and unyielding as frozen steel.

"So," Lucy said, tapping ash, "tell me your story. And I'll tell you where we go from here."

After a moment's hesitation, Dan began to talk. He told his story for the second time, not withholding anything except for the fact that Alex was hiding the bag of data and prototypes. He found his heart rate increasing when he spoke about the plane crash, as anger surged through him in the retelling, and again when he described the attack at George and Sally Bear's home. Finally, he shared about the numbers he had found on the gunman's phone and his suspicions about Robert Krum. Through it all, Lucy just sat and listened, not taking notes, simply smoking her cigarette impassively.

He finished, and she stubbed her smoke out in the center of the sweet bread. "Quite a story."

"Now it's your turn. Your turn to talk."

Lucy shrugged. "Not a lot to tell. I live for coffee, relaxing bubble baths, and long nights at the gun range." She grinned, and this time it looked real, though it was very hard to tell. Did she let him see through the first act on purpose, just so she could fool him with the second?

"You said that following your instincts isn't popular in your office, but you do it anyway," Dan said. "You sound like a bit of a renegade."

"Takes one to know one, eh, doc?" She broke off a piece of the sweet bread, flicked ash off it, and nibbled at the corner. "You don't exactly follow the rules at Amarillo Medical Center."

He started to ask how she could possibly know that, but of course she had done her homework on him. Had probably spoken to half a dozen people at the hospital, and he could only imagine that Dr. Golden Shaw had found plenty of less-than-glowing things to say about him.

"Here's the thing, Dan," Lucy said. "I've been investigating Robert Krum for a long time, with dead end after dead end. The man knows how to cover his tracks, and he's got pockets deep enough to pay off or get rid of anybody who might speak against him."

"So you think I'm right. He killed Kim Konno and tried to kill me, too."

"What I *think* doesn't make a bit of difference. What I can prove in a court of law, that's what interests me. It's clear he's a crook, overcharging people for their insurance and denying most medical claims, but I can't put him away for nearly long enough on that." She leaned across the table, closing the distance between them until it would appear to any passerby that she was imparting an intimate secret—and perhaps she was. He found himself leaning in as well, watching her lips move, the words soft.

"I can't prove it yet, but I believe he's heavily involved in the medical black market for organs and tissues," she said. "Cities around the world, people are disappearing. There's a thriving ring, connected not just to corrupt funeral homes and crematoriums, but to tissue banks, and to wealthy clients so desperate for an organ transplant for their loved one that they don't ask where it came from. People are vanishing, undesirables nobody cares about—poor, homeless, prostitutes. A single body can generate over $200,000 in organs. It's huge money for Krum."

For a moment, Dan could not decide how to respond. It was

horrifying—and it was far worse even than he had imagined. He had suspected Krum was willing to let one researcher die, perhaps get rid of a couple other loose threads, in order to get his hands on artificial organs that would change the face of medical care and spell a fortune for him. But to wilfully take lives around the world as a routine part of doing business? It meant that the misery Dan had endured these past days was no more than a blip on the radar for a man like Robert Krum. Destroying someone's life was just another day in the office.

Lucy was watching him in that calculating way again, her blue eyes almost shining. "I feel the same way," she murmured at last.

Dan realized then that she had steered the whole conversation in this direction, had intended from the very start for him to ask the question that could not, now, be kept inside. Despite this, he couldn't help asking it. "So what can we do?"

"Well, funny you should ask," she said, as if a little surprised by the question, "but Krum depends on partnerships with corrupt doctors who will do his black market dirty work for him. Disgruntled physicians and surgeons who got tired of working ninety-hour work weeks and seeing their income drop every year while the insurance companies get fatter and fatter." She didn't say it, but the *Sound familiar?* tone was implicit in her voice.

Clear as day, he knew then why she had agreed to meet him alone. "You want me to infiltrate his organization."

"You'd have my support. Contacts to get you in, a new identity, documents, a background to match that would hold up when Krum checks you out."

"That's insane." Dan rubbed his temples, amazed he was even having this conversation. "I'm a doctor, not an undercover agent."

"You sound like McCoy on *Star Trek*."

"I'm not kidding! I can't just fly off to some other country and start hacking up bodies for criminals. No."

"Not asking you to," she said. "With your skillset, you'd probably be put to work implanting the organs into the new recipients."

"Probably?"

"Look, I'm not gonna lie to you, Dan." She folded her arms on the table, meeting his gaze squarely, and he saw the iron will again, behind her eyes and in the set of her jaw. "It's dangerous. If any of these people realize you're trying to get information, and passing it to me, they'll kill you on the spot. So, yeah, I'm asking a lot. But this guy has to be stopped."

Dan shook his head. "Why me, though?"

She began to tick off the reasons on her fingers. "Because they're expecting agents like me to try this. They're not looking for you. You have the skill to do the needed medical procedures and gain their trust. You have the knowledge to know what to look for in their records. You have the expertise and credibility to ensure powerful testimony in court when you testify to what you saw. You have a personal reason to want to take Krum down. You have motivation to get your life back. And you have training from your time in the Marines, so you can defend yourself if it comes down to it."

She let her line of reasoning settle, like a weight pressing onto Dan's shoulders. And when the pressure was such that he felt himself starting to give in, she threw down the final piece. "And, because this is a man who will not forgive you for taking the hearts and running... and he knows who your wife and daughter are."

Dan felt his final resolve giving way. He balled his fist on the table, squeezing it with his other hand until the knuckles popped. Lucy could see in his expression that she had won, but she only nodded and sat back in her chair.

"I'll help you every step of the way," she said. "I'll also put a protective detail in place to keep an eye on your family, discreetly. And as soon as you find proof of Krum's involvement, either in the black market ring or in the fire in Austin, I'll get you safely out and you can go back to your life." Reaching into another jacket pocket, she pulled out a wallet and produced a thin stack of bills, which she passed to him. "This should cover a motel for tonight, if you're getting low on cash. And go to Walmart to buy some new clothes. The ones you've got on look like you've been in a war. Tomorrow morning, you're flying to Mumbai. I took the liberty of booking your flight—or rather, a flight for Dr. Steven Richards. Before you leave, I'll bring you everything you'll need. Clothes, IDs, passport, untraceable cards, and a clean phone. By then, a full background for Steven Richards will be available online, going deep enough that it should convince Krum. I'll give you more instructions when I come by tomorrow. Do you have a place yet?"

Dan swallowed, his throat dry. "Yeah. The Desert Inn. Room 22."

"Good. I'll see you at 6:30 tomorrow morning. Rest while you can."

She stood, straightened her jacket, and scooped the remains of the sweet bread and wrapper off the table. Lucy tossed them into a nearby wastebasket. She started down the sidewalk, but Dan called after her.

"One other question," he said. He looked up and down the street, but could still see only locals and a handful of tourists going about their business. "Did you really come alone like I asked?"

"Guess you'll never know," Lucy said. She pulled out a pair of dark sunglasses, the rims shiny gold, and popped them onto her face. "Oh, and I have one more question for you, too."

He stood from his chair, turning to face her, and she grinned again. "Any chance your motel has a continental breakfast?"

Chapter Eighteen

The knock sounded on the motel room door at 6:30 on the dot, three quick raps. Dan was already showered and dressed, sitting on the edge of the bed with his hands on his knees and fighting to still his restless thoughts. He had barely slept, finally abandoning the pursuit around four a.m. The room was cold. The thermostat was broken, and his hands trembled slightly, which he attributed to the low temps. Normally his hands never shook.

At the knocks, he jumped up and swung wide the door, realizing his mistake immediately. It was Agent Brown, sure enough, but of course he should have checked. She wore the same outfit as the day before, but now her blouse was rumpled, like she had slept in it. She held a cardboard tray that supported two steaming coffees and a couple of breakfast burritos, and a grey carry-on bag was slung over her shoulder.

"Did you even look through the peephole?" She scowled at him. "I'd think your paranoia would be in overdrive by now."

"Sorry," he said, stepping back so she could enter and locking the door behind her. "Guess I'm not used to having international criminals gunning for me."

"Well, you better get used to it fast. We've got an hour." Lucy put the tray and bag on the bed and sat in the room's only chair, crossing her legs. "No continental breakfast, by the way. I checked. So help yourself."

Not really feeling hungry, Dan unwrapped one of the burritos and passed her the other. He took bites as she talked, and so did she, speaking around mouthfuls of eggs and chorizo.

"Everything you'll need is in that bag. I want you to leave everything else with me—your wallet, phone, anything that's yours." She took a sip of the coffee and hissed through her teeth at the heat. "When you step out of this hotel room, you're leaving Dan Parker behind."

Dan unzipped the bag and rummaged through the contents. On top, in a clear baggie, were a passport and a new wallet. The passport held the same photo of him that he was used to, but the name read Steven Richards. In the wallet was a new driver's license similarly updated—current photo, new information. It listed the home address for Steven Richards in Brooklyn.

"I don't talk like a New Yorker," Dan said, tapping the license.

"You grew up in Texas and did your residency in the Midwest. You only moved to New York four years ago."

Dan flipped through the cards in the wallet—a gym membership, a savings card for a pizza joint, a movie rental place, a grocery store, all of them with Brooklyn addresses. If someone snooped through his wallet, it would be convincing. It also held several hundred U.S. dollars and about fifty thousand rupees.

"You've thought of everything," he said.

"Bon voyage, Dr. Parker." She smiled. "And salaam, Dr. Richards."

* * *

He had of course flown countless times before, but the lurch in his stomach when the airplane's wheels left the ground was something he hadn't felt since he flew for the very first time, a young man on his way to Beaufort, South Carolina, and the Marine Corps Recruit Depot on Parris Island. He hadn't thought of that trip in a long time. Scarcely more than a boy, but determined to serve, to protect and heal. He'd been raw and naïve, but on a different flight a handful of years later—this one returning to the States—his nerves were unshakable and he had felt nothing would surprise him again.

Well. So much for certainty. Staring out the window as the ground dropped away, New Mexico spreading out below him like a patchwork quilt as the plane tilted to aim for the east, Dan knew that never in his wildest dreams could he have imagined this journey. His whole life had been a series of high-stakes decisions and life-and-death consequences, but the weight of his responsibility had never pressed more heavily. Laura. Marla. Countless people around the world. All depending on his ability to find the needed information and pass himself off as someone that he thankfully wasn't—a corrupt, disgruntled, bitter doctor.

He had acted just once, that turn in *A Midsummer Night's Dream* in his senior year of high school, at the urging of his mother. What was the part? Something cozy-sounding. Snug, that was it. Snug the joiner, a dim-witted character with few lines. A lifetime ago.

His concerns had certainly shifted since then. Before leaving the motel room, he had convinced Lucy Brown to let him leave a message with his old phone for his wife. A part of him was grateful when she didn't pick up, though he longed to hear her voice. He left what he hoped was a convincing voicemail about the

week-long international medical convention he'd been required
to attend at the last minute, how he was all recovered from the
crash, had helped Alex's father, and thought getting back into
work concerns would help him, and how he was having trouble
with his phone and she shouldn't worry if she couldn't reach him.
They would sort everything out when he got back, he said, and it
would all be better. And he loved them and wanted more than
anything to be with them again. That part was the truth.

During the flight, he thought over Lucy's directions, few
though there were. He was to follow the lead of her contact in
Mumbai, who would try to keep tabs on him once he was embed-
ded in Krum's organization. And, if possible, this contact would
pass off a camera to him for documenting what he saw. He was to
witness all he could and gather as much evidence as possible.
Next, Dan set to studying the information that she had instructed
him to memorize—*internalize completely* had been her phrase—
before he landed in India. She had downloaded a file to his new,
clean phone and made sure he knew how to delete that file before
stepping off the last plane. It held a wealth of background
information about Dr. Steven Richards: where he had gone to
school (Midland, Texas), who his childhood friends had been
(Fred and Ted, twins from down the street), what had happened
to his parents (father ran off with a secretary, mother died of lung
cancer fifteen years later), and on and on it went. Magazine sub-
scriptions, favorite restaurants, musical tastes. Fitness and hobbies
(reading, gym, boxing classes). Dating and marital history (divorced, no kids). Trained in CV surgery in Houston, had several
malpractice events and lost his Texas license, which hopefully
made him fit the profile that appealed to Krum. They had created
an entire life, and buried enough artificial confirmation in the

world to create the digital footprint that the majority of human beings on the planet create.

He had plenty of time to study. A fairly short flight to Dallas, a brief layover, and then a nine-hour overnight flight to London, where he sat in the airport for two hours, had breakfast, and boarded another nine-hour flight to Mumbai, where by the time of his arrival it was just after midnight the following day. He was twelve and a half hours ahead of New Mexico time now, which made his internal clock set precisely opposite to the sun. He had slept a little on the planes, but he was still exhausted and jet-lagged, unshaven and disheveled, as he stumbled out of the gate and into the concourse of Chhatrapati Shivaji International Airport.

But he knew this other man's life story, backward and forward. And when an Indian man in a dark jacket approached him —extending a hand and asking, "Dr. Richards?"—Dan answered without hesitation.

"That's me."

* * *

The man's name was Pravek Singh, or at least he said it was, and he was Lucy's man in Mumbai. He was not FBI, nor CIA, though it was unclear to Dan what in fact he was, then. He had been in place as an asset here for two years, but Singh refused to insert himself very deeply into Krum's network, unwilling to take the risk. He maintained his cover as a low-tier criminal, coordinating shipments of other black-market goods and occasionally crossing paths with Krum's men, enough to pass steady but only nominally useful intel to D.C. He knew where to find Krum's people, though.

R D SUTHERLAND

Singh was medium height, middle-aged, and not prone to small talk. Dan gave up trying after the first three exchanges resulted only in nods or shrugs. Singh had a car parked outside the terminal, a blue sedan, and he drove the two of them away from the airport and then south toward Dharavi.

When it was clear that Singh was not inclined to conversation, Dan stared out the window, at the masses of people crowding the streets, at the endless stretches of buildings, at the cluttered avenues overflowing with taxi cabs, carts, and pedestrians, always people, people everywhere, on the sidewalks, between cars, on bicycles, in doorways. The city changed. He saw market stalls, cafes, vendors hawking their wares; it changed again, and he glimpsed the slums, abject poverty stretching as far as the eye could see.

"We're getting close," Singh said, startling him.

"To where?"

"Your stop. You're looking for a man named Tagore. He tipped you off about an opportunity for a man with your skills in this area. You came to find out more."

"Where will I find this Tagore?"

"You won't. He's dead."

Dan couldn't help sitting up a little straighter. He had scarcely been off the plane an hour and his contact was dead.

"Lucky for you," Singh said, "because that means he can't contradict your story. Which means maybe you can pin the tip on him."

"How am I supposed to get an introduction to Krum's men?"

"By asking for Tagore. That will get you noticed. They're looking for a few highly skilled men because four of Krum's top

156

guys here disappeared a couple days ago. Tagore being one of them. But you, Dr. Richards, don't know that."

"Right," Dan said, already feeling the water rising over his head.

"Try the bar at the end of the street," Singh said, pulling to the side of the road about two blocks from it.

"You coming with me?" Dan pulled the door handle.

Singh laughed. "Friend, I complete my part of this when I hand over your bag. And then you should give me a tip, so if anyone's watching it looks like I'm just picking up cash as your driver."

They both got out, and Singh opened the trunk and passed the carry-on bag to Dan, who slipped a bill into his palm. Singh nodded briskly, climbed back into the car, and drove off without a backward glance.

Dan hefted the bag and walked down the sidewalk, shouldering his way through the crowds. He thought that Singh needn't have bothered with the subterfuge; he didn't see how anyone could see anything in the throng of people. He could smell strange scents from unknown herbs and spices, the reek of the homeless and unwashed, the refuse in the gutter. Bright colors and indecipherable symbols surrounded him, words scrawled on signs and walls in Marathi, Gujarati, and Hindi, with the occasional English word slipping in—Coca-Cola, eat, beer, girls. People tried to sell him things, tried to entice him to stop to eat or shop, or begged for a few rupees. He saw a girl with no hands, a man with no legs, countless without shoes. He wanted to help them all. Dan forced himself to keep walking. He reached the bar, a run-down establishment that did not even seem to have a name, and stepped inside.

Dive bars look much the same the world over, and this one did not break the mold. It was dimly lit, with a few patrons at stools at the bar and a few others scattered around tables. Shelves of alcohol, a few drinks on tap, local brews he didn't know. The clientele were mostly Indian, but he saw a few who seemed to be Europeans, if he had to guess. The bartender was a young local who barely looked up when he entered.

Dan stepped to the bar and placed his hands atop it. "First time in Mumbai. Got a beer you recommend?"

The guy shrugged. "People like Kingfisher. Or Haywards. We have Kalyani Black Label, Knock Out, whatever you want."

"Kingfisher." Dan waited while it was poured, asked how much, and passed across a generous tip. As the bartender picked it up, Dan slid a second bill onto the bar, bigger than the first, but kept two fingers on it. The guy glanced at him. "Looking for someone. Maybe you've seen him? Tagore."

The bartender stiffened. "Sorry. Don't know him."

"You see a lot of people, I'm sure," Dan said, drawing another bill from his wallet and placing it atop the other. "Think hard."

The young guy stared at the bills on the stained wood for a long few seconds. Finally he leaned over the bar, his voice low, his eyes moving around the room before settling on Dan. "He's dead. No good reason you'd be asking about him. Told you what I can." He put his hand on the bills and Dan let him take them.

Dan drank his beer, and the bartender moved down the bar and then, out of the corner of his eye, Dan saw him disappear into a back room. He waited, but the bartender did not reappear. Dan finished the Kingfisher and judged that perhaps seven minutes had passed. He could see no one in the bar paying him any attention whatsoever, so he stood, picked up his bag, and walked out the exit.

A fist slammed into the side of his head with enough force to knock him clear off his feet. As he fell toward the ground, strong arms caught him, roughly hauled him back onto his feet even as stars danced in his vision, and dragged him around the side of the bar to an alley. He was slammed against the wall. His head cracked back even as another blow drove into his ribs. A second punch connected with his jaw, and he tasted blood. Then Dan let long-dormant instincts take over.

There were three men. Big, burly, leading with their fists. The closest drew back and threw a furious punch toward Dan's stomach—but rather than block, Dan twisted to the side at the last instant, and the man's coiled fist slammed into the brick wall instead. The man screamed, drawing back his bloody and broken hand. The second man threw another punch at Dan's head, and Dan blocked with his forearm. He then grabbed the other man's wrist, pulled him off balance, and drove his elbow into the man's throat. The man collapsed, wheezing for breath. The third man drew a gun and leveled it at Dan's head.

Dan stilled. He raised his hands. The man with the broken hand, who looked American, was cursing and cradling it to his chest, while the other massaged his throat and watched.

"Just looking for someone," Dan said. "Got a tip that there were opportunities for a man with my skillset, and Tagore was the person to see. That's it."

"You'll see him, all right," growled the American, glaring at the Indian man with the gun. "What you waiting for?"

"And what skillset would that be?" the man with the gun said.

He was dark-skinned, mid-thirties, with a neatly-trimmed beard. He spoke with perfect, unaccented English.

"Surgery," Dan said, and let that hang in the air only a second before adding, "and organ transplants, in particular."

The man with the gun did not react at all, and the weapon remained trained on Dan's forehead. Five seconds passed, ten. The other man's eyes revealed nothing, dark and thoughtful.

At last the gun lowered, and Dan released a small breath.

"Fortunately for you," the man said, "we might have an opening."

Chapter Nineteen

When the hood was yanked off of Dan's head, it took a moment for his vision to focus. He was in some kind of converted industrial space, the bottom floor gutted and now being used for warehousing—pallets of crates and boxes filled the far side of the large room he sat in. He was bound to a metal chair, hands zip-tied behind his back, while a harsh, yellow bulb shone down on him. At the periphery of its circle of light, he could see the men who had brought him here, having put the hood over his head and then trundled him into a car for a short, perhaps ten minute, drive in silence. All of them held guns now.

A different man, a new face, stood over him. His head was shaved, his face angular, his jawline sporting the shadow of a beard. He wore khaki pants and a short-sleeved shirt, and though his hands were in his pockets there was nothing casual about his expression.

"Dr. Richards," the man said. "I'm Lee Brandt. Why are you in Mumbai?"

Dan fought to keep his composure. They were surely watching for the smallest reason to kill him as either a threat or a potentially weak link. "I crossed paths with Tagore a while ago," he said carefully. "We were never close, but we saw eye to eye when we talked about what the medical industry has done to doctors in the last twenty years." Dan slipped further into the role, lifting his chin, refusing to let any fear show. "We pour years and fortunes into our educations. We train like Olympic athletes. We save lives every day. We're the best and the brightest our society can produce. We work harder than anyone on the planet, and for what? To see our income *drop* every year, while others are buying the latest Maserati. And we're just supposed to take it? Keep working with a smile?"

Lee clicked his tongue. "Poor man. You have to sell your house in the Hamptons, is that it?"

Dan chuckled bitterly. "No, my wife took that. But Tagore hinted that I didn't have to keep getting ripped off. He implied there was... other work, if I was willing to bend a few rules. I tracked him here and thought I would offer my services."

"As what?" Lee crouched to look him in the eyes. "What exactly do you think those services would be?"

Dan lowered his voice. "I'm not stupid. We're close to Dharavi, an endless mine of people who will never be missed. Carting around organs worth tens of thousands or more. Meanwhile good people wait years before getting a donor, if they're lucky, and this human garbage just lives and dies with it? It's a waste."

Dan cringed inwardly at his own words, but he saw the silent connection in Lee's eyes, the unspoken agreement. The man waited while Dan continued. "I can transplant whatever you need. None of the hack jobs you usually get on the street, which means your high-paying customers will survive. Neat incisions, scarring to a minimum. Very worth your while."

For a long moment, Lee watched him in silence. Eventually, a woman called out from behind him, from a smaller room: "Story checks out, at least so far. Trained in cardiovascular surgery in Houston. Divorced. No kids. Was well-respected, but had several malpractice events and lost his license in Texas, looks like."

Lee appeared unconvinced, standing and crossing his arms. "Seems a little convenient that Tagore isn't here to vouch for him. The safest thing is to—"

Dan did not find out what Lee felt was the safest thing to do, as a door behind him burst open and a small group of people hurried inside, two of the men supporting a third between them who was hunched over, a dark red stain spreading across his shirt.

"Got jumped near the slum," one of the men said. "Thakur's men. We took out two of them, but Basu's shot."

Lee and the others approached the newcomers as Dan's eyes swept over the wounded man. He was pale and had already lost a lot of blood. Lee examined Basu's injury, lifting up his shirt to see the gunshot wound. He cursed and shook his head, stepping away. "He's done. Dump him with the others."

"I can help him," Dan said.

Lee's head whipped around. "You think I'm cutting you loose? I don't know you. Tagore's not here to ask. You can join Basu, who was stupid enough to get shot."

"Let me show you what I'm capable of," Dan said. "You get to keep your man. Then, if you want to shoot me in the head after that, fine."

Lee looked from Dan to the bleeding man, who was hanging limply now with his arms hooked around the other men's shoulders. It looked like he might have already lost consciousness.

"I don't think he's going to make it," Lee said. He stepped around, drew a knife from his belt, and sawed through Dan's zip-ties and the cord binding him to the chair. "And if he dies, you'll find out quickly what *I'm* capable of. Both of you see tomorrow, or neither of you do. Consider this your working interview."

Dan stood, rubbing his wrists, and moved toward the other men. "I need a clean place to operate. And I need someone to help me."

"There's a room converted to an operating suite in the back." It was the woman from the side room, who had emerged to hover in the doorway. She looked Indian, her black hair secured back and her dark eyes watching without concern. "We do the transplants there. It has what you'll need."

"Lead the way."

The woman jerked her head at one of the men. "Go get the others." Then she turned and led Dan through a door and down a hallway, while two men brought the patient. The corridor was grungy underfoot, completely bare, and Dan worried about the conditions he would be working in. They went around the corner and down another hall until they passed through a doorway, and Dan let out a slow breath, hardly believing what he saw.

Inside was a sterile, well-equipped operating room—tile floor, sanitized surfaces, overhead LED lights, a stainless steel operating table, and multiple monitors next to the anesthesia machine. Of course, they would need all of this to operate on their customers shelling out a fortune for black market transplants, but still, it surprised him by how clean and complete it was. Dan only had a moment to take it in before the woman led him down the hall into an office that had been turned into a dressing room, which was likewise spotless and had been outfitted with multiple open lockers.

"Take off your clothes," the woman ordered, already handing

him fresh, clean scrubs. He changed in front of her and she didn't look away, her hand extending to take his dirty clothes before dropping them in a bag. She led him through another door to a stainless-steel scrub sink.

"Only two minutes to scrub," she said. "Then hurry to the OR."

She departed, and Dan began to scrub. The motions were so familiar, he had done this a thousand times over, and yet he might as well have been scrubbing on the moon for how foreign it felt. What was he doing here? What if this man died on the operating table despite all his best efforts? It would mean a quick end to this trip. An unmarked grave. He pushed the thoughts down, the two minutes were up, and he headed straight back to the operating room.

The wounded man, Basu, was already prepped and lying on the operating table. He had been placed in the lateral thoraco-tomy position—on his side, with his arms up and out of the way. The "others" the woman had asked for had arrived quickly, and Dan could tell immediately what role each would serve; a nurse anesthetist had intubated the patient and attached him to a respirator, while a circulating nurse was finishing up washing the chest with chlorhexidine and painting with betadine, leaving the skin that reddish-orange shade Dan knew so well. A scrub tech stood ready. If it weren't for the fact that he could face his own murder if the patient died, Dan might have been in a hospital back in his home state. Of course, that was a pretty big *if.*

Dan gowned and gloved, moving quickly. He helped the scrub tech rapidly place sterile drapes over the man, leaving the chest area exposed. Instinctively, Dan extended his right arm and opened his hand. Before he could say anything, a scalpel was placed in it. Good. They would work as a team. He made a long, curvilinear incision in the chest, just above the man's fifth rib. Before Dan could ask, a Bovie cautery handle appeared in front of his hand, and he grabbed it and cauterized the small bleeding vessels. With the Bovie on cut, he dissected through the thick, red chest muscles, and then the intercostal muscles, which ran between the ribs to move the chest wall for breathing. He cut through the pleura, membranes lining the thorax and enveloping the lungs, entering the right chest cavity.

Not a word had been spoken. *These people have done many operations before*, Dan couldn't help thinking. They were too efficient, too experienced, for it to be otherwise. They knew what they are doing, but did he? Dan wasn't so sure. Here he was, operating on a criminal that the world would likely be better without. How many people had this man killed? How many more would he kill if put back on the street?

The assisting tech grabbed the suction and removed the pooling blood from the chest, which allowed Dan to examine the lung. He struggled to focus. *Just remember*, he told himself, *it's your job to save lives, not to decide who gets to live.* He examined the lung, determining the extent of the injury. It was a substantial gunshot wound—the bullet had barreled right through, exiting the back of the chest. He saw blood being pumped out of a branch of the right lower lobe pulmonary artery, and oozing from the raw surface of the lung where the bullet had ripped through. The man would die soon if nothing changed.

Whatever else it meant if the operation succeeded, right now this man was his patient. Dan let his training take over. He put out his hand and a hemostat arrived; he clamped the bleeder. With a strand of 3-0 silk he tied off the bleeding vessel, his fingers tying three knots so fast they were a blur. In his peripheral vision he saw the assisting tech look at the scrub nurse, eyebrows raised, and both nodded.

He kept working, intently focused. Multiple other vessels were ligated—tied off—or cauterized. Seeing several areas of air leaking out of the raw, damaged lung, he asked without thinking for COSEAL, an absorbable spray agent used to seal the lung. As soon as the words left his mouth, he was sure that he was expecting too much, but a moment later it was handed to him.

As he applied the spray agent, he was struck once again with how efficient, equipped, and experienced were the people in this room. They had to be this good in order to do successful heart transplants, but these people could work in any operating room in the world. And here they were in some back-alley, converted facility, working for criminals.

So are you, an inner voice whispered, and he felt a small twinge at the base of his neck. His shoulders were tight with pressure, a headache starting just behind his temples. He checked the monitors, and all parameters and vital signs were normal. Looking across the table at his assistant, Dan said, "Do you want to close?"

The tech nodded and put out her hand, instruments and sutures flying across the table from the scrub nurse as the chest was closed. Dan watched, impressed again, until they were finished. The man would live. So would he, at least for now.

Going back to the dressing room, Dan found that every piece of his clothing had been removed and replaced, probably to avoid the possibility of some kind of surveillance or tracking device if he was not who he claimed to be. The bag he had been carrying, which contained his passport among other things, was likewise absent, as was his wallet and every other item he had entered India with. Not a stitch, not a penny, was left to him.

Replacement clothes were on a hanger, his approximate size, and in the corner of the dressing room he saw a shower. He pulled off the scrubs, feeling a strange dirtiness that had never followed an operation before, wishing he could shed it as easily as the scrubs. He stood in the shower, which had poor pressure but at least was hot, feeling the water spray down on his tight muscles and trying to relax.

He thought of Laura. Of Marla. And then of Kim Konno, his last moments spent in a blaze of fear and pain. Now here he was saving the life of a killer. Guilt and anxiety fought to claim him until both were replaced with anger, which gradually melted down to a hard core of determination. This had to work. He certainly hoped that Lucy Brown knew what she was doing.

Thirty minutes later, he emerged from the shower, dried off and got dressed, and went to the door. It was locked. Possible reasons for this swirled through his thoughts, most of them terrible. They had discovered his real identity. They had guessed his true reasons for coming here. They had changed their minds about letting him leave if the patient lived. They were opting to be careful and would dump his body in a ditch behind the slum.

The door opened. Lee Brandt stood there, his expression flat, his hands behind his back. Lee met his gaze and held it, and Dan did not look away.

"The techs and nurses say you passed," Lee said. "So you can stay for now. You're going to earn your keep, and if you don't, you're done."

Lee turned and walked down the hallway. Dan closed the door and followed.

Chapter Twenty

It was not a large group—a fairly small number of people were involved, given the scope of what they did here—and yet they stayed very busy. There were the medical staff he had already met and a few additional nurses and techs, who together seemed to handle all of the operations. There were several men who covered security, some of whom Dan had fought with at the bar. There was Lee, the man in charge, and Ina, the Indian woman who had led Dan to the OR, who appeared to be a kind of manager, facilitating logistics and resources. Then there was Dr. Jennings, a surgeon already on staff at this facility, if one could think of it in that way—on staff.

Jennings had been brought recently from another facility, somewhere in Asia from what Dan could gather, to help fill an unexpected gap in personnel. There was no mention of what had happened, but four of the top people handling things here had disappeared. *Been* disappeared, Dan thought, was more likely.

Dan met Jennings in a break room, where Lee led him to introduce him to the rest of the staff. Ina sat typing at a laptop, and the nurses and techs were scattered around the table or seated in chairs along the walls. Jennings was a tall, lanky white man with an impeccable appearance, a reedy, crisp voice, and a European accent he could not quite place, British mixed with Swedish perhaps. Dan hated him instantly, in a way he could not recall ever feeling from a first impression.

"I don't recall your name, Richards," Jennings said, his arms staying crossed despite Dan's outstretched hand. "And I'm very familiar with the literature."

"I don't recall your name, either," Dan said. "But then, I'd be foolish to claim I know every surgeon in both hemispheres."

Jennings smiled thinly. "I hear we have you to thank for bringing Basu back from the grave. The nurses say you were adequate."

Adequate? Dan chose to smile back. "They're an experienced bunch. They made my job much easier."

Jennings turned his back on Dan, stepping to a coffee pot to pour a mug of thick, dark liquid. "No doubt. With a staff like that, a trained monkey probably could have done the operation."

"You've been operating here, I take it, so you would know."

Lee, who had been watching from a chair at the table, laughed. "It's like a playground squabble at medical school. But maybe you can get along, for what we're paying you."

Ina, the manager, spoke wryly beside him. "And maybe one of them will slice the other's throat with a scalpel while he sleeps."

Jennings raised his coffee mug in Ina's direction, an approving salute, and took a sip. Dan took a seat at the table and was introduced to each person in turn. Most were Indian, but a handful were from other countries. Lee explained that a few of his men were currently in the field, doing acquisitions work.

"Acquisitions?" Dan asked.

"Fresh product," Lee said, and Dan recalled his own words:

An endless mine of people who will never be missed, carting around organs worth tens of thousands or more.

"Product I can handle on my own," Jennings said, leaning back against the counter.

"But you can't be two places at once," Lee said. "You can't harvest and transplant at the same time. We have a recipient scheduled tonight, and we're also expecting a fresh load of product, which needs to be cut and packed."

"I'll take the transplant," Jennings said.

"You'll take what I tell you to. The nurses said Richards was more than *adequate*. This is an important client, and I'm putting him on it. You're harvesting."

Jennings said nothing, but when he put down his mug and strode from the room, Dan caught a look cast his way that was nothing short of murderous. Ina's prediction—a scalpel in his sleep—did not seem unlikely.

"Not sure it's a good idea to antagonize him," Ina said after Jennings had left. She did not sound concerned, simply stating a fact.

Lee shook his head. "Not much choice. The parts are flowing here, and we need more hands. Boss wants us picking up slack from some of the other sites."

Ina nodded and shut the laptop. She tucked it under her arm and rose from the table, beckoning for Dan to follow her. Dan started to open his mouth, but something told him that any questions would be met with suspicion, so he followed Ina from the break room. They took the stairs up a level, to what had previously been a suite of offices and conference rooms for whatever company had used the building before. Many of the rooms

R D SUTHERLAND

had been converted to sleeping quarters, and halfway down the corridor she produced a ring of keys and unlocked a door.

Inside, the room was sparsely decorated but clean. There was no window, but it held a bed, a chair, a lamp, a desk, and a portable sink and washbasin. A closet held hangers with a couple of changes of clothes. There were no books, no television, no computer. Ina followed him in and shut the door behind them. In the quiet and seclusion, away from the others, the atmosphere seemed to change, and he found her watching him closely with large, dark eyes.

She was undeniably attractive, about six inches shorter than he was and wearing a button-up white shirt and beige pants. She set down her laptop on the desk, and his eyes lingered on it but a second before coming back to Ina.

"You're going to need a friend here," she said. She let those words do their work as she stepped farther in, going to sit on the edge of the bed. Dan turned, wishing she would leave and he could keep the laptop. It was the only possibility he had seen here for reaching out to Lucy, not to mention being able to search for information he could use against this black market ring.

"I'm always looking for friends," Dan said. "But sometimes it takes a while to know who those are."

Ina smiled, one hand drifting up to fidget with the top button of her shirt. "You can't recognize friend from enemy? You seemed pretty sure about Jennings, and you only just met."

Dan reminded himself that his alter ego, Richards, was divorced. And immoral. And looking to serve only himself. Ina patted the bed beside her. Dan stepped closer, his heart speeding up, thinking of Laura an ocean away, while FBI agents watched her from a distance so no one harmed her. He sat on the bed beside Ina, their sides not quite touching.

"You'll be locked in," she said. "Every entrance and exit is also locked, every window covered. No phones allowed. No contact with anyone outside this facility." She reached up to tug her hair loose, so that the long, dark locks spilled over his shoulder, and she leaned close until her lips brushed his ear, her voice nearly purring. "But I have keys to the building. And I have the only computer. Lee thinks he's in charge, but I run everything here."

Dan tensed, his eyes closing as her mouth lingered at his ear, her breath warm against it, her hand moving to rest on his leg. And then he felt the blade, its point cold and sharp, push against his side with enough force to pierce his shirt, digging under his ribs just enough to break the skin. A red spot of blood the size of a nickel bloomed on the fabric.

"Which is why you should know I don't have friends *or* enemies, Dr. Richards," Ina said against his ear, her tone cold now, her breath withdrawing as she leaned back sufficiently to reveal the knife in her hand. "Only people still serving my purposes, and people who are dead. Do we understand each other?"

Dan nodded, wordless. She kept the knife pressed into his side a second longer, and then drew it back and tucked it deftly away again in a sheath behind her back that he had not even seen.

"Good." She rose from the bed. "Keep it in mind, or Jennings killing you in your sleep will be the last of your worries." Ina walked to the door, picking up her laptop on the way. "Your first transplant is in two hours. Someone will come to get you when it's time."

She shut the door behind her. Dan heard the click of the lock.

* * *

The two hours passed slowly. There was nothing to do but sit in the chair, stare at the wall, and wonder if other choices in his life might have led to a different, better, chain of events. He searched the room, checking each drawer of the desk, looking under the bed, examining each corner and crevice, but Krum's people had left nothing. There was little to do but wait.

At last the door was unlocked and opened without a knock or other warning. Ina stood there, regarding him as impassively as she had before. She led him back down the hallway, down the stairs, and to the same dressing room as before, where he changed into fresh scrubs before going to the sink to scrub his hands and forearms.

When he was ready, Ina escorted him to the operating room, where the same team of nurses and techs was assembled to support him in the transplant. On the table was a young Middle Eastern woman, Pakistani if he had to guess, perhaps late twenties or early thirties. Her whole life ahead of her. Sitting ready, a cooler containing a heart packed in ice. Someone's unwilling offering.

Dan took a steadying breath and stepped to the table. "Let's begin."

Chapter Twenty-One

It had been a long time since it was anything more than a massive stone tower to her, the largest in the world in fact, rising over 550 feet in the air. A testament in marble, granite, and blue-stone gneiss to men's egos, their ambition and pride. Would Washington have approved? Lucy Brown wasn't certain. But one thing was sure; the bright-eyed optimism she had brought to the capital as a fresh graduate—armed with a degree in criminal justice and a desire to leave the world better than she'd found it— had gone the way of the dinosaur, about the time of her twenties. Extinct. Now she couldn't look at the monument without feeling the urge to roll her eyes and quicken her pace.

But the people. She still felt something when she saw the people, something beyond cynicism about nations and power. They gathered at the base of the obelisk, from all nations, every culture and people represented from day to day as they stared up at it in wonder and awe and something else, something that had changed radically for her over the years—patriotism. A belief that symbols like this still represented something important, something worth fighting for.

She watched them now, crowds of visitors snapping pictures

with their phones, standing before the famed D.C. landmark, reading the plaque, waiting their turn to ride the elevator to the top. She sat on a bench with a windbreaker on, wondering how the next half hour would go. It could really go one of two ways.

Well, she was about to find out. She saw Krum approaching from the direction of Constitution Avenue, dressed in a pinstripe suit. He would have fit in at one of the swanky steakhouses in Georgetown or Capitol Hill, rubbing elbows with Washington's elite power brokers, but here he looked out of place amid the joggers and picnicking families whose blankets dotted the grass despite the chill in the air.

Krum approached and took a seat at the other end of the bench, one arm stretching along its back, the other hand smoothing down his tie. He looked away from her, watching the green spread of the mall.

"I was glad to get your call, Agent Brown," he said.

"Frankly, I wasn't sure you would come." She looked directly at him, refusing to treat the meeting like a clandestine arrangement. And she doubted anyone was watching, except perhaps Krum's own men who were no doubt stationed around the vicinity.

"Of course. You'll find I'm nothing but a friend to the bureau, and to the American people."

"How reassuring." She kept her tone neutral, aware that sarcasm rapidly crept in even when she didn't intend for it to. "Ellen Blake at the FDA tells me that Health Now is going to be financing transplants for artificial hearts."

"That was the plan," he said. "Sadly, I hear that Worldwide Medical Research in Austin has burned down, and its chief researcher perished in the fire."

"A tragedy," Lucy said. She watched him closely. "My suspicions are that someone wanted to steal the research, and then set the fire to cover his tracks."

"Or *her* tracks." Krum widened his eyes a little. "We must be politically correct. We're in the capital, after all."

Lucy gave a tight smile. "This research could be priceless to the right person, or organization. Worth killing for, perhaps."

"Perhaps well worth it," Krum said. His mouth didn't smile, but it was in his eyes—a cold, hard delight at the idea of Lucy bleeding out on the floor if the occasion presented itself. She could see it.

So she stood, folding her hands behind her, and took a couple of steps away, intentionally turning her back to him. She would *not* be intimidated. If he was going to have her killed, it would not be here on the National Mall, anyway.

"We've learned that Kim Konno met with a trusted friend and colleague, and we can't help wondering if Konno passed anything to him," she said. "Something that might have survived the fire because it was already moved."

"Any reason you're telling me this, Agent?"

"You were going to be the project's financial backer. I thought perhaps you heard something, or someone might have reached out to you."

"No, nothing."

"Dr. Parker hasn't contacted you?" She turned as she asked the question, and she saw zero surprise in his eyes at the name. She knew then and there that Krum was onto Parker, knew he'd survived. Krum knew she knew it, too; she saw the flash of anger, quickly controlled.

"No. Has he reached out to the FBI?" Krum said. "Since we're trading information."

"He was in a plane crash," Lucy said. "He vanished after that. We spoke before and I told him he's wanted for questioning, but he's in the wind."

"So he could be anywhere," Krum said.

"He was in New Mexico, the last we knew." She sat again, crossing her legs at the knee. "But you know that, since you sent a couple of mercenaries there to kill him."

This time, he controlled his expression, even his eyes, and gave nothing away. His tone was even-tempered, almost amused. "That's quite an accusation. I trust you have some evidence?"

"Just having a conversation," she said.

"Seems to me that you're awfully concerned about Parker. That you think he's the key to this."

"Actually, I'm not too concerned with him. Probably a case of wrong place, wrong time. Even getting the hearts back is not high on our agenda." She drew out a pack of cigarettes, tapped one out, and lit it. "I'll tell you, Robert. I'm really more concerned with illegal organ harvesting and transplanting on the international black market."

Krum stiffened. His hands flexed in his lap, as if he might signal for something. Or to someone. Lucy suddenly wondered if she had crosshairs settled on her forehead right now, a sniper hidden on a nearby rooftop—the Holocaust Memorial Museum, perhaps, or the National Museum of American History. The thought made the hairs on the back of her neck stand up.

Krum recovered himself. "Not sure how that's your concern. Seems like it would be Langley's prerogative."

"Well, we're working together," she said, taking a long draw.

"Cooperation is rare in the government, but it does happen." Lucy blew a thick cloud of smoke between them. "In fact, we're closing in on a massive underground network, one that extends around the world. If, hypothetically speaking, a key figure in such a ring were willing to come forward and testify, to help us by exposing the whole network for prosecution, well... I'd be in a position to arrange some clemency."

Krum was angry now, too angry to hide it. A vein by his temple beat a steady rhythm like a drum, while his jaw locked tight. Lucy continued.

"We could offer a stay in a white-collar Federal penitentiary, one of the nice ones. More importantly, we could take the death penalty off the table, if he were willing to cooperate with us."

"You mean if he turned himself in and handed over his entire organization, despite the fact you've got no proof," Krum said, in as steady a voice as he could manage.

"Or her," Lucy said, and smiled. "Got to be politically correct. And I did say it was hypothetical."

She took another drag on her cigarette and blew the smoke slowly out, watching it drift. Krum was quiet. Maybe deciding whether to have her shot dead in public after all; he was clearly furious. *Not the way you thought this meeting would go, Rob? Thought you'd pump me for new information on Parker?* She took another drag.

"You should be careful, Agent Brown," Krum said at last.

"Is this the part where you pretend to be concerned for my safety, when really it's just another threat?"

"You shouldn't think of this situation as just another threat," Krum said. "Not at all. Because the kind of person who could do what you're describing? He wouldn't take kindly to interference.

He'd have the resources to remove you from the equation, you and your family, your parents, everyone you love." Krum made sure to hold her eyes, his own almost shining. "He'd carve you apart. Not just for profit, but for fun. He'd sell your parts to the highest bidder, and whatever bits and pieces wouldn't sell, he'd feed to his dogs."

Krum stood. "Not just another threat, at all." He straightened his coat. "So don't wade into waters too deep for you, Agent Brown."

She shrugged, blew out another large cloud of smoke, and leaned over to stub out her cigarette on the ground. "I'm a good swimmer."

"I suppose we'll find out. Good luck with the case."

Krum walked away, and down the path she saw a man step away from a food vendor's stall and move toward a parked sedan. There were doubtless others. And perhaps the crosshairs she'd imagined were not simply paranoia, after all. What was the prob-ably-apocryphal quote? *Just because you're paranoid doesn't mean they're not after you.*

She had not really expected him to take the bait and strike a deal, but Krum was nevertheless rattled, otherwise he wouldn't have tried to scare her. When people were rattled, they made mistakes. And he had revealed that he knew about Parker, which meant she needed to be extra concerned about Krum finding out about Parker's undercover work, infiltrating his organization. Possibly, too, she needed to step up the security around Parker's family, and the Bears. She made a mental note to add a bit of extra manpower, if she could get the pull for it, for watching them and also her own parents. Krum didn't strike her as the type to make threats he could not back up.

Lucy reached into her pocket and switched off her phone, which had been recording their conversation. Krum had been careful not to say anything that could be incriminating. And she hoped she had given nothing away about Parker that Krum did not already know.

Because Parker did not need to be put in any extra danger. Lucy stood, tugged her windbreaker a little tighter, and started for the Metro entrance at 12th and Independence. She hoped she had adequately prepared the doctor before he left. Krum would not hesitate, she believed, to do precisely what he had promised— to carve up his enemies and scatter their parts. It was what he did daily to people he had not even met, wasn't it?

Be careful, Dan, she thought as she pulled out her Metro card. *Be more careful than you've ever been in your life.*

Chapter Twenty-Two

It was something he had done countless times before—opening the chest of a patient on an operating room table, the patient under deep anesthesia, while a surgical tech assisted him. Yet, it felt so strange this time, something undeniably *off*, and it took a couple of minutes before he realized what it was: there was no relationship.

The young Pakistani woman on the table was no one to him, a complete stranger. They had never met; he had never introduced himself, had not had a chance to explain the operation, had not answered any questions. There was no connection, no established trust, just an unconscious patient and an operation that needed doing.

His motions became automatic as he cannulated the ascending aorta and the superior and inferior vena cava, the two large veins carrying deoxygenated blood into the heart—the first from the upper body, the second from the lower. Then he motioned for the perfusionist to start cardiopulmonary bypass.

Dan did not even know the reason this woman was getting a transplant. She looked like she was in her early thirties at the oldest, and completely healthy otherwise. It must be cardiomyopathy.

But how did she get to this place? What was she doing in an illegal makeshift clinic in the middle of India? She might as well be one of the cadavers he practiced on in medical school. An unknown. Maybe that was how Jennings and the others were able to live with themselves, by refusing to recognize the humanity of these people. With no connection, no relationship, they could pretend there was nothing more than the operation itself.

But Dan couldn't, not even if he wanted to. There was always more.

On bypass, he clamped the ascending aorta, and the superior and inferior cavae, and cut across the aorta, cavae, and pulmonary artery. Spilled blood was suctioned up and returned to the heart-lung machine. After dividing the aorta, pulmonary artery, superior and inferior vena cavae, and the left atrium, Dan removed the still beating heart out of the young woman's chest. He handed it to the scrub nurse, who wrapped it in a towel and gave it to the circulating nurse. The donor heart was passed to him after being taken out of the sterile ice bucket, the organ a healthy red, dark veins criss-crossing it like tributaries from a river. So full of the potential for life. Or death.

Dan accepted the heart. He cut open the left atrium, then he trimmed the aorta and pulmonary artery to fit the recipient. When it was ready, he started suturing the new heart in place. First, the donor's left atrium was attached to the recipient with a running 3-0 Prolene suture. The superior and inferior cavae were then sutured, then the pulmonary artery, and last the aorta. After placing a small profusion catheter in the donor's ascending aorta, he glanced at the perfusionist.

"Start a slow, low pressure delivery of warm blood." The perfusionist nodded and began the delivery. The blood would flow through the coronary arteries and warm the heart.

The donor heart started to beat slowly, a rhythmic pulse, and Dan unclamped the aorta. After waiting about five minutes for the new heart to be warm and fully functioning, he signaled the perfusionist to very gradually come off bypass. The monitors for heart rhythm and blood pressure displayed normal rhythm and normal blood pressure. It was looking good. Dan instructed the anesthetist to do a transesophageal echo so he could check each cardiac chamber and each suture line. As he had hoped, everything was normal.

Dan turned to the anesthetist. "Did you give the first dose of antirejection medications?"

"Yes, when the operation started," she said. "That's our usual practice."

Dan removed the aortic and caval cannulas, and he started closing the chest—stainless steel wire sutures around the sternum, then absorbable sutures on the pericardium and deep subcutaneous tissue. Finally, a beautiful subcutaneous plastic skin closure. The new heart beat with a strong, normal rhythm. It fit exactly into the space previously occupied by the sick heart. With a good closure of the sternum and tissues of the chest, the young lady would soon forget she had a transplant. The six-inch-long incision would become invisible.

"I want to go with her to the recovery room," Dan said, "to make sure everything is all right."

He thought he might meet resistance, but the anesthetist nodded. "That would be good. Sometimes the surgeon leaves and has no idea of the post-op care."

"Not me."

In the recovery room, an equally clean space, Dan observed the patient. The woman seemed to be doing well. After a couple of minutes, Ina appeared silently at his elbow; he hadn't heard her come in. She said nothing, just watched the patient with him in silence as she started to wake up. The woman still showed normal vital signs and rhythm. No bleeding.

"Any thoughts after your first case?" Ina said at length.

You're all sociopaths, Dan thought. "You've got a solid team and a good facility here. Successful transplants aren't simple to pull off, but she looks like she'll be just fine."

"You care a lot about the recipients." It didn't quite sound like an accusation, but he could hear the suspicion.

"Protecting my investment. If they die, it's bad business."

"Mm-hmm," she said, with a disbelieving tone. "Speaking of, I notice you haven't asked about your share."

Dan folded his arms. "I'm assuming we'll negotiate after my trial period's over."

"Something like that. If by negotiate you mean we tell you what you'll be making, and if you resist, I'll shoot you in the head." She smiled as if it were all a joke. "But there's plenty to go around. Always more product where the last batch came from."

Dan kept his gaze focused on the recovering patient, with effort. "Quite an operation you've got here. There must be more I haven't seen. I'm curious how you get the patients antirejection medications, and how they're tissue typed for compatibility."

Ina turned and beckoned him to follow her. "Let's go for a walk." He trailed her into the hallway and through the building. "Our system is very unique," she continued. "The boss is very efficient. We can visit the lab, it's just a block away."

"This boss of yours must be quite the leader," Dan said,

hoping she would say his name, or give him anything else to go on.

"He's your boss now, too." Ina's eyes slid toward him. "That's all you need to know."

It felt good to be outside for a few minutes. A broad stretch of blue sky, countless people hustling past, cars packed and honking, stray dogs. There was a strong, pervasive smell on the street—a mix, perhaps, of curry, sweat, and excrement—but a slight breeze eased the heavy, drowsy warmth from the sun, and Dan felt his spirits lifting. At least he was out of the cool, sterile operating room.

They walked on, Ina keeping one hand on the crook of his elbow, as if she were simply concerned they might get separated. He had no doubt she had her knife ready, and probably a gun. After a block, they came to a one-story, well-maintained office building surrounded by a strangely mixed jumble of high rises and deteriorating structures in a slow collapse of decay. A few beggars sat out front, a couple of women and a young boy with hands outstretched, but Ina steered Dan by them and into the building. The receptionist at the desk nodded in their direction, and Ina took him past and then into a back room.

A middle-aged Indian man sat working at a computer, and he rose when Ina entered. He was balding, with wire-frame glasses and a pleasant face. Ina gestured to him and then to Dan.

"This is Dr. Bhavin Aadarsh," she said, "Ph.D. in biochemistry. Bhavin, this is Dr. Steven Richards, a new CV surgeon on the team."

Bhavin smiled and extended his hand. "A pleasure, Dr. Richards."

"Good to meet you, too," Dan said. "I was hoping you could

tell me how you get antirejection medications for the heart transplant patients."

Bhavin looked to Ina, just a furtive glance, and she nodded. "It's very simple," he said. "We give free vaccinations for the usual maladies around here. Polio, measles, smallpox, typhoid, diphtheria, pertussis. Tetanus, influenza. Freely available to anyone who asks. So we have thousands and thousands of people that come to us. We vaccinate and also draw blood from each of them."

Bhavin sat at his desk again and indicated a couple of chairs opposite him. Dan sank into one, but Ina remained standing.

"For those between ages twenty and thirty-five we do tissue and blood typing," Bhavin continued. "When we get a blood sample from a possible recipient, we look through the computer database and find a near-perfect match. Then we notify Ina, and she makes all the arrangements for the recipient and donor."

"What about the medications?" Dan asked.

"The usual. Steroids, antimetabolites, and immunosuppressants. We can get those from the black market in bulk quantities, so they're cheap. When the patients leave, we give each of them two weeks' worth of medication, which should last until they find a cardiologist that works with us. There are many who do, and we give them a list."

Dan fought to keep his expression merely curious, although he was gripping the arms of the chair. "How do you find the donors again? I would think a lot of the people around here who would come in for free vaccinations might not have regular addresses."

Bhavin raised a finger. "You're right! We require a name and as many details as possible about where they live. Sometimes it's landmarks, or a description of a certain part of the slum. Under a certain bridge, in an alleyway. We tell them it's in case we need to follow up, and a requirement for the vaccines, if they're reluctant."

"Very clever," Dan said.

"Lee Brandt has a team that knows this area well and specializes in finding these people when they've been selected," Bhavin said. "They have some persuasive ways of getting others to tell where people are, or of tracking them down. Of course, sometimes they make a bit too much fuss, and then we see things like that unfortunate article that—"

Ina cleared her throat forcefully. "That'll do, Dr. Aadarsh."

Bhavin silenced immediately, and Dan thought he saw fear in the man's eyes. Dan stood, extending his hand again. "Very helpful to know. You run quite an impressive operation here."

"Yes, it's really something," Bhavin said, shaking Dan's hand once more.

It certainly was. Dan was glad that the conversation was finished. He had learned what he needed, but it wore on him to continue pasting on a mildly interested expression rather than punching the man in the face. Ina took him by the elbow again and guided him back onto the street, back into the sights and scents of Mumbai.

"Now you know how we work," Ina said.

"Except for you," he replied. "Still not sure what you do around here."

It had come out more angrily than he intended, but she laughed it off, apparently amused. "I keep us all from becoming meat ourselves. That's what we all are, is it not? Dead meat walking. Years or days or minutes left."

Dan followed her down the street, back toward the main facility. The crowds were thick and Ina gripped his arm as they walked. He subtly looked for street signs, trying to fixate their position, but saw none. Someone bumped into Dan as his eyes roved, jostling him. He felt something pressed into his palm. As Lucy's words came back to him, he dropped the item into his pocket without looking as a man disappeared into the crowd. It might have been Singh; it was hard to tell. Ina pulled him forward, unaware, and soon they were stepping into an alley and through a side door that she unlocked. Dan forced himself not to react to the pass-off that had just occurred.

"If you're hungry for dinner, head to the break room," she said. "There's food in the fridge. Maybe even a bottle or two of Kingfisher."

"What, are we celebrating my first case?"

"Nothing like that. But it might be your last night, may as well drink up. By now, Lee will have told Jennings that, based on how you did with that operation, he's putting you on all the transplants and keeping Jennings on harvest duty." Ina pulled her hair back from her face, twisting it into a bun and securing it with a long, straight hairpin. Dan could see no compassion in her eyes.

"Like I said," she added, "dead meat walking."

Chapter Twenty-Three

Dan had heard it plenty of times—that, given enough time, people could get used to anything. Eventually, their minds desensitize them, and what once was shocking becomes banal. The horrible becomes ordinary. It had been a coping mechanism while he was in the Marine Corps, and to a degree while in medical school, too.

After two weeks in Mumbai, carrying out transplants, his situation began to get familiar... familiar enough that the feeling of desensitization disturbed him. He would be suturing an artery, or even sitting in the break room, and for a moment almost forget that he was here against his will, only present to build a case for tearing all of this down.

And it *had* to be torn down. That was abundantly clear.

Each day was much like the one that went before. Jennings continued to wish him slow death through word and look, the other doctor visibly resentful of Dan's skill and workload. Lee continued to give Dan the majority of the transplant cases. And the situation was made worse when Dan made recommendations to improve the process, guessing that this would ingratiate himself to Lee and Ina and relax their guard around him.

Dan had made suggestions to them to adjust the timing of the transplant process and increase efficiency. Now, the donor—and Dan hated the term, as if these poor, doomed people had any choice in the matter—was taken to a shower at gunpoint, washed with chlorhexidine and betadine, given a broad-spectrum antibiotic, and at the same time the recipient in the other area of the building was also taken and given a similar shower. Although in different operating rooms, both the donor and recipient were put to sleep at the same time, prepped and draped. Both operations started simultaneously. The donor heart was harvested by Jennings and cooled with cardioplegic solution, injected into the aortic root to cool and preserve myocardial cell function. Meanwhile, Dan opened the recipient's chest and placed the person on bypass, then explanted the heart. The heart to be donated was wrapped in a sterile towel and placed in a sterile basin, then carried to Dan's OR. The circulation nurse unwrapped the towel, and the scrub nurse took it and handed it to Dan.

Because of Dan's efficiency and suggestions, they were now able to do six or seven transplants a day. Business was booming. Lee and Ina began to give him more freedom to move about the facility. And Dan found himself alternating between a numb haze of familiarity and a flood of extreme anxiety and guilt, so strong that he lost his appetite and had to force himself to choke down a few bites here and there. He stopped sleeping more than a couple of hours a night.

After the first few days, Jennings stopped making snide remarks and simply left the room whenever possible once Dan had entered it. Dan found the man's silence, and the cold vacancy in his eyes, more frightening than the previous bluster and insults.

"Don't turn your back to him," Ina warned him one night,

over a plate of biryani in the break room. "I'm telling you, he'll gut you, trusting that Lee will keep him on anyway."

"Would he?"

"Most likely, yes," she said.

Dan considered this. "I thought you didn't care what happened to me."

"I don't. But you're still useful to me, so I don't want you dead yet."

Dan believed her. If the time came that Dan was discovered in a pool of coagulating blood, cold and stiff, Ina would feel only passing annoyance at an asset no longer available. But he took her warnings to heart, and on the occasions that he and Jennings shared a room, Dan was careful not to give the man any chances. He would not even accept a drink from the other surgeon, from the possibility of poison. He was probably being paranoid, but there was no telling.

Dan watched for chances to take photos, now that he had a camera. This was what Singh, if it had been him, had secretly passed to him on his way back from the lab with Ina. He had managed to snap a few pictures, but it was horribly difficult; whenever he was someplace that photographs would be important evidence—such as the operating room—there were invariably other people present who would notice. He was forced to bide his time and wait for an opening.

One particular evening (he could not even be sure what day of the week it was, so minimal was his contact with the outside world), he was sitting at a table in the common area when Basu approached him. Basu, the man who had been shot, and whom Dan had operated on his very first day here, had not spoken five words to him since that time. Everyone else, at the moment, was absorbed with busywork, or eating, or talking to others, but Dan was alone as the man slid into a chair opposite him.

"I haven't forgotten what you did," Basu said. He was fairly young, muscular, with a short black beard.

"Just doing my job," Dan said. "Don't mention it."

"Maybe back in the States." Basu shook his head. "Not here. Here, your job is to take body parts and sew them into new bodies. Like Dr. Frankenstein."

"Not quite how I'd—"

"You could have let me die," Basu continued. "Lee was going to. I heard him. I was halfway gone from blood loss already, but I heard him. He was ready to have me tossed in a ditch, until you spoke up."

Dan listened, hearing the gratitude, seeing it in the man's eyes. It affected him, even knowing what the man must have done to be a part of this operation. "Well, old habits die hard, I guess. You needed the help."

"Yes, I did," Basu said, and sighed. "Didn't even see it coming."

"Who were those guys that got the drop on you?"

"Thakur's men," Basu said, and when Dan stared at him blankly, he added, "Indian mafia, if you will. Organized crime here in Mumbai. India's a major transit point for heroin from the Golden Triangle. Plus opium, Mandrax, diamond smuggling from South Africa. Even money laundering. Thakur's got his hands in all of it. Most other black market outfits pay a fee to him for protection, insurance money, you know. A piece of the action, and Thakur leaves them alone."

"But not us?"

"Lee'd be happy to, just to get them off our backs. But the word comes straight from the top—not a penny. The boss doesn't want to share any of the profits, so Thakur has been out for our blood more and more."

This was helpful information, but Thakur's men were not the criminals he needed background on. Dan considered his next words carefully. If Basu shut down, he could lose a valuable source, and maybe his only chance to confirm what was going on with this medical ring.

"Nobody will tell me about him," Dan said. "Our boss."

"We're not supposed to say anything. Those are the rules."

Dan leaned forward over the table, his voice lowering. "Seems to me I have a right to know, seeing as how I work here. I've put my life and career on the line like everybody else. I'm facing prison time, or worse, same as you if we ever go down."

Basu folded his arms, a guarded expression on his face now. "Sorry, but Lee says we can't even say his name."

"You mean the guy who wanted to let you die?"

That barb struck home, and Basu visibly wavered.

"I'm not asking for much," Dan pressed. "Just a little context, for the man who saved your life. Just between us."

A long moment of silence settled. They could hear other conversations in the room, along with the sound of people eating and drinking. Basu frowned, and Dan thought his chance was gone. But then the man angled toward him, speaking quietly.

"His name is Krum," Basu said. "He's the one at the top."

"Of what? The Mumbai operation?"

"All of them."

"Where are the others?"

"I don't think you need to know that."

Dan offered a reassuring smile. "It's job security for me. Jennings wants my head, and I don't know how much longer I can keep peace with him. If I have to leave, I'd like to know other options for where I can go to keep doing this work."

Basu cursed under his breath and ran a hand into his hair. "Fine. There's Tokyo, Beijing, Sao Paulo. Mexico City. New York. Those are the ones I know about."

Dan nodded, mentally filing it away. "Thanks. It's good to know my choices."

"Yeah. But listen, you didn't hear it from me. Any of it."

"Of course," Dan said. "I wouldn't want to have to sew up another bullet hole in you again."

Basu chuckled, but it was clear the other man did not find this amusing in the least. To be honest, Dan didn't either.

Lee and Ina walked by, carrying plates to the sink, and Basu rose from the table. Ina gave Dan a long glance, assessing, but she continued on without a word.

Basu left the room, and Dan finished his dinner before walking himself back to his room for the night. He was not escorted every time now, but within minutes he always heard someone locking the door. Probably Ina.

He had searched his room carefully but had not discovered any hidden cameras or microphones. This did not, of course, mean they were not present. To be cautious, he had kept the camera hidden under the mattress since bringing it back. Twice now, he had snuck it out to take photos of the facility, and he had managed to take pictures of the operating room and scrub room while they were not being used. But he knew more evidence was needed. He decided it was worth the risk to start carrying it in his pocket. He could testify himself, having now heard from Basu, and he could give the information about the other cities to Lucy Brown—but without more to go on, it was still very vague.

What am I doing here? The thought hit him, at least once a day, along with a nearly overwhelming urge to find a way to escape—to give the FBI what he knew and ask for protection for himself and his family. But he didn't want that life, not really... to be always on the run, to ask Laura and Marla to give up everything they knew and cared about, for however many years it took for the FBI to stop Krum and to see the case through the courts. Without a smoking gun, Krum might go free, and then where would he be?

Besides, here at Krum's facility, the doors were locked at all times. Was there a way to escape this place, even if he wanted to?

He wondered what Laura was doing. She must have tried to contact him, perhaps had found out by now that the conference excuse was a lie. She might assume that he was having an affair, or had run off and left them, or maybe that he was involved in something corrupt himself. Maybe that he had given in to the pressure at work and chosen to turn tail and flee rather than face it. A coward, taking the easy way out. Maybe she wondered if he was even still alive.

I miss you, Laura. He had never missed her so much in his life. He wanted to hold her, to tell her how much he loved her, that none of this—none of what he did anywhere—mattered as much to him as their marriage, that no other person's life was as important as their life together. That was a message a long time coming. Would he have a chance, now, to tell her?

Dan lay down on the bed, staring at the ceiling, his heart rate refusing to slow down. He thought of his daughter, growing up so fast. What if Marla had to go the rest of her life without her father? What if he never made it home?

"I am coming home," he said, realizing belatedly he had

spoken it aloud, but if someone was listening in, there was nothing he could do about it now. *I'm coming home. Come hell or high water, I'm going to beat these people... and I'm coming home.*

Chapter Twenty-Four

Human capital.

It was a term that Robert Krum had grown quite fond of. Some economist from the University of Chicago had popularized the phrase, and that man used it in the sense of knowledge, attributes, habits, even the creativity held within people, and embodied in their ability to use it to perform labor and produce economic value. All well and good, but that was quite a *limiting* understanding, wasn't it? There was far more to humans that could be mined for economic value, after all.

Krum stood in the living room of his condo in Madison Square Park Tower, before a wall of ten-foot chamfered floor-to-ceiling glass windows looking out across the New York City skyline, lit orange by the sunset's glow. He had grown accustomed to the sight, almost bored by it, and yet he had to admit—the view was unparalleled. Corner exposures, 360-degree views, 777 feet in the sky with wisps of cloud drifting past; at the nexus of Flatiron, NoMad, Gramercy Park, and Chelsea, he could gaze down upon the tiny, ant-like creatures scurrying about their little lives, making whatever miniscule contributions to society they could.

Microscopic drops donated to the endless river of mankind's history. Human capital.

How many of them lived and died with no meaningful change to the course of that river? How many could have never existed in the first place, with no discernible difference to any pattern of human events? He saw rows of taxi cabs, pedestrians wending their way down sidewalks, lights illuminating down the streets. Meaningless busyness, flickers of life, soon gone. The ones with a shred of value were those that contributed to something more permanent, something of real worth and lasting structure— like the building he stood in now. He would never know the names of the people who built it, yet it was enough that he could enjoy their labor, it was *something*, and at least that gave their lives some simple validation.

Custom stained floors. Optimized vantage points. Integrated appliances, custom cabinetry, imported stone, nickel fittings, the finest marble and steel. Curated homes, individually crafted by a London designer. Five bedrooms, five and a half baths, over seven thousand square feet, and the penthouse sat empty most of the year, between his solo visits. He had not even had an opportunity to use the majority of the Tower's exquisite amenities, from its private dining room to the dedicated attaché, a concierge who could secure any reservation, could arrange for the most exclusive chef to prepare his dinner, or for a favorite author to read in the Tower's private library. At least, that's what the brochure had claimed; he had bought the place mainly for the views and the prestige.

New York—that hive of life, that hub of cultures and peoples, that thriving metropolis and crossroads of the world, a throng of humanity. Of human capital. The perfect reminder of why he did what he did, why it mattered, why it was fully justified. He had not made these rules. He had not built this building, had not set its price tag, and could not be blamed for playing the game to win. It was the only game there was. And without a winner, at the top, the lives of all the losers mattered even less.

The doorbell chimed.

"Let him in," Krum said.

One of Krum's men, who had been standing silently in the foyer, opened the door. A plump, middle-aged man entered, his face wearing the wide-eyed expression of a street urchin who's just been ushered into Buckingham Palace. He kept his hands to his sides and stepped into the penthouse, openly staring.

"Dr. Walters," Krum said. "A pleasure to see you again."

"I told you before," the man said, shaking his head at the view as he stepped into the living room, "just Bruce is fine."

"Bruce, then. Thank you for coming."

"I really don't know what else I can tell you," Bruce said. He glanced with concern at Krum's man, who had taken up his post again by the door.

"Don't worry about him. And I thought of something I failed to ask you about before." Krum led the anesthesiologist from the living room to a dining room, where a chandelier hung over the mahogany table and the glass walls continued to dazzle. Krum gestured to a seat, and Bruce took it. Krum pulled a bottle of champagne from a bucket of ice and poured them each a glass.

"What are we celebrating?" Bruce had looked nervous when he arrived, but it seemed to be melting away. He accepted the champagne flute readily.

"Our upcoming success." Krum sat opposite Bruce and raised his glass. They drank. "That flash drive has been immensely valuable. The data was, as we had hoped, all about construction of Konno's artificial heart."

"Not just Konno's," Bruce cut in.

Krum's eyes narrowed. He forced himself to relax. "Of course. In any case, the data is incomplete. It's only a fraction of what's needed to replicate the hearts."

"So find the hearts," Bruce said. "Problem solved. Doesn't take a genius."

Krum had the urge, then and there, to hurl the man through the nearest floor-to-ceiling window, and he had a sudden mental image of the doctor's body tumbling down sixty-four stories, finally flattening on the street with the tiniest flash of red. It made him smile. "I've tried. But I can't find them, so I need the rest of the data."

"It's probably gone in the fire," Bruce said.

Krum ignored this. "When you took that flash drive from Konno's office, were there others?"

"I think so. I was in a hurry. And I figured they were probably back-ups, all had the same thing."

"How many were there?"

"Four, maybe, in all. About that."

"The same type as the one you took?"

"I think so."

Krum sat back in his chair. It was what he had expected, but it helped to have it confirmed. Now he was certain what he was looking for—a handful of additional flash drives, which would complete the picture and allow manufacture of the hearts. And Dan Parker, wherever he was, almost surely had them, or knew where they were.

Krum pressed a button on an intercom. "We're ready to eat."

Within a minute, the man from the foyer carried in a tray and began laying down plates, cloth napkins, and silverware. Dinner was a pasta dish, topped with chicken risotto and truffle shavings.

"Looks delicious," Bruce said. He glanced at the hired man, and then at Krum. "It doesn't have nuts, does it? I have a peanut allergy."

"Oh, really?" Krum raised his eyebrows. "Thankfully, no. No nuts."

The hired man withdrew, and they tucked into the pasta. Bruce ate hungrily, and for a couple of minutes neither spoke.

"Did Konno ever say anything to you about the flash drives?" Krum asked. "Or backing up data, steps he might take for security, anything like that?"

Bruce shook his head, slurping up the pasta. "Just that he was being careful. He didn't seem to trust me."

"Can't imagine why." Krum took another sip of his champagne. He let the other man eat, and then when it seemed the appropriate time to ask, he said, "Are you feeling all right?"

Bruce's skin had become flushed, and he wiped the back of his hand across his forehead, which was growing damp with sweat. His hand slid down to tug at his collar, and then rest on his chest. "Not sure," he said.

Krum pushed back his chair, watching the other man. Bruce's breathing started to become labored, a noisy wheeze settling into it. His hand clamped harder against his chest, and his eyes became wide. He tried to gasp something out and waved at Krum, who stood, dabbed at the corner of his mouth with his napkin, and came around the table to him.

"Epi," Bruce wheezed, and he fumbled in his pockets until he produced a device about the size of a pen, an epinephrine auto-injector. Bruce flipped off the cover and lifted it over his thigh.

Krum's hand locked onto Bruce's wrist. He held the other man's arm immobile. Bruce stared at him in horror, his lips starting to swell, the sweat running down his throat. He fought to bring the injector down, but Krum was too strong, and his breaths were coming more and more weakly. Krum wrenched the injector from Bruce's hand and slid it across the table, and then Krum held the man in his chair and watched dispassionately as he struggled to breathe. Bruce fought, but his strength was failing as his oxygen ran out, and when it was clear the man's death was imminent Krum released his hold.

Bruce fell out of his chair, sprawling on the custom flooring. He started to crawl toward the end of the table where the injector lay, but it was clear he would not make it, and Krum didn't bother to intervene. He picked up his champagne flute and sipped, watching until Bruce, wheezing, collapsed to the floor. He gave a last, pained gasp for air, and then he lay still. Krum turned back to face the windows.

The information about the flash drives had been moderately helpful, but not too surprising. Still, he had also been able to tie up another loose end, which was always a sound business practice. He heard his hired man enter and waved the flute in the direction of the anesthesiologist's body.

"Take him to his hotel room and make all the arrangements," Krum said. "He ordered room service, failed to realize it was cooked in peanut oil. Sadly forgot his injector while traveling. Don't miss anything."

"Yes, sir."

A few minutes later, Krum was alone. Soon, he knew, his

condo would be wiped down, any trace of Bruce Walters's presence gone. He likely could have hired the Tower's attaché to do some of this, he reflected—after all, if sixty-five million dollars couldn't buy discretion, what could it buy?—yet he preferred to utilize his own men. You never knew when some fool would cling to an outdated moral code and claim that he or she couldn't be bought. Better to use his own people, who were also less complicated to dispose of themselves if it came down to it. He had confidence that everything would be perfectly arranged for the anesthesiologist's death—timing of the room service order, fingerprints, everything—so that the police would readily judge it an unfortunate, allergy-related accident. One less tie between Krum and Worldwide Medical Research in Austin.

Receiving the flash drive of Konno's data from Walters had been, he had thought at the time, a great coup. Yet it was only a fraction of the needed data, and the hearts were unbelievably complex. He needed the rest of the data. If only he could get the other drives, it would not be too difficult to arrange a place to manufacture the hearts for sale; or he could sell the research to Lockheed, General Dynamics, or some other entity that had manufacturing facilities already in place. But only if he had a complete blueprint to sell.

Which brought him back to Dan Parker. Parker must know where the drives were. The man had to be found. Krum's people could overpower the FBI agents and take Parker's wife and daughter hostage, but from what he knew, Parker had had no contact with them in weeks. Wherever he was, he was off the map, off the grid. He probably would have no idea that his family was even in danger, and Krum would have stirred the hornet's nest of the Bureau. No, the doctor himself had to be located.

Krum turned his back on the windows, on the colors dancing across the glass facades of skyscrapers. On the clouds drifting lazily past while lit by the last rays of sunlight. On the crowds of people far below, so small as to be nearly invisible.

But they were there. Ready to be yielded up as human capital. And Parker was out there somewhere, too. Walking past the table, where the rest of Bruce Walters's dinner sat uneaten, he thought of the man's final moments, his bulging eyes, his red face, his swollen lips, the panic and desperation at the very end. Each person had a role to play in the great game. And if Dan Parker refused to play his, then he would only wish that death would come so quickly for him.

Chapter Twenty-Five

Another transplant. Another operation down. The same motions: open, cannulate, bypass. Clamp, cut, suction, divide. Remove the still-beating heart, like an offering to an ancient, pagan god. Accept the new heart, and try not to think where it came from. Trim, suture. Warm, defibrillate. Rhythm and pressure. Off bypass. Echo. Remove cannulas. Close.

Rinse and repeat.

He felt it wearing away at him, each day, whatever had once divided him from these murdering people becoming steadily more of a moot point. Did it matter to the people who had unwillingly given their lives, their bodies, that he was here to stop it if he could? Would it matter to the recipients, with their new lease on life, whether he had a choice in their illegal rescue?

A cog in a terrible machine. Grinding, cutting, wearing him down until a cold, hard core was all that was left. It was all that was left inside Ina—he could see through her eyes to the deadness within. All that was left of Jennings, too, and Brandt. All of them. He wasn't sure how much time he had remaining before it was all that was left inside himself, too.

He liked to think he was different from them, better... but

when he scrubbed out, washing away the blood, it seemed to him that those words had little real meaning here. If they ever had, if they still did when he arrived, they didn't hold the same power now.

He needed to get out. Before it was too late.

"Richards." It was Lee Brandt, from the doorway. Dan finished scrubbing out before he turned.

Lee was disheveled, his normally combed hair in disarray, sweat stains under the arms of his shirt. He looked impatient and frustrated, beckoning Dan out into the hallway.

"Come on, you're helping with harvesting." Lee started walking, not looking back.

Dan's insides tightened into an uncomfortable coil. If he'd thought he was no longer feeling anything, this was a painful reminder—things could get much worse. "No, Jennings handles that," he said. "I do the transplants."

"You'll do what you're told," Lee snapped. "You have no idea the pressure I'm under to keep the numbers up. I've got my hands full just dealing with Thakur's men, and I've got a lot of donors waiting and recipients on the way. You'll help take care of it, or I'm not responsible for what happens to you next."

Still, Dan hesitated, but when Lee looked back at him, the seriousness of his expression backed up his words, and Dan relented. "Lead the way."

Lee guided him out of the building, locking the door behind them, and onto the street, but they went in the opposite direction from when Ina took him to the lab. They turned quickly down another alleyway and through a door into a building, but Dan barely had time to make any impressions of it—an unremarkable, three-story brick structure—before they were inside. Lee took him down a hallway and pushed him through a door into a cold room.

Two people looked up at his entrance—Jennings and Ina. The rest of the people in the room were all under IV sedation.

"Jennings, show Richards how the hearts are harvested. See if he has any more suggestions for this part of the process to make it more efficient, then put him to work," Lee said. Without waiting for a response, he left and pulled the door shut behind him.

"You've got to be kidding me," Jennings said.

There were three stainless steel operating tables in the room, which was clean, sanitized, and frigid. People were unconscious on all three tables, on respirators and IV lines. Buckets of ice stood ready. Jennings was in scrubs and holding a scalpel, positioned next to one of the donors, while Ina sat in a chair by the wall, holding a semi-automatic rifle in her lap.

"What are you doing here?" Jennings demanded. "First you take the transplant work, now you think you can take this, too?"

"Just going where I'm told," Dan said, surprised at how much it still bothered him to see the unconscious individuals on the tables, to think about harvesting from them, or to wonder how recently they were walking the streets, going about their lives. Because of these people. Because of the organization he was now in effect a part of.

"We still don't know you," Jennings growled. "You could be anybody."

"Easy," Ina said, but she did not move from her chair.

"We can't trust him," Jennings said. He strode swiftly toward Dan, the scalpel gripped tightly. "He might be the one tipping off Thakur's men."

Dan took a step back, his hands rising. "I'm not tipping off anybody."

"It was better without you." Jennings got closer. Dan backed up until he bumped the door. Ina was watching, still not moving, as Jennings went on, his voice rising. "You can't keep taking what's mine and expect me to do nothing. That's why I'm here in the first place. It was people like you. Took everything from me, but no longer. You hear me?"

Jennings was in Dan's face now, his spittle flying, only inches of separation, the scalpel raised up between them. One quick slash and Dan's throat would be slit open, pouring out, all of it ended. He was not ready for that, but he was ready to fight. His hand tightened into a fist as he locked eyes with Jennings.

"I've heard enough," Dan said.

But before he could make a move, the door slammed open behind him. It crashed into Dan with such force that he was knocked to the side and onto the floor. His shoulder and side hit hard, and from the floor he saw three armed Indian men rush through the doorway, already firing. Their shots blasted into Jennings, hurling him back to land in a heap. Ina jumped up from her chair, her rifle swinging to aim, and the burst of fire from its barrel took the first of the gunmen down. The second fired at her, and Ina staggered back, but she fired off another burst and the second gunman dropped as well.

The third gunman entered at a crouch, aiming immediately at Ina. Dan drew back his leg and kicked hard, connecting just behind the man's knee. The man's legs buckled and he dropped, a spray of bullets hitting the ceiling. He rolled onto his knees, sweeping his gun back toward Dan. Another gunshot echoed in the room.

The third man slumped to the floor, and Dan looked up to see Ina, one hand braced against the wall, the other leveling the rifle. Blood was soaking her shirt, spreading across her chest and abdomen. The rifle dropped from her hand and she collapsed.

Dan rushed over to kneel beside her, the floor already growing red and slick. He opened Ina's soaked shirt, finding a bullet entrance just to the left of the sternum and below her breast. Blood was being pumped steadily out of the wound. Her eyelids were at half-mast.

"Thakur," she said faintly. "I knew this... was coming."

Dan felt her neck and found a thready pulse. He wanted to help her, but there was little he could do. From what he could see, the bullet had struck her left ventricle. Like most gunshots to the heart, it was only a matter of time, and not much of it.

He stepped over to Jennings to see if there was any more that could be done for him, but there was no pulse, no sign of life. He was gone. He checked the three attackers, Thakur's men, and found they were all dead as well. Returning to Ina, he found her breaths light, weak, her color fading.

"You were never... one of us," she said. Her eyes were tight with pain.

"That's not fair," Dan said. "I did everything I could."

She almost smiled. "Meant it as... compliment. You never... bought into this... did you?"

He put a hand on her shoulder. Before he could answer, the woman's breathing stopped, and then her eyes dilated. The light was gone out of them, and the spark that meant a living human being inhabited this flesh—it had left. He had seen it so many times before. And despite the circumstances, Dan knew he would carry her with him like the others, the ones back in the hospital he had not been able to save, and there would be no way to lay that down.

"No," he said. "I never bought into this."

He reached into her jacket and found her keys. He put his hand to her face and gently closed her eyes. It was time to do what he had come to do.

Chapter Twenty-Six

It was an opportunity. A terrible, bloody, horrifying one, but an opportunity nonetheless. He had the camera in his pocket; it was small enough to be unnoticeable if he kept it there, and they'd had no cause to search him since his first day. He took it out now and began to document what he saw, snapping a quick series of photographs of the room, the tables, the unconscious people on IVs, the ice buckets, Jennings, Ina, the dead gunmen. When he was done, he dropped the camera back into his pocket.

He felt a strong urge to run, so powerful that he had to wilfully force himself to stay. But if he left now, he knew he would regret it for the rest of his life, however long that might be. He went to the three people receiving IV sedation in preparation for becoming unwilling heart donors—two local men and a woman. He stopped the IVs and waited, the seconds and then minutes ticking by unbearably, interminably, sweat beading on his forehead. Any moment he expected more of Thakur's men, or Krum's, to burst in and start shooting. He searched around the room and found scrubs and blankets for the people on the tables, and then he went between them, lightly shaking to help them awake as they came off the sedation.

"Wake up," he said, not even sure if they spoke English. "It's time to go."

He took them off their respirators as they stared at him with wide, terrified eyes, their faces paling as they took in their surroundings. He helped them sit, pulled them off the tables as they shakily stood, and thrust scrubs and blankets at them.

"Hurry, go," he said, ushering the bewildered people toward a back door. "Just run."

They reached the door, and he pulled it open and pushed them through, one after another. The last, the woman, met his gaze and paused only long enough to put her hand for the smallest instant on his shoulder.

"Thank you," she said, and then she and the others were gone.

He shut the door and ran the other way, back to the door Lee had brought him through. Once on the street, he slowed a little as it struck him that here was another opportunity, as well—the first of its kind since he was jumped at the bar. He could leave. He could flag down a taxi cab and head to the airport, taking the photographs and his testimony to the FBI. He could escape and never look back. Dan pushed through the crowds, people jostling by, and saw Krum's building to his left, and a line of taxis to his right.

It would be so easy.

A hand grabbed his arm, and Dan spun, his arm twisting out of the grip even as he brought his free hand across in a hard jab. It connected with the other man's jaw, and the man staggered back as Dan prepared to fight or run.

"Get a little jumpy on the inside?" the man said, rubbing his face.

"Singh," Dan said. He lowered his hands. "Sorry about that."

"Come on. Lucy sent me to pull you out. She wants you to come to the States and testify with whatever you've got. Things are getting too hot here."

"You're telling me." Dan reached into his pocket for the camera, but then hesitated.

"There's good reason to think Thakur's men could attack Krum's operation soon," Singh said in a low voice. He took Dan by the arm again, guiding him toward the taxis. "Lucy doesn't want you caught in the middle of it."

"Thakur already hit. Five people are dead in the building I just left."

Singh swore under his breath. He continued to pull Dan toward the street. "This way, I've got a car. Let's get out of here."

Dan drew his arm out of the other man's grip once more. "I've confirmed that Krum is the boss. And that he's over other operations in New York, Tokyo, Beijing, Sao Paulo, and Mexico City. I've got photos of some of the rooms."

"That's a lot more than we had before. We can talk more in the car." Singh turned and took two steps, then looked back when Dan didn't follow.

"I've got the keys to the building, to all the rooms," Dan said. "This is my chance to do what I came for. To get the evidence that will take Krum down without question, no matter what billion-dollar legal team he has. I'm not leaving without it."

Singh stepped close again, his tone urgent. "Look, I applaud your courage. You've gone above and beyond what anybody could ask of you. But Thakur is already out for blood, and Krum will be on the warpath when he finds out what happened here, if he hasn't been tipped off already that an attack was coming. You go into that building and start digging around, I can't guarantee you're coming back out."

Dan nodded. "I understand. Give me ten minutes. I'll meet you here."

Without another word, he turned and left Singh standing there on the sidewalk. Dan hurried back to the building, to the side entrance. He pulled out Ina's keys and found the right one. He unlocked the door and stepped inside.

It was deathly silent within. His footsteps sounded unnaturally loud. As he passed the common room, he saw a couple of the nurses and a few of the men who did security and acquisitions, talking quietly. They looked up, stared at him a moment, and looked back to their meals or conversations. He did not see Lee Brandt.

Dan knew where he needed to go. Once he was out of sight, he headed straight for the office, the one that he had first seen Ina working in when the hood was pulled from his face on arrival. She went into it frequently, often with folders or a stack of papers, and she invariably locked it behind her. Dan had never seen the inside except through the door when she passed in or out.

He reached the office. There were several keys on the ring, and it took him longer than he would have liked to find the right one. With each second, each wrong key, he feared someone would walk up behind him, feared he would hear Lee's voice or the click of a safety flicked off. At last the key slid in, the lock turned, and the door opened.

It was dark inside. Dan didn't want to draw attention by letting light spill through the shades, but he could not very well search in the dark, so he shut the door and flipped the light switch. It was a small, simple office, with a desk, Ina's laptop, a bookshelf, a filing cabinet, a paper shredder, and a wastebasket. He flipped open the laptop, and a log-in screen appeared. Neither the username nor password was pre-filled. He did not even know her last name, much less have any clue what she would use. Time was wasting. Frustrated, he flipped it closed again.

He searched the desk drawers, looking for anything useful. He found pens, matches, rubber bands, a planner dated two years ago, paperclips, and a box of .45 caliber bullets. No flash drives, no CDs, nothing useful he could stuff in his pockets. Feeling the tension tighten a knot at the base of his neck, he stood and began rifling through the shelves, which mostly held books in languages he couldn't read. There were also notepads, some of them covered in chicken-scratch notes, as well as medical manuals. There had to be something here, *something*. He began tossing the books off the shelves, looking behind them, hoping for something hidden. Nothing.

The paper shredder was full, but everything in it was thoroughly cut to pieces and unrecoverable. Who knew what critical piece of evidence lay in the bin, now in tiny strips? He pushed it aside.

He thought about carrying the laptop out, just making a beeline for the street with it. But if anyone in the building saw him with it, anyone at all, that person would raise the alarm, and he would not make it out of here alive. He would have to pass by the common room again to reach the exit to the street. It would be suicide.

The filing cabinet. His eyes settled on it, and he rushed over. His fingers tugged at a drawer, but it wouldn't budge. Locked. He fumbled for Ina's key ring, and sure enough there was one key smaller than the others, brass, and when he fit it to the lock it turned. The cabinet had three drawers, and while one was empty, the other two were stuffed with files. Again, it was far too much to carry inconspicuously. He grabbed a folder at random and flipped it open.

It was a chart of accounts, with columns of numbers and abbreviations running down either side of the page. There was no time to parse it; he pulled out the camera and snapped a photo. He flipped rapidly through the pages, snapping pictures, and then began to go through folder after folder, as rapidly as he could, taking photographs of anything that looked important—medical charts, donor records, lists of prescription medications, payments, receipts, correspondence, budget forms, recipient rosters. Perhaps Ina had worried about being hacked online, had felt safer keeping it on paper, because it all seemed to be here. On one set of pages, a series of shipping manifests, he saw addresses for multiple cities, and they were instantly familiar: New York, Mexico City, Sao Paulo, Beijing, Tokyo, and Mumbai. The address in Mumbai had to be the building he was now standing in. His heart sped up even more, and he could hardly hold in a triumphant laugh. *I've got you, Krum.* Lucy Brown would not only have all the records he was documenting now, but she would have the exact address for every one of Krum's other locations around the world, and with this evidence, she could get legal authority to bust down every door within a week. It would all come crashing down.

Dan photographed the page and a handful of others, and then he replaced the folders in the drawer. He felt he had enough, and he did not want to push his luck. Voices had been audible out in the hallway a few minutes before, and at any moment someone could bang on the door—or come rushing in to put the place on lockdown, having discovered the massacre at the harvesting facility. Dan relocked the cabinet and stood. After a moment's hesitation, he hurriedly put the books back on the shelf so the room did not look like it had been ransacked. Ina could have told that they were not in their original spots, but she would not be alive to share this information. Dan took one more look at the office, confident that his investigation would go unrecognized, and flipped off the light. He opened the door.

Just outside the doorway, a man stood with a pair of armed guards flanking him on either side. The guards were aiming their guns at Dan, but this was not the main thing that caught his attention. He knew the man in the middle, recognized his face from pictures he had seen.

It was Krum.

Chapter Twenty-Seven

"Dr. Dan Parker," Krum said, with a smile. He extended his hand. "What a pleasure to finally meet you."

Dan's gaze flitted from one of the armed men to the next. There was no way he could overpower four. Worse, Krum knew his identity. With this realization, horrible as it was, came a small, unexpected relief—that he could slough off Dr. Steven Richards forever, never again pretending he felt nothing. He did not have to act. He did not have to hide how much he despised these people.

"Robert Krum," Dan said. "A man who's gotten wealthy off the blood and misery of others. A filthy sewer rat in a fancy suit." He did not shake the offered hand. "It's not the slightest pleasure meeting you."

Krum's fake smile faded, and in its place came a sickly, self-satisfied sneer, full of poison and anger. "You think you're smart. You think you're made of steel. But you're in way over your head here."

As Krum spoke, Dan recalled Dr. Shaw's words in the Chief of Medical Affairs office back at the hospital, what seemed like a lifetime ago—*Chest surgeons think they're bulletproof, and you're worse than most. You think you're God's gift to surgery and can do anything you want. But here's the catch—you can't.*

How right Shaw had been. There had been a part of him that thought he could do whatever needed to be done, and he would somehow pull it off, get away with it, make his own rules and follow these alone. He still wasn't sure that had been wrong. But it was naïve. And here, again, he thought he could go in, get out, and beat the system. Bend the rules. Win the game.

"Are you listening to me?" Krum said. "You thought you were outsmarting me, maybe had some control, but you've got no idea what real power is."

People like Krum, they had *built* the game. They had designed its rules. How could he think he could beat them at it?

One of Krum's men guided him to a chair, and as they bound him to it with zip-ties again, he felt a sense of déjà vu; it was the same chair he had been bound to when he'd arrived here.

"You believed you were putting one over on me," Krum continued, standing with arms crossed and a smug expression on his face. "But I knew all along who you were, what you were do-ing, from the first day you got here. You and that idiot FBI agent, Lucy Brown."

At that, Dan couldn't keep a flicker of recognition and dismay from his expression, though he tried to hide it. Krum saw it and laughed.

"You actually thought you could just come in here, pose for a while, and walk out. All the time you've been serving *my* ends, *my* needs. I needed a good surgeon to fill in with transplants, and I needed to find you to ask you some questions. You and Agent Brown helped me kill two birds with one stone."

"I don't believe you," Dan said, and he didn't. It didn't add up. Why would Krum have waited so long to confront him? If he was desperate enough for the artificial hearts to burn down the Austin facility, bomb his plane, and send men to attack him on the reservation, why would he sit back and bide his time, with the added risk of Dan escaping?

"Believe what you like," Krum said. "I was just waiting, letting you put more cash in my pocket with every operation, until I had the leverage I needed." He pulled out his phone, pressed a button, and held it up for Dan to see. "Take a look."

The first photo showed Dan's house. Krum swiped to the next, which showed a close-up of Laura, while the third showed Marla, sitting quietly in a chair, possibly outside. Krum only left each photo up for an instant before pocketing the phone again.

"I've got all the leverage I need," he said. "You're going to cooperate, or your family is dead. You're dead. And I'll still eventually get what I want."

If Krum had gotten to his family.... Panic surged in Dan, and he struggled against his bonds. At the threat to his wife and daughter, a fury rose up in him that he hadn't felt in a long, long time—and as he pulled against the ties, muscles straining, he let out a scream of frustration that had been building for weeks. The bonds held. He sagged back against them, breathing hard.

Krum smiled. "So then. I have one of Kim Konno's flash drives with the data for the artificial hearts. I need the others. I believe Konno gave them to you, and I believe you either hid them or gave them to someone else. You're going to tell me where to find them."

"If you so much as touch my family, I swear—" Dan growled.

"I'll do a lot more than touch them. I'll break their necks and toss them in a ditch." Krum gave a half-shrug. "Or, actually, I'll hire someone to do it."

"Let me speak to them," Dan said. "I want to talk to my wife and daughter."

"Not possible."

"I'm not telling you anything until I know they're all right."

"You're not the one dictating terms, Dr. Parker. Tell me how to get the flash drives, and then we'll talk about your family."

For a moment, Dan could hardly see for the red haze clouding his vision, his thoughts, the blood thundering in his temples as he continued pulling against the zip-ties until they cut into his skin. But then he forced himself to calm, to think, to listen to his instincts, honed over years of talking to people during traumatic situations—of reading their body language and discerning what they were really trying to say.

Krum was lying. Dan was sure of it. Krum didn't have his family. He had taken those photographs from a distance, or had someone do it, using a telephoto lens. Laura and Marla had not looked frightened; why take pictures before they were captured, if Krum had them? Lucy had said they would be protected. The most likely answer was that Krum couldn't get to them, but wanted Dan to think he could.

And Krum probably hadn't known until this very day that Dan was working undercover in this facility. Maybe Ina had sent him something with the new recruit's photo on it, or just his name; maybe Krum had finally gotten around to checking him out online personally and had seen through the FBI's changes to his appearance, guessing that he was Dan Parker. Maybe Krum had been called in to personally deal with the situation with Thakur's men, and he had found Ina dead, her keys missing, and someone emerging from her office—and had only pretended to be expecting Dan.

Whatever the case, Dan might not have a lot of options, and he did not wish to even risk his family's safety, but he did not think Krum was holding all the cards he said he was.

"Let's talk flash drives, then," Dan said. His voice was calmer, and he sat straight now, no longer fighting against his bonds. "There are three others. You won't find them without my help."

Krum nodded, pleased, and pulled over another chair. He sat down directly opposite from Dan, so close their knees almost touched. "Go on."

"I'm not telling you everything," Dan said. "You'll kill me the moment you have all the information you need."

"I'll kill you if you don't," Krum said, stiffening again. "And your family."

"We're doing this my way, or not at all. You're taking me with you to get the drives." Dan took a breath, but kept his voice firm. "We're flying back to the U.S., where I'll set up a meeting with the person who can get them. You won't know the specific location until we're on our way there. I'll hand the drives to you personally, or it won't happen. And then you let me, and my family, go."

Krum stared at him for a long minute. He didn't rub his jaw, or rest his chin in his hand, or even fold his arms. But Dan could see his enemy's mind working, the calculations taking place— cold, hard math, estimating odds and risks, determining his best chance for profit. Finally, Krum turned and gestured to one of his men.

"I have someone who should join this conversation," Krum said. As Dan watched, Krum's man disappeared into a nearby room, and a moment later he came out with another man, this one wearing a hood. Krum stood and pulled the man's hood off.

It was Singh. His hands were tied and his mouth gagged, his eyes wide with fear.

"Mr. Singh, I believe it is," Krum said. "Dan here is telling me the terms of his cooperation. He's pledging to get me the flash drives. But I'm a little worried about whether he'll come through." Krum reached to the belt of one of his men and withdrew a long knife with a serrated edge. "He may try to play both sides, a bit like you did, Singh—acting like a local thug, but doing it only so you could try to stab me in the back. Like this."

Without any more warning, he plunged the knife into Singh's back. Dan shouted, trying to rise, as Singh screamed into his gag. The men holding him wouldn't let him fall. Krum wiped the blade off on Singh's shirt, slid it back into its sheath, and then pulled a gun from behind his own back.

"I think trying to double-cross me is a very poor idea," Krum said.

He pressed the barrel of the gun to Singh's temple. He pulled the trigger. Krum's men released him, and he dropped.

Dan stared at the floor, feeling sick with anger all over again. Krum walked slowly back to the chair opposite him and sat again, keeping the gun out, letting it rest atop his knee. He gave a small smile.

"We can try it your way, Dr. Parker," he said. "But I trust you understand what will happen if you try to cross me."

Dan breathed in, out, in, out, calming himself. He needed to keep a clear head. "I need a phone," he said.

Krum pointed at Dan's ties, and one of the men cut him free.

Dan rubbed his wrists, and Krum handed him a phone. "Set up the meeting for the flash drives."

Dan entered Alex Bear's number and began to type a text message to his friend. Krum stepped around and watched over his shoulder.

Alex, it's Dan. I need the flash drives, which means I need to take you up on that favor. Bring them and meet me where I got thrown from my horse that time. Tomorrow, 2 p.m.

He pushed 'send' and passed the phone back to Krum. "It's done."

"And where are we flying?" Krum asked.

"New Mexico. I'll tell the pilot more as we get closer."

He stood, and Krum did as well. They were faced off, eye to eye. Dan saw plenty of deception in the other man's gaze, but no idle threats; he would continue to kill without hesitation.

"I have a car and a private jet available," Krum said, and started walking. "Let's be on our way."

Dan followed him, the other men falling into step on either side, guns ready. Krum stepped over Singh's body and headed for the exit.

Chapter Twenty-Eight

The jet, a new Gulfstream G650, offered the epitome of luxury. Every detail, every surface and texture, every aspect offered ultimate comfort and convenience. Sitting in a plush, oversized seat, with a glass of Scotch in his hand and the plane's engines so smooth that he might have imagined himself in a posh resort, rather than at thirty thousand feet, Dan felt sickened by it all. Not that such things existed; by knowing the human cost that had made such a thing available to a man like Krum.

They had talked little on the drive to the airport, in a tinted luxury SUV, or on the plane ride thus far. Perhaps Krum thought that his execution of Singh had made his point clearly enough. They had made a necessary stop in London to refuel as they followed the great circle route, and they would be making another stop in Maine and then heading on to New Mexico. It would be a long flight back to the U.S., and Dan was exhausted, but he found it difficult to sleep even after darkness had settled over the ocean outside his window and the interior lights of the plane were dimmed. Krum had treated him more like a business associate he was wining and dining than like his captive, but the men with their guns were never far away.

Dan was glad to be going home. But so much could go wrong.

Somewhere over the Atlantic, Krum left his seat near the front of the plane and came back to Dan. He had a bottle of fifty-year-old Scotch in his hand. Dan had left his first glass mostly untouched, letting the ice melt, but Krum gave him a fresh glass and poured another even when Dan shook his head.

"I know you can't afford this on your salary back at the hospital," Krum said. "You'd be smart to drink it while you can."

"I don't need things like this," Dan said, setting the glass to the side.

"Of course you don't. No one does." Krum poured himself a glass as well and sat across from Dan. "But you want them."

Dan started to open his mouth to argue, but it felt disingenuous at best, an outright lie at worst. A part of him *did* want these things, this luxury, the standard of living that Krum enjoyed. Who wouldn't?

"And why shouldn't you?" Krum went on, as if reading his thoughts. "You've worked hard enough. With your education, your training, and your contribution to society, you should be living the high life when you're not on your feet for fourteen hours straight saving people's lives."

"You don't know what I want." Dan turned to the window, to the darkness outside the plane.

"I think we want similar things. To improve people's lives, to make a mark in the world, and to expect a healthy return in the process. The difference is only how much we're willing to do to get it."

"I don't operate on people to make a buck," Dan said.

"Oh don't you? So you would willingly give up your salary

and work for free? Admit it, you'd like to be rewarded more for what you contribute."

Well, sure, it would be nice, Dan couldn't help thinking. He reached for his glass and took a swallow. The Scotch was smooth, rich, one of the best things he'd ever tasted.

"There's another point I bet we agree on," Krum continued. "And that's the value of those artificial hearts. They'll change the world. They'll make a difference for countless people's lives."

"You're acting like you care about people's lives," Dan said.

"Of course I care. I want their lives to matter, to mean something. Every life has a value to it, but most are wasted. Thrown away. Never used for any greater purpose." He paused. "Has it occurred to you that, with these artificial hearts, I'm effectively putting myself out of a job?"

At that, Dan looked at him. Krum looked serious. "What are you talking about?"

"Think about it. If artificial organs become widely available and affordable enough, there won't be a need for anyone to wait for years on a donor list. Or to spend hundreds of thousands for a black market organ."

Dan shook his head slightly and took another drink. Krum leaned on one elbow, propping a foot on the opposite knee. "You're a talented surgeon, Dr. Parker. And Kim Konno trusted you with this project. He trusted you to get it out to the world. I can do that. I *want* to do that, even with what it will mean to the business I'm in. I can get out of that and sell these hearts instead."

"You won't get out of it," Dan said.

"Come work for me, and I will. Work on these hearts. Oversee their development and manufacture. You have my word that I'll pull out of this messy business I've been in, and sell artificial organs instead. We'll make a fortune. You can have your own jet like this." He swept his hand around them, and smiled.

It felt as if the world was being offered to him on a silver platter. And as much as he hated the fact, some of what Krum said had resonated in uncomfortable ways. His eyes drifted over the teak and Italian leather, the $30,000 bottle of Scotch. It was almost enough to make Dan forget the blood that had brought them here. Almost.

"I could never do it," Dan said, "never work for you."

Krum dropped his leg down and sat forward. "You can work for me, and have every luxury you've ever dreamed of, or you can get in my way, and I will crush you. Why should you put your life on the line any longer? Why should you keep giving everything, day after day? Society no longer values you and your work. Nobody cares about you. People love their entertainers and sports stars in a way you'll never be loved."

Dan wanted to stop him, to cut him off, but he had to look away. He gripped his glass, wishing he could tune the other man out.

"People are endless fodder." Krum was almost yelling at him now. "They're self-serving, foolish, an unending supply of stupidity and greed, and they're hardly worth saving unless you get something out of it. You know that it's true!"

Krum stood on his last words, towering over Dan, holding the bottle of Scotch like he might smash it across Dan's skull. Slowly, Dan stood, until they were eye to eye again.

"That's what you'll never see," Dan said. "You're a corrupt businessman, and a killer. You stab people in the back. You think that's all a knife is good for." Dan pushed his finger into Krum's chest. "But you can't understand because you've never seen the other side of the knife, the side I hold every time I cut to *heal*. To save. To bring someone home to their kids, their husband, their wife. I do get something out of it." It was as if the words had been building up in Dan, and now that they were tumbling out, there was no stopping them. "The most important thing on the planet is life. Most people understand that, which is why there's such an outpouring of help and sympathy for the victims of floods and tornadoes, or fires, or mass shootings. I had those feelings in medical school and they are only stronger now. Doctors understand that. But you never will."

Dan drew his hand back, and Krum watched him appraisingly. Silence descended in the cabin. At last, it seemed, they understood each other, and Krum set the bottle of Scotch back down.

"You may want to catch up on your rest," Krum said at length. "We've got a big day coming up, and I have a feeling you'll need your strength."

He turned and walked back to the front of the plane. Dan sank back into his seat, breathing hard. He rested his forehead against the cool glass. Outside, far below, an ocean of black.

Chapter Twenty-Nine

Dan watched the miles roll by through the tinted window of the SUV. One of Krum's hired mercenaries sat next to him, watching him like Dan might try to wrest away his gun, or shove open the door and tumble out onto the road. The doors were probably locked. And anyway, the time for escape had long since past. He was committed to this course of action, wherever it took him.

Krum sat ahead of him in the passenger seat, while Lee Brandt drove, peering through aviator sunglasses. More of the mercenaries had joined them at the airfield when the jet landed, and they followed in a second SUV and a pickup truck behind that.

Outside, the majestic peak of Sierra Blanca rose into the sky, and he remembered the cold night he had spent huddled in a cave on its rocky slope. Had that man he had helped, the one who had fallen off the cliff, survived? Was his adopted little girl improving by now? Dan hoped so. And Alex's father—had he lived? Had the experimental oxygenator worked?

So much was unknown. He could not guess what was waiting for him at this meeting, only hope that Alex came through.

He would not have to stay in suspense much longer. The

rolling hills and thick forests outside the window were familiar, Ponderosa Pines and New Mexico cedar, and he knew they were getting close to the reservation when they turned onto Highway 70. Soon they passed a sign that read "Welcome to the home-lands of the Mescalero Apache Tribe."

"We'll turn off in about two miles," Dan said. He had been feeding directions to Lee since they had left the airfield. Lee seemed irritated at being forced to rely on his captive passenger, his hands tight on the wheel, but he followed Dan's prompts.

"Remember," Lee said, "we smell a trap, we see that your contact called the cops or Feds, we see *anything* we don't like, and we're gone. And the last thing you'll hear is your family's screams. You got me?"

"You've been pretty clear," Dan said. "Both you and the guy holding your leash."

"Hey," Lee said, twisting around to point a finger at Dan. "I'm on nobody's leash. I'll put you in the ground if you say the wrong word out here."

"Down, boy," Krum said dryly. "You'll follow my orders."

Lee turned back around, furious, but said nothing else. Dan smiled.

They passed a church, and then a sign that said *Frybread for sale.* "Turn off the road here," he said, and pointed. "There's a good dog."

Lee cursed him but pulled the SUV off the highway, where it drove off-road across scrubland of grass and bushes between hills and stands of trees. The second SUV and the pickup truck followed them, all the vehicles rocking lightly across the ground. They left the highway and wound around a hill, and soon the road was out of sight.

Dan could barely make out the trail that wound into the forest, which would eventually lead to a river. Many years ago, he and Alex had been riding not far from here, and Dan's horse had spooked at a rattlesnake sunning on a rock, rearing so abruptly that Dan was thrown off. Once the snake departed and Dan was safely back in the saddle, Alex could not stop laughing. He would remember the spot.

They drove about five more minutes, and then Dan said, "A hundred yards farther on. Just around this hill."

"Then this is where we change rides," Krum said.

Lee stopped the SUV and flipped the door locks, and both he and Krum got out. Lee came around to Dan's door and opened it, a gun out and trained on him.

"This isn't the meeting spot," Dan said, alarmed.

Lee grabbed him by the back of his shirt collar and pushed the muzzle of the gun against his head. "Walk."

Krum and Lee marched him past the second SUV, to the pickup truck, where three of Krum's men had climbed out of the bed and were walking past them to take empty seats in the lead vehicle. Two men remained in the pickup, both in the bed. Once their guns were trained on Dan, Lee climbed into the cab, and Dan was forced to follow Krum, climbing into the bed of the truck. One of the gunmen kept his weapon on Dan, while the other scanned the hills.

"Let's get my data," Krum said. He crouched near the cab, holding the side for balance, a bag now at his feet.

Behind the wheel, Lee spoke into a radio, and all three vehicles started forward in unison. Dan knelt, one hand on the side of the pickup, fighting down fear. They drove around the hill and into a plain strewn with rocks and holding one visible figure, a man standing in the middle of the open space. Alex Bear stood in a grey shirt, light jacket, and jeans, holding a small bag like one might put a pocket camera in. He watched the approaching vehicles.

When they were still some sixty yards away, Dan heard Lee through the open window speaking into his radio again. "Vehicle one, take that stand of trees on the far side. Vehicle two, the hill to the right."

The pickup braked to a stop. The first SUV peeled off, circling widely around the plain, looping around to approach a thick copse of trees from the far side. The second SUV turned in the opposite direction, driving to the right to circle around and scout out a hill overlooking the field.

They're looking for an ambush, Dan realized. *Krum's too careful. He's making sure Alex didn't mobilize the reservation police or the Feds.* And if Krum was smart enough to avoid any trap that Alex had planned, it meant that Dan could easily lose any upper hand he had. The pickup truck sat stationary, not pulling toward Alex. Dan wasn't sure what they were waiting for. And then he heard it—the sharp reports of gunfire, not from one direction but two, the woods *and* the hill.

"Floor it," Krum called to Lee.

The pickup truck shot forward. It accelerated fast, roaring toward Alex, and as they drew closer, Dan could see the surprised look on his friend's face. More gunfire was sounding now, and he couldn't be sure but he thought some of it was striking the ground around the pickup. It looked as if Lee meant to mow Alex down, just drive the truck right through him, and Dan saw Alex tense as the same realization hit him, about to throw himself to the side. At the last second, Lee slowed a little and steered so that the pickup drove directly past Alex, close enough to touch.

Close enough to grab. The two men in the cab were ready, and they reached over and took hold of Alex, hauling him up and into the bed of the truck as it kept moving. As soon as he was in, Lee accelerated again, and now Dan was sure that bullets were flying at the truck—one of them splintered the windshield, another blasted off a side-view mirror.

The truck turned, tires kicking up grass and clods of dirt, and headed back toward the main road. Alex was shoved down in the bed of the truck, one of the men pointing a gun at him while the other checked him for weapons. The man found a gun and knife and tossed both out of the truck. He dragged Alex up to sitting as they left the field, facing Krum.

"*Da'anzho*," Alex said.

"What did you call me?" Krum demanded.

"He said hello," Dan said.

Krum braced himself on the side as the truck picked up speed again, bouncing across the ground, and leaned in closer to Dan. "Tell Tonto here to be a good little Indian and hand over the drives."

"I speak English, you idiot," Alex said. "I don't need a translator." The small bag was still in his grip, and he unzipped it and opened it enough to show the flash drives inside before passing it to Krum.

"Now pull over and let us out," Dan said. "You have what you came for."

Krum ignored this, and the truck continued to tear around the hills and toward the highway. Krum reached into the bag at his feet and pulled out a laptop, which he flipped open. He pulled out the first flash drive and plugged it in. Dan watched him, but his face betrayed nothing. Krum pulled out another drive and checked that one. Dan looked at Alex, and saw that his friend's face was pale; in his eyes, a warning.

The flash drives must be blank. The real ones were somewhere safe. Dan didn't know what to feel at this—terror, relief, desperation, gratitude. He had only seconds to process it before Krum had tried all of the flash drives and dropped the laptop to the bed of the truck. He produced a gun of his own and pushed it not against Alex's head, but against Dan's.

"You have three seconds to tell me where the actual drives are, or I blow his head off," Krum said. "One."

"Wait a minute," Alex said, holding up his hands.

"Two."

"I can get them to you!"

"Three."

Dan saw Krum's finger tightening on the trigger. At the same moment he heard Lee's cry of alarm from the cab, and the truck swerved violently to the side, braking hard. There was the sound of exploding tires, all four in rapid succession, and something tangling with the wheels. It all happened so fast. Lee lost control, the passengers were tossed about in the bed of the truck, and then the pickup slammed head-on into a tree and Dan was hurled into the cab's rear window hard enough to shatter it with his shoulder. Alex was knocked roughly onto the floor, one of the gunmen was thrown out of the bed entirely, and Krum and the other man crashed into Dan and the cab.

Smoke rose from the engine, and inside the cab Dan could see Lee slumped to the side, his forehead bloody from colliding with the dash. Krum and the man beside him groggily pushed themselves up. Krum had lost his gun over the side in the crash, but the mercenary reclaimed his weapon from the bed before Dan could snatch it. As Dan withdrew himself from the window, feeling a blaze of pain down his shoulder and arm where the glass had sliced him, he glimpsed the spike strip trailing from the back of the truck where it had tangled after the truck drove over its iron points. And beyond, Dan saw someone walking toward them from around the last hill, the direction of the highway. The woman had her gun up and braced, jogging straight at them.

"Lucy," Dan said.

Chapter Thirty

The mercenary next to Krum recovered first, wiping blood from his eyes and straightening, his gun swiveling around to fire at the FBI agent who was closing fast. He fired several times as she closed, and Lucy ducked but kept coming, and then she slowed and returned fire. Three shots. The man staggered back, his legs hit the side of the truck, and he fell over the edge.

Krum, unarmed, flattened in the bed of the truck and started to crawl, right past Alex. Dan's eyes shot to his friend. He was motionless, and seemed to be unconscious from striking his head, but he was breathing. Krum grabbed the edge and lunged over the side of the truck away from Lucy, out of sight. Dan pulled himself up, leaning on the side to see where Lucy was, and he saw that the mercenary who had been thrown clear of the truck had crawled to his gun, pushed himself up, and started firing at Lucy. She dropped to one knee, aimed, and fired back. The man dropped his gun and fell, dead.

That was when Krum came around the side of the pickup truck, wielding the gun the other mercenary had dropped. He stepped into the open, and as Lucy stood and her eyes swung to find him, he shot her twice, directly in the chest. She was knocked off her feet. Lucy landed hard on her back and did not move again.

Krum pivoted toward Dan and began firing. Dan threw himself prone in the bed of the truck as bullets impacted with the metal, some ricocheting off, some piercing and leaving holes far too close to his body. Through one right by his face, he saw Krum look back at the road, consider a moment, and then take off running for the woods, away from the highway.

He thinks Lucy will have back-up waiting at the road, Dan thought. But as he waited for a few seconds longer and none appeared, he was sure that no one else was coming. For whatever reason, Lucy had come on her own, and all of Alex's friends with the reservation police were engaging the SUVs full of Krum's men, or were dead. There was nobody else. Krum was getting away.

His eyes fell on something protruding from under the laptop bag. The gun that Krum had dropped. He scrambled over, the movement sending pain through his shoulder and arm, his head throbbing, and he snatched it up and then used his good arm to vault over the side of the truck. He nearly landed on the man that Lucy had shot dead before being gunned down herself. Straight ahead, he saw a copse of trees, perhaps a minute's run away, and Krum about to disappear into them.

It wasn't a choice. This had to end. Dan took off running, ignoring the pain. Just before Krum vanished from sight, he raised the gun and fired twice. Krum darted into the woods. Dan pumped his arms and legs faster, calling on reserves he didn't know he had—the endless hours on his feet, the marathons—and he closed the distance between them rapidly. He reached the woods, the trees stretching high, the light lower, softer here where it was filtered through their many branches. Krum was visible again, closer now, and he turned around and fired at Dan—three shots that went wide. Dan fired back, missing as Krum ducked behind another tree.

Dan ran closer, but slowed when he did not see Krum running any farther on. He was lying in wait. Dan skirted to the left, trying to circle silently around, but try as he might, his footfalls caused too much sound on the fallen leaves and brush. He reached a small cluster of trees that he believed was roughly parallel to Krum's position. Before he left its protection, he popped out the gun's magazine to check his remaining ammunition. The sight made him want to drop to the ground in despair.

The clip was empty. Which meant he only had one round left, in the chamber.

That was plenty of excuse to turn and leave now. He could make a run for it, maybe reach the highway, flag someone down, and try to get back to his old life and forget this ever happened. Things would never be the same, but maybe he could at least make it out of this. Survival was something, wasn't it? He tried to rationalize to himself that it would be understandable to walk away. To survive. Wasn't that what being a doctor was all about? Trying to facilitate survival?

No, not survival. Living. There's a difference.

He stepped out from the tree and saw that Krum had done the same. Dan raised his gun and fired, but even as he did he knew the shot was going to miss, Krum already flinching away, and sure enough it flew past Krum's ear. Krum fired, and the bullet shredded bark inches from Dan's head. They both retreated to safety after the exchange, stepping back to the trees they sheltered behind.

You're out of ammo, Dan. He was sweating, breathing hard, still gripping the empty gun. *Now how are you going to keep living?*

Maybe he could make it back to the edge of the grove. There was still time to escape. He chanced a quick look, leaning around the tree. And he saw something out of the corner of his eye that almost stole his breath.

It was now or never. Dan stepped out from behind the trees.

"Hey!" he shouted. He aimed the gun at Krum's hiding spot and pulled the trigger. It clicked, clicked again, nothing happening, and as he stood there pulling the trigger on an empty weapon, Krum emerged with a triumphant grin on his face. He took three steps toward Dan and raised his gun.

"What a waste," Krum said.

From the edge of his vision, Dan saw the figure running toward them, and as Krum's finger squeezed the trigger, she fired. Two shots blasted into Robert Krum, the impact pushing him off his feet to land on his side, blossoms of red already spreading across his chest. Despite the blood, Lucy Brown kept her gun trained on him as she approached. She didn't relax her aim until she had kicked the gun out of Krum's limp grip.

"I saw you get shot," Dan said.

Lucy tugged the collar of her shirt down, revealing a black vest underneath. "Forget diamonds, Kevlar is a girl's best friend. Don't leave home without it."

Dan walked up as Lucy knelt to check Krum's wounds. She shook her head slightly; nothing to be done. The dying man coughed, his lips red, and he lay back, hands moving weakly to his chest. He tried to speak, but no words would come out. He coughed once more, his eyes fixing on Dan. At the end, there was no ego or cruelty in them, only despair. He grew still.

Lucy rose, and for a moment they stood looking down at the man who had terrorized on four continents, now dead in the dirt.

"Yes," Dan said quietly. "What a waste."

* * *

Lucy ended up giving Dan a ride to the hospital in Alamogordo, where Alex was taken by ambulance, along with the surviving reservation police who had fought with Krum's men. After an initial examination, it seemed Alex had a mild concussion but no other apparent wounds aside from a few scratches. After seeing Dan's shoulder injury, the paramedics wanted to take him in the ambulance as well, but he waved them off and insisted he would be fine until they reached the medical center.

"I've been monitoring all of Alex's calls and messages," Lucy explained. "So I knew when you reached out to him."

"You can do that?"

She fidgeted in her seat. "Well. I pulled a few strings. Anyway, I called him, explained as much as I could, and told him I could help. But he stressed that we couldn't mobilize a lot of manpower, or Krum would spot it. He preferred to call on a handful of friends he had on the reservation police who he thought would be better at keeping a low profile."

She didn't sound like she had entirely approved, and in a way, he couldn't blame her—the plan had not exactly worked out. "He was just trying to keep me from getting shot," Dan said.

"I know. And I've been getting pushback for the way I've handled this case, so I couldn't have gotten much support for a last-minute ambush on an Apache reservation, anyway. I told

Alex that me and my trusty spike strip would hang back in case things went wrong." She looked at Dan with a wry smile. "Boy, did they go wrong."

"Don't look at me." He started to raise his hands with a *not my fault* gesture, but it hurt too much. "This whole undercover operation was your idea."

"And a good one. We found your camera on Krum's body. With the pictures you took, we can find his operations around the world and shut them all down, bring everyone in them to justice. It's over."

"And my family?" Dan asked. Until the question left his lips, he hadn't realized just how desperately he needed to know for sure, how much fear he had been carrying around with him.

Lucy looked at him again and smiled. "They're safe."

Dan closed his eyes and leaned his head back. The knots in his neck and shoulders began to loosen. "Thank you."

"You're the one that deserves thanks," Lucy said. She reached over and patted his hurt shoulder without looking, and he winced. "You did good, Dr. Parker. Now you can go back to your hospital, back to life as usual."

Something in the way she said it made Dan realize that she knew, as well as he did, that this was perhaps not a lie, but not exactly truthful either—he might go back, but life would not go on as usual, maybe not ever again. Some things could not be put back how they were. And yet, all the same, he was glad to hear her say it.

Chapter Thirty-One

"And the garage?" Dan asked. He was walking back and forth in his bedroom, trying not to smile, the phone to his ear.

"Dad wants to get right back to cleaning it," Alex said. "Says he'll wear a face mask this time. After nearly dying from Hanta virus the first time around. Unbelievable."

"I can believe that," Dan said. "Sounds about like your dad."

"He'll make a full recovery, thanks to the oxygenator we used on him. Of course, my mother says he's just too hard-headed to die."

"Runs in the family," Dan said, sure that Alex could hear the grin through his voice now. "That's how I knew that concussion you got in the truck crash wouldn't do any lasting damage."

"Wasn't really hurt, I just felt like taking a nap. I knew a super spy like you could handle it."

Dan laughed. "You know me." He looked toward the door as Laura entered, holding a handful of papers. She sat on the edge of the bed, waiting for him with a strange expression on her face.

"Speaking of," Alex said over the phone, "I guess you're kind of a big-shot now. You know yet what you're going to do with your new-found fame?"

"I have a pretty good idea," Dan said. He smiled at Laura, and she gave a tentative smile back. "Listen, Laura's here, I gotta go. Give your parents my best, and keep some for yourself."

"Peace, my friend," Alex said.

Dan disconnected and dropped the phone in his pocket. Laura patted the bed next to her, and he sat on the blue-checked comforter. For a moment, he had an uncomfortable flashback to the room in Mumbai, and Ina. Walls closing in. He shook it off, his eyes falling to the sheaf of papers that Laura held.

"What are those?"

"Offers," she said, flipping through her notes. "I wrote down all the voicemails that we got from people wanting to interview you. Talk shows, magazines, newspapers. Some big names." She passed the stack into his lap.

Dan just held it, looking down but not really focusing on the words. He started to page through them, but stopped. Her hand slid over and rested atop his.

"Aren't you interested? Isn't this what you've always wanted, to be treated like a celebrity?" Her voice was gently chiding, almost teasing, but he could sense the undercurrent of insecurity. "Haven't you wanted to be loved and adored, and *paid*, like one?"

Dan stood and walked to a wastebasket on the other side of the room. He tossed the papers into it. It hurt much less than he'd expected. "I guess I've realized a few things about what I want."

Laura spread into a smile, and when he stepped back to her she wrapped her arms around him and laid her head against his chest. "I think we all have," she murmured.

He stroked her hair. It felt better than he could have imagined to be back home with her. He could smell the shampoo she had used, something with lavender. Dan breathed it in. Here in their bedroom, as elsewhere in the house, the evidence of the horrible ransacking remained in places, but they had begun to replace broken items and to put their home back together.

"I've been worried about you," she said quietly. "Even after you came back."

"I'm home now. I'm safe."

"When I saw you at the airport, I hardly recognized you. Your face is so thin." She reached up, placing a cool palm on his cheek.

He took her hand in his. "I lost a few pounds, that's all."

"It's not just that. I watch you when you think no one's looking. I see the look on your face, like you're still seeing it, whatever happened over there. Sometimes I catch you staring off into space."

Dan didn't know what to say. His hand dropped away from hers.

"I called Dr. Shaw," Laura said. "He told me he'd seen veterans with the same symptoms. He said you need time away from the hospital, that we should go to familiar places. Spend lots of time as a family."

"I'm fine," Dan said, more roughly than he had intended. She dropped her hand away, but Dan reached for it and held it. He drew a deep breath. "I'm sorry," he said. "Those are good ideas."

She was quiet. After a while, she said, "It's not just me you need to spend time with, either."

"I know. Where is she?"

"Out in the yard."

She stepped away from him, but her hand reached back to take his, and he followed her downstairs. Dan found Marla in the shade under a sprawling oak tree, with a stick in her hand, while a young border collie stared at her expectantly, legs braced, tail wagging.

"Fetch!" Marla said, and threw the stick across the yard. The dog tore after it, snatched it up, and then looked back at the girl as if unsure what to do next. Marla patted her knees and called to the dog—"Rico! Come!"—but he just watched her with a quizzical expression, head cocked.

A bag of treats sat on a picnic table nearby. Dan picked it up as he passed by and carried it over to his daughter. "Here," he said, taking her hand and pouring a few treats into it. "Hold one out and try calling him again."

Marla tried once more, with an extended treat this time, and the dog raced back to her, dropped the stick at her feet to get his mouth free, and gobbled up the treat, licking her hand. Marla laughed. "Good boy, good boy!"

"Keep enticing him back with the treats until he learns the game, and then you can just praise him, and pretty soon he'll fetch just for the fun of it," Dan said.

"Cool." Marla tried again, tossing the stick, and when the dog looked back at her, held out another treat. Rico carried the stick to her, tail bouncing back and forth. Dan watched as she repeated the process a few more times.

"It's weird to have you home," Marla said to him.

Dan looked to the side, trying to hide the disappointment he felt, but it melted away when he caught her beaming at him.

"It's a good weird," she said.

"It's a very good weird," Laura added, sitting at the table. Dan walked over to join her, and they sat and watched their daughter playing with the dog. A few leaves drifted peacefully down as a breeze rustled through them.

"I'll make us a picnic lunch," Laura said, patting her knees and standing. "And maybe we can all go to the park together?"

Familiar places. Time together as a family. "Sounds wonderful," Dan said. And it did.

* * *

A few hours later, back at the house, Dan rose drowsily from his armchair and stepped to the door to pluck his key ring off the hook.

"Where are you going?" Laura asked from the couch, where Marla was curled on the other end, the young border collie in her lap.

"I need to go to the hospital for a bit," Dan said.

Laura frowned. "I thought you were taking the week off."

Marla jumped off the couch so quickly that the dog sprawled on the floor. "That didn't last long," she muttered, heading for her room without looking at him.

"Whoa," Dan said. "I am taking the week off. But I haven't had a chance to talk with Shaw since all of this happened. I need to make sure I still have a job when I go back, okay?"

"Okay," Marla said, turning back, then added, "Sorry."

"Don't worry about it. Just have that circus puzzle ready to start when I get back."

Marla's eyes widened. "The two-thousand-piece one?"

"I think it's time. You both up for the challenge?"

His daughter grinned; his wife cocked her hip.

"Bring it," Laura said.

Dan drove to the hospital, and pulling into its parking lot felt familiar in a reassuring way. He couldn't help wondering if this would be his last visit, though. While in India, he had missed his scheduled appearance to defend himself to the committee; he might not have a place at Amarillo Medical Center anymore. He didn't want to have to move, to uproot his family, to try to start over somewhere else. He wanted another chance here, to do things differently. But time had proven that he didn't always get what he wanted.

Dr. Golden Shaw had his office door open when Dan reached it, and everything in the room looked precisely the same as it had the last time they had talked. The Chief of Medical Affairs had the same shirt and tie on, the same harried look on his face, his hands interlaced on the desk in front of him in the same authoritative fashion. Dan sat and waited, not sure how to begin the conversation.

"Quite a turn of events," Shaw said at last.

"Pretty crazy," Dan agreed.

Shaw scowled. "You've put me in a strange position. I stand by everything I said before. You can't work in this hospital if you're going to be some cowboy that only plays by his own rules." He flattened his palms on the desk, leaning back and sigh-ing. "And yet, I'm glad for how everything turned out, and the hospital is certainly getting a lot of attention. You know, before you came in, I just got off the phone with a reporter from Channel 8?"

Dan thought he might have imagined it, but no, looking closer, it was clear—Shaw was actually puffing out his chest. "That's... that's really something."

"Sure it is," he said gruffly. "And, it's thanks to you, I suppose."

Dan started to say something else, but Shaw's expression told him it was better to wait until the chief had had his full say. A moment later, Shaw continued.

"Given the truth that's come out, and everything that's happened, I can hardly chase a national hero from the hospital without giving you another chance. The rest of the committee agrees with me." Shaw paused. "You're being reinstated with full privileges."

Dan let out his breath. He reached across the table to vigorously shake the chief's hand. "That's terrific. You won't regret it."

"See that I don't. Now go on, and enjoy your time off." He paused, adopting a falsely casual tone. "Actually, you should take an extra couple of weeks. There's no need to rush back to work."

Shaw had never been subtle, and Dan frowned. "I don't think that's really necessary."

"You don't? Huh. All that you've been through, and you still think you can do everything."

Dan's mouth opened to argue, but the words bit deep, and he closed it again. No, he could not do everything. But he could do some things. "You might be right. Maybe some time away will be good." He stood, and at the door he turned back, his hand on the frame. "I did want to ask you for something else. A favor."

Shaw stiffened. "Look, just because you're a star now doesn't mean I can give you extra perks."

"I just wondered if I could start serving on the executive committee after my time off." Dan had never shown the slightest interest in being part of the group that, among other things, was responsible for setting and implementing policies for the hospital.

Taken aback, it took Shaw a few seconds to collect his thoughts. "Why, sure, I mean, of course you can. I'll make the arrangements."

"I figure that if I think something's not right and want it to change, I'd better be part of the long-term solution, working as a team to make things as they should be." He patted the doorframe. "Thanks, Chief."

Shaw, still surprised, just nodded, and Dan strolled down the hallway—not for the last time. He would be back. And before he reached the exit, a voice called out to him, one he knew well.

"Well, look who decided to drop in," she said. "Have a nice vacation overseas?"

He turned to see Holly Martin standing by the water cooler, holding a cup, the corners of her mouth twitching. "Oh, it was so relaxing," he said. "The parts that I wasn't getting shot at."

"Quit your whining, they clearly had terrible aim."

"Missed you, too. You manage to pull off any successful operations without me there?"

"You weren't there?" She blinked. "Sorry, I didn't notice."

Dan laughed. "You run any halfs in the last few weeks? I was giving you a chance to finish the marathon without somebody making you look bad."

She fell into step beside him as he continued down the hall, and she ran a few paces in place. "Oh, I could beat you right now, old man."

"Let's go, then." He ground the toe of his shoe on the floor, assuming a runner's stance.

A nurse in scrubs rounded the corner in front of them at top speed and nearly collided with them both. The nurse recovered herself, and then she gasped out, "Dr. Parker! You're back! Thank goodness. Dr. Williams is taking back the lung resection he did earlier, and the patient is bleeding. Can you help him?"

Some things never change, Dan thought, but then someone else spoke up before he could.

"Dr. Parker is off-duty," Golden Shaw said from behind them. "Dr. Stinson can help, he just finished a CAB operation. He's in the recovery room, go ask him."

"Thank you," Dan said, unable to hold in his relief.

"Of course," Shaw said, strolling briskly down the hallway. "We're a team."

The nurse and chief disappeared around the corner. Dan looked over at Holly.

"Slacker," she said.

"You better believe it. Time to do a two-thousand-piece jigsaw puzzle."

"You can put together a puzzle with two thousand pieces?"

Dan walked down the hallway, and at the door he turned and waved. "One way to find out."

Epilogue

There had to be a catch. There was always a catch.

Ellen Blake had spent the day touring the impressive facility, meeting with department heads and supervisors, learning the specifics of the operation, and examining for herself the ins and outs of manufacturing. Of course, this was simply the tip of the iceberg; the bulk of her inspection duties for the FDA were carried out before she ever arrived, in other forms of due diligence, or in hours spent in an office poring over paperwork and being stepped through records at the facility in question. Less than glamorous stuff. But necessary, she supposed, and it still beat the Janus-faced bureaucracy she had to deal with the rest of the time on Capitol Hill.

Besides, it wasn't the part of the iceberg *above* the water that sunk the Titanic, was it?

There was always a catch.

She finally had a few minutes to herself, and she stood in a hallway at a glass partition overlooking a segment of the manufacturing wing. The level of technology was staggering. Yet she wasn't quite focusing on it, notepad and pen held motionless, her mind wandering.

This was a particularly interesting and unique situation, given the dubious origins of the case. On the heels of her initial interest in Worldwide Medical Research, she had met with Robert Krum, who had—she could admit it now—scared her with the coldness of his calculations, the feeling that something was not quite right. Then she had placed that call to FBI Agent Lucy Brown, who assured her they had it under control.

Then she had called, and warned, Kim Konno. And then Konno had died mysteriously in a fire. It didn't seem the FBI had it under control, after all.

Agent Brown had called her six weeks ago, finally following up on their initial conversation, and had given her bits and pieces of information—little more than she'd gleaned from the newspapers, really—that raised more questions than answers.

"So I was right about Krum," Ellen had said. "And he was responsible for the fire at Worldwide Medical, wasn't he?"

"We are investigating leads that suggest possible involvement," Agent Brown had replied.

"It's so bizarre," Ellen said. "I knew he was off, but what I'm hearing on the news—did you have a chance to question him?"

"Sadly, he... ah... resisted arrest."

"I appreciate the follow-up," Ellen said. "Does this have anything to do with the memo I got today about Worldwide's remaining assets?"

"Not my jurisdiction," Lucy said. She paused. "But I know some people who feel pretty strongly about getting this research out to the world."

Ellen herself had become one of them. And here she was, six weeks later, in a gargantuan building that housed the means to efficiently produce working, superbly engineered, highly effective artificial hearts. She was looking right at them being made.

The Konno Heart, a medical marvel. If all went according to plan, they would soon be available worldwide. Surgeons wanting to implant would come to the factory to learn the exact techniques and precautions for successful implantation. Medicare and other insurance companies—Health Now was long since out of the picture—had agreed to cover the costs. The manufacturing facility was using sterile technique and employed many of the PhDs that previously worked for Konno in Austin.

"Amazing, isn't it?"

She looked up sharply, then relaxed. It was a consultant the company had hired, after a few strong suggestions from high places, with Agent Brown's office likely among them, if Ellen had to guess. The company was plenty big enough and had its own consultants—it had outbid both Boeing and Lockheed-Martin, after all, other contenders with their own manufacturing facilities already in place—but this consultant was familiar with the research prior to its new management.

They had met that morning, and the man had been very friendly. He'd explained to Ellen that this was an ideal arrangement for him, only the commitment of a few hours here and there, the occasional day trip, but it let him keep his finger on the pulse of the research and the development of the hearts—something he said he had a personal stake in. If half of what the sensational news stories had reported was true, she could understand why.

"Dr. Parker," she said, extending a hand. "Good to see you again."

He shook it warmly. "Call me Dan. Admiring the view?"

"It's incredible. I still can't believe it's really possible." She tapped her pen against the notepad, where earlier she'd underlined a scribble to herself—*Too good?* "It all seems too good to be true. The hearts, all this. I'm used to there being a catch."

Dan's expression darkened, his eyebrows drawing together as he folded his arms. "Of course there's a catch. There was a huge price to pay. People died for this research."

Ellen nodded and lowered her eyes. "Of course. I didn't mean any disrespect." For a moment they stood in silence, both their gazes drawn to the manufacturing floor beyond the window. "You know, I tried to warn him. Konno. I called him, after I met with Krum, hoping he would be careful enough."

"Then you may be the reason he moved all the animals off-site, and called me to come get the prototypes. You might be the reason all of this is here." Dan unfolded his arms, and he tilted his head toward the elevator at the end of the hall. "Come with me, I want to show you something."

She followed him up three floors, and a few minutes later she found herself in a room containing, among other things, a scale model of what appeared to be a lovely, garden-filled park. The model was large and intricately detailed, taking up a third of the room. She walked around it, admiring the carefully cultivated artistry of the planned space.

"What is this?" Ellen asked.

"The leadership here approached me for my thoughts on doing something to honor Kim Konno," Dan said. "It was a nice thought, naming a building after him or something, but we settled for a memorial park that's going to be built next spring."

"Good publicity," Ellen said.

"No doubt. But still a nice way to honor Kim."

"I didn't know him well, but I'm sure he would have been proud."

Dan smiled. "I did know him well, and it's not what he would want. So we scuttled plans for a park in his name." Dan walked around the model, his eyes roving over the cherry blossom trees, the benches, the paved walkways, the koi pond, the flowers. "He'd be proud when this starts actually impacting lives. Kim would say that anything else is just science for science's sake, and he never had much use for that. No time for medicine that didn't have real human impact. It was why he was so careful with his own work. Do it slow, do it right, like his father told him, as he used to tell me."

Ellen followed him around the model until they reached the planned entrance to the park, where now she could see the small recreation of the sign that would be supported by an arched entryway: *The Tadami Konno Memorial Park.*

"His father was one of those whose life would have been impacted by one of these artificial hearts," Dan said softly. "A good man, lost too soon. We honor Kim... by honoring him. And by making sure that the sacrifices of people like Kim Konno lead to real change in the world."

"They will," Ellen said. She put a hand on the edge of the model. "I believe this will change the landscape of medical care for a lot of folks. It's going to help so many people to survive serious conditions."

Dan Parker stood still, looking at the sign and the model of the park. He smiled, turning to face her. "Not just survive. Live."

Ellen followed him out. As she walked, she crossed out her previous note to herself, and Dan reached back before the door swung shut. The light clicked off.

About the Author

R D SUTHERLAND practiced thoracic and cardiovascular surgery for thirty years. Now lives in the Dallas metroplex with wife Carolyn and dog Happy. Having fun with children and grandchildren.

38170901R00144

Made in the USA
San Bernardino, CA
07 June 2019